Fallen Star

ALSO BY SUSANNAH NIX

Chemistry Lessons Series:

Remedial Rocket Science

Intermediate Thermodynamics

Advanced Physical Chemistry

Starstruck Series:

Rising Star

Fallen Star

Fallen Star

SUSANNAH NIX

Haver Street Press

FALLEN STAR. Copyright © 2019 by Susannah Nix

FIRST EDITION: March 2019

ISBN: 978-1-950087-99-0

Haver Street Press | 448 W. 19th St., Suite 407 | Houston, TX 77008

Edited by Julia Ganis, www.juliaedits.com

Cover Design by Sarah Hansen, Okay Creations

1

"So it's really Scotty Deacon?" Carmen asked.

Grace Speer looked up from her desk in the empty bullpen of the *Sunset Limited* production offices. It was late, and nearly everyone else had called it quits for the day, except Carmen Vargas, who'd just wandered over from the costume department office down the hall.

"It's really Scotty Deacon." Grace's lips curled a little as they formed the words. "He's coming in tonight to meet with Joe." She glanced at the clock on the wall. "In about ten minutes."

After months of searching, a string of disappointing auditions, and two failed negotiations, the producers had finally cast the lead of *Sunset Limited*, the indie neo-noir thriller that was due to start principal photography next month in New Orleans.

Grace could only assume the decision to give the part to Scotty Deacon had been made out of desperation. It was the only reason she could think why they'd agreed to cast a washed-up former teen heartthrob who hadn't worked in years.

"Huh." Carmen held a pad of costume sketches in one hand and a cup of coffee in the other as she leaned against the edge of Grace's desk. "I thought he was dead."

Grace had thought the same thing until she'd seen his name on the short list for *Sunset Limited*.

Scotty Deacon had been one of the rare Disney Channel stars to make the transition from tween heartthrob to big-time box office hunk—until a messy drug habit, a string of DUIs, and enough bad behavior to earn him his own episode of *E! True Hollywood Story* had derailed his career. After getting himself fired from the set of a Michael Bay film four years ago, Deacon had been blacklisted in Hollywood and dropped off the radar completely. Grace could have sworn she'd heard something about an overdose a couple years back, but she must have been mixing up her former child stars.

"Only figuratively," she told Carmen. "He's looking to make a comeback, apparently."

Carmen's eye roll conveyed her skepticism. "And we're the chumps who get to take a chance on the drug addict? Lucky us." As costume supervisor, Carmen had to get up close and personal with all the actors, but especially with the lead, who would be in nearly every scene of the film and would therefore require the most costumes and costume changes.

"Recovering addict," Grace corrected. "Joe says he's been working the program for two years now. Turned over a new leaf or something."

Not that she believed a word of it. She trusted Joe Lincoln—he was one of her preferred directors to work with—but he had an optimist's tendency to think the best of everyone that Grace didn't share. Because she liked Joe so much, she hated to think of him being taken in by a self-destructive burnout whose dumpster fire of a personal life could bring the entire production to a screeching halt.

What surprised Grace was that Joe's producing partner and wife, Nichole, had ever agreed to cast Deacon—an actor with a well-documented history of showing up to set so high he couldn't say his lines without an earpiece when he even bothered to show up at all. Nichole was the pragmatic business-minded half of the partnership who kept the ship afloat and cleaned up messes before they could turn into full-fledged disasters. The fact that she'd agreed to take on Scotty Deacon meant he'd either made one hell of a convincing case for himself, or they were so desperate Nichole hadn't had any other choice.

"I thought he was uninsurable," Carmen said, dragging a chair over from a nearby desk.

That was the main reason Deacon hadn't worked in four years. Once the insurance companies determined you were high-risk, the insane premiums tended to dissuade producers from taking a chance on you.

"Everyone's insurable if you've got enough money to pay for it." Grace cut a glance at the closed door to Joe's office and lowered her voice. "A friend of his put up the bond out of his own pocket."

Carmen's eyes widened as she fiddled with the height adjustment on the chair to accommodate her short frame. "Who?"

"Robbie Scarborough."

"Wow. Okay, then."

Robbie Scarborough had hit it big around the same time as Scotty, and for a while the two of them had run in the same pack of young Hollywood actors charmingly nicknamed the "Coochie Squad"—until they'd had a big falling out a few years ago. But if Robbie was personally bankrolling Scotty's comeback, they must have patched things up.

"Must be nice to have a friend willing to risk a few mil to get you a job, huh?" Carmen said sourly.

"Yeah," Grace agreed, unable to imagine a friendship worth handing over that kind of money. "Must be." She clicked her retractable pen as she glanced at the clock again. "The schedule's already tight, and I know the budget's stretched to the max, so if Deacon starts pulling his usual crap again..."

Carmen shook her head as she sipped her coffee. "Didn't he throw a chair at a director once?"

"Yeah, he did." Grace had done some reading up on Deacon after Joe told her he'd been cast in the lead, and what she'd learned had only intensified her misgivings. The guy hadn't just thrown a chair at Jerry Duncan, the two of them had gotten into an on-set shoving match that had devolved into a full-on brawl before the crew managed to pull them off each other.

Grace's job as script supervisor required her to be the director's near-constant companion, sitting next to him and taking meticulous notes on every take—time codes, lenses, camera movements, props, costumes—to ensure continuity when the footage was cut together in editing. That meant watching the actors closely and noting every detail of their performance: every action they made, when it happened and where, how they were sitting or standing, when and how they handled the props.

When an actor forgot a line or stage direction, Grace was the one who fed it to them, and if they deviated from the script or a previous take, it was her job to point it out. That could involve a lot of interaction with the talent, particularly if they were prone to flubbing lines or missing marks.

A bad apple could make her life a living hell for the duration of the shoot, and Scotty Deacon was one giant honking Red Delicious. If he decided to start throwing furniture or punches on this set, Grace would be right smack in the line of fire.

Carmen shook her head. "Gonna be an interesting shoot."

"I honestly don't know what Joe and Nichole were thinking," Grace said as she clicked her pen. "The guy's never been more than a pretty face, so why take such a big risk on him? There are dozens of actors more talented and more professional than Scotty Deacon. Why not pick one of them instead?"

"They must have their reasons," Carmen said with a shrug. "We'll just have to trust them."

"Yeah," Grace replied without zeal.

Trust wasn't something that came naturally to her. She'd always been too much of a worrier and control freak to embrace the concept of blind faith. As much as she respected Joe and Nichole, she'd sooner trust a clown hiding in a sewer grate than put her fate in the hands of someone like Scotty Deacon.

———

Scott Deacon stood in the hall outside the production office, frozen in place. He was early for his meeting with Joe Lincoln, which he'd been feeling pretty proud of until the sound of his name had stopped him in his tracks.

Two women inside the office ahead were talking about him, and in less than flattering terms.

He ought to be used to it by now. He had a string of critical and box office successes under his belt, he'd been inducted into the Academy when he was only twenty-six years old, and he had a star on the goddamn Walk of Fame, but all anyone seemed to care about was his mistakes. He had been branded a fuckup by the world at large, and a fuckup he would remain until he'd proven himself otherwise.

That was the whole point of doing this two-bit indie film for union scale. To show the world that Scott Deacon was clean and sober and willing to show up on time every day to do the work. To prove he still had talent and a career left in him.

Scott knew he had a lot to make up for, and he couldn't blame anyone for being reluctant to put their trust in him after all the shit he'd pulled over the years. All most people knew about him was what they'd read: the coke binges and drug psychosis, the run-ins with the law, the multiple stints in rehab. They didn't have any reason to believe that was all in his past, didn't know how hard he'd worked these last two years to finally get himself clean and stay that way. No one was writing articles about healthy, sober Scott Deacon, because the everyday struggle of recovery wasn't as entertaining as his drug-addled antics had been.

He'd known going into this job that everyone would be scrutinizing him with mistrust, waiting for him to revert to his old habits. He'd been prepared for that, but that wasn't what had stopped him cold in the hall outside Joe Lincoln's office.

The guy's never been more than a pretty face. There are dozens of actors more talented and more professional than Scotty Deacon. Why not pick one of them instead?

Hearing his own worst fears about himself voiced aloud by a stranger was a real punch to the diaphragm. Whoever the woman was, she'd landed a solid hit on Scott's deepest, darkest insecurities—the ones that woke him up at night in a cold sweat.

In his lowest moments, he was convinced he'd never had any real talent in the first place. That the successes he'd achieved in the past had been the net effect of luck, connections, and unearned confidence, and now that all three of those magic elements had abandoned him, he'd be revealed for what he really was: a no-talent waste of space.

Fame had been part of Scott's life for almost as long as he could remember. It had been a protective sheath woven into the fabric of his reality that had shielded him from certain kinds of scrutiny and a lot of the harsher realities of the world. When you were famous, it stopped mattering who you were underneath the fame, because the fame was all anyone cared about or reacted to.

But when that fame slipped away, it left you stripped bare and defenseless in the stark glare of an unforgiving world. Learning to cope with the back end of fame these last few years had been almost as difficult as learning to cope without drugs.

Navigating his recovery and his new reality as a celebrity washout was like kayaking over unfamiliar rapids. He didn't have any control over where the river went or how rough the ride was, so he had to exert his control in whatever small ways he could, by learning safety maneuvers and equipping himself with gear to cushion the blow. He'd had to learn coping mechanisms to manage himself and fill the empty spaces the fame and the drugs used to occupy in his life.

Scott had felt like he'd been doing a pretty decent job steering through the rapids lately, but hearing that woman's words just now, when he was about to meet with the man who'd be directing him in his first film in four years, was like having his kayak overturned by a rock hidden beneath the water's surface.

His hand moved reflexively to the pocket where he used to keep his pills. There was nothing there but gum now. He popped a piece with a shaking hand, trying to pacify the lingering itch for pharmaceutical intervention. Spearmint was a miserable substitute for the soothing, glorious numbness of an opioid high. Without that tranquilizing buffer to protect him from the real world, his brain felt like it was being dragged over a cheese grater.

He closed his eyes and put a hand against the wall as reality came crashing down around him, crumbling his thin veneer of confidence to dust.

Before anyone inside the office could see him, Scott turned and retreated back the way he'd come, back to the safety of his car where he could pull himself together in private.

GRACE WAS STILL CHATTING WITH CARMEN IN THE OUTER office when Scotty Deacon finally showed up for his meeting with Joe—fifteen minutes late, of course.

After working ten years in the entertainment industry, Grace liked to think she was immune to celebrity. She'd dealt with enough of them, both major and minor, that fame and beauty no longer made much of an impact on her.

But even she had to admit that in person, Scotty Deacon was something extraordinary. It wasn't just his good looks, which were the kind of off-the-Richter-scale gorgeous she'd encountered plenty of times before. It was his *presence*. She couldn't put it into words, but there was something about him, some sort of hypnotic intensity that worked like a supermagnet to pull all the focus in the room.

When Deacon's six-foot frame filled the doorway, he commanded attention without saying a word. Grace found herself sitting up a little straighter as his dark eyes skated over her and Carmen—then quickly dismissed them as insignificant.

"Joe Lincoln?" he demanded in a brusque, *I don't have time for niceties* tone that dared anyone to waste his time with intrusive chitchat.

Grace lifted her eyebrows along with her pen, and pointed toward the space's only office, which had a piece of white printer paper taped beside the doorframe with the words *JOE LINCOLN* written in large black capital letters.

"Get me a water," Deacon threw over his shoulder as he started for Joe's office. "Sparkling if you have it."

Charming. Grace could already tell working with him was going to be as much fun as a pap smear with a cold speculum.

"Which one of us were you talking to?" Carmen replied coolly as she leaned back in her chair. If her eyes could shoot knives, the back of Scotty Deacon's head would look like a cutlery starter set right about now.

He stopped and turned, fixing them both with a look that reeked of disdain. "I don't care. Whichever one of you is Joe's assistant."

Grace crossed her arms and met his gaze evenly. "That would be neither of us."

One of the first things she'd learned as a script supervisor was not to let herself be intimidated by anyone's entitled, imperious bullshit. Her job and the success of the entire film depended on her not being afraid to speak up when she had something to say, so she couldn't afford to be meek or passive.

What Grace's job *didn't* entail was taking water orders from washed-up cokeheads. If she gave ground now, it would set the tone for the rest of their working relationship, and he would go right on snapping orders at her and expecting to be obeyed.

Before Deacon could reply, the office door opened and Joe Lincoln peeked out. "Scott! I thought I heard your voice out here!" Despite being recently lauded by TheWrap as "the next great black director," Joe had a down-to-earth attitude and a friendly demeanor that tended to put everyone at their ease. But even his natural warmth couldn't quite take the chill out of the room.

Grace watched as Deacon turned to greet Joe and his scornful expression shifted into an ingratiating smile, smooth as the slide on a dimmer switch. She and Carmen exchanged a look as the two men shook hands.

"You guys all introduce yourselves already?" Joe asked, turning to Grace and Carmen.

"Not yet," Grace said, affixing a saccharine smile to her face as she got to her feet. She could pretend to be nice when the boss was around too.

Joe addressed Deacon as he gestured to Carmen. "This is Carmen Vargas, our costume supervisor."

"Nice to meet you," Carmen said flatly as she stood and shook hands with Deacon.

"And Grace Speer, our script supervisor."

"Hi." Deacon's voice was warm as popcorn butter, though his eyes grew distinctly cold as they focused on Grace.

She kept her expression neutral as she accepted the hand he offered. "So you're the famous Scotty Deacon."

"I prefer Scott."

"Of course you do," Grace said. "My mistake, *Scott*."

"I'm glad you all could meet." Joe's dimples peeked through his salt-and-pepper beard as he surveyed the three of them. "Since you're going to be spending a lot of time together when production starts."

Scott's eyes bored into Grace with unsettling intensity. The dark, brooding mystique he'd adopted as his post-puberty persona was on maximum display, his hazel-green gaze narrowed and his angular jaw set in a hard line. Most actors looked smaller in real life than on-screen, but Scott had bulked up considerably in his time away from the spotlight, and he struck an imposing figure in person.

Grace's smile grew even wider and more artificial as she stared him down, grateful for every one of the five feet ten inches that put her almost at his level. "Wonderful."

"Can't wait," Carmen said beside her.

Scott turned to Joe, affecting his genial expression again. "Shall we get started?"

"Absolutely! Can I get you a water or anything?"

"No thanks," Scott said as he followed Joe into the office. "I'm good."

"He seems nice," Carmen said dryly after the office door had closed behind them.

"Yeah, he's a real treat," Grace replied, turning to gather her purse. "I'm going home." She'd seen more than enough of Scotty Deacon for one night, and would rather ingest a gallon of live bees than hang around until he came out of Joe's office.

After bidding goodnight to Carmen, Grace collected her things and headed down to the parking lot. The production had rented a suite of second-floor offices in a dire-looking office park in Culver City, sandwiched between a Public Storage and a tile wholesaler. As she stepped outside, she saw an electric blue Tesla that probably cost more than the balance on her student loans parked diagonally across two spaces.

It had to be Deacon's car. Because of course he'd drive something that flashy and park it like a total asshole.

That was who she'd be working with on a near-daily basis for nine weeks in New Orleans starting next month. The guy who couldn't be bothered with common politeness unless the director was standing there, who'd assumed she was an assistant and tried to order her around like a servant, and who'd gifted her with a malevolent glare simply for refusing to be intimidated by him.

Scotty Deacon could get fucked.

2

Grace had been to New Orleans a handful of times before— for Mardi Gras once in college, for Jazz Fest a few years ago, and most recently last summer for an ill-advised bachelorette party that had turned into a forced death march around the French Quarter in high heels. It had always seemed like a nice enough place to visit as a tourist—French Quarter death marches with women she shouldn't be friends with anymore aside—but she wasn't sure what it would be like to actually live there for two months.

The production was using mostly local hires with the exception of a few principal cast members and department heads, and they'd put the out-of-towners up in rented accommodations around the city. The house the production company had rented for Grace turned out to be in Audubon Park—like, actually *on* Audubon Park itself. Literally, her front yard opened directly onto the park, which was not too shabby at all.

The house itself was small—just a cozy one-bedroom cottage —unlike the sprawling edifice immediately next to hers, which looked like an actual, honest-to-god castle, complete with gray stone blocks, Gothic arches, and leaded glass windows. The two houses appeared to have been built at the same time and shared architectural elements, only the castle was about eight times as large as Grace's little house.

They were actually adjoining, the travel coordinator had warned Grace, connected by an interior door in a shared wall between them. But there were secure locks on both sides, she'd promised in her email, so there was no worry about uninvited visits from whoever happened to be living in the mansion next door.

It was still a little weird, Grace decided, eyeing the wooden door in her living room that connected the two houses. The "secure lock" was nothing more than a simple slide bolt that looked about twenty years old. But it was probably fine, as long as the people next door weren't crazed ax murderers or total assholes.

The rest of the house was pretty great. It was fully furnished, and whoever did the decorating had a flair for mixing eclectic vintage and modern elements in a way that complemented the Tudor-influenced architecture. Besides the combined living and dining area, there was a kitchen and laundry room downstairs, and a bedroom, bathroom, and small office nook upstairs. Best of all, a pair of French doors in the bedroom opened onto a gorgeous balcony overlooking the park.

Grace dropped her bags next to the bed and ventured out onto the balcony, inhaling a lungful of the balmy Louisiana air. It was ridiculously lush and green here compared to Los Angeles or Arizona, where she'd grown up. The park was ringed by immense, billowing live oaks whose green limbs were festooned with strands of Spanish moss reminiscent of the Mardi Gras beads she'd seen hanging from the trees and street lamps on her drive through town. There was a shady jogging trail that ran past her front yard, and the bright green lawn beyond the trees was covered with picnickers taking advantage of the temperate spring weather.

Yeah, okay. Maybe it wasn't so bad here.

She spent the next couple hours unpacking her bags and familiarizing herself with the house before hitting up the nearby Winn-Dixie for some groceries. When she got back, there was music coming through the wall from the castle next door—and not just any music, but some truly god-awful death metal—confirming the place was indeed occupied. Too bad. It would have been nice—and quieter—if it had been empty.

Grace had spent most of her adult life living in apartments and sharing walls, so she wasn't inclined to begrudge someone the right to listen to their terrible music at a completely reasonable hour of the day. Anyway, she could barely hear it when she turned the TV on, so it was fine. Whatever.

The music finally shut off around nine, which she took as a positive sign that her neighbors were decently considerate. She stayed up another hour and a half to watch *The Daily Show*, then got into bed and spent some time reviewing the scenes they would be shooting tomorrow.

It was the first day of principal photography, and she was always anxious before her first day on a new set. She liked to make extra sure she was extra prepared.

Which she was. She totally had this. It was going to be fine. It always was. What she really needed to do was stop psyching herself out and get a decent night's sleep.

Grace made herself close her laptop and turn out the light. She lay in the strange bed and stared up at the swirly patterns in the plaster ceiling of the unfamiliar house. The wildlife sounds in the park had really ramped up since nightfall. Above the din of the crickets she could hear a chorus of frogs and an owl and—what even was that weird clicking sound?

Jesus, was that an insect? How big was that thing? She probably didn't want to know.

The sheets on the bed were scratchy and they made her skin feel raw. It was possible she was allergic to the detergent. Or maybe it was the air. The whole city was basically covered in mold, and god only knew what kinds of weird plants they had here. Just her luck, she was probably allergic to the entire state of Louisiana.

The mattress on the bed was too firm, and it kind of slanted to one side, which made her feel like she was in persistent danger of rolling onto the floor. As Grace lay in her slanty bed trying to sleep, she thought about the way the light in the bathroom had flickered when she first turned it on, and wondered if it was the sign of an electrical problem that could cause the house to catch on fire while she slept. You never knew what kind of wiring night-mares were hiding behind the walls in these old houses.

What if the local crew didn't know how to do their jobs tomorrow? What if none of the cast knew their lines? What if she screwed something up and let everybody down?

Maybe she should pull up Google Maps and double-check the directions to the soundstage one more time. Just to make sure she knew how to get there. Just in case.

No. Stop thinking. Just relax and go to sleep.

She took a deep breath and counted slowly to five as she exhaled.

When she got to four, the death metal started up again next door, even louder than before.

Unbelievable.

Grace rolled over and reached for her phone to check the time. 12:08. On a weeknight, for crying out loud. What kind of monster blared death metal after midnight?

Grumbling under her breath, she dragged a hoodie on over her T-shirt before stomping downstairs to give her neighbor a piece of her mind.

"You're going to be on your best behavior, right?"

Scott pressed the phone to his ear, scowling as he stared at the unnecessarily large painting of a nude woman that was hanging in the living room of his rental house in New Orleans.

"We already had this conversation," Scott told his agent, trying not to sound as irritable as he felt.

"And now we're having it again." Sabrina Keeling's English accent was clipped with impatience. "I want to make sure you understand what an enormous favor Joe and Nichole Lincoln are doing you by giving you this chance. I cannot underestimate exactly how indebted to them you are. No one else was even willing to have the conversation, much less hire you."

"I get it," Scott mumbled, turning his back on the ridiculous nude.

"If your mate Scarborough hadn't put up the bond—"

"I *get* it."

"Is this the patented Deacon charm you're planning on taking to your first day on set tomorrow?"

Scott gritted his teeth. "No, this is my *stop hounding me, Sabrina* voice. I'm stressed out enough as it is."

He was fucking terrified, in point of fact. Christ, he couldn't even remember the last time he'd gone to work sober.

"Good," Sabrina said. "I want you to be impressed by the precariousness of your situation. I worked hard to make this happen, so don't make me look like an arsehole."

"And I appreciate that, but—"

"Why can't you just stop there? 'I appreciate you, Sabrina.' End of sentence."

"*But*," Scott persisted stubbornly, "let's not pretend the extra press generated by my comeback isn't going to give Joe Lincoln and his obscure little film a nice PR boost."

"Only if you don't fuck this up. You fall on your face, Scotty boy, and both you and Joe Lincoln will be paying the price together. And do you know what people love even more than an underdog? Watching an underdog crash and burn."

Great. No pressure. Scott really needed to find an agent who was better at pep talks. Except Sabrina was the only agent who would touch him after his flameout, and she'd only taken him on as a favor to Robbie, who was one of her clients. They'd both stuck their necks out for him, and if he blew this it would make all of them look bad.

"I'm clearheaded, focused, and serious about the work," Scott said, tamping down his resentment as he paced across the house to the kitchen. "Things will be different than in the past."

"Glad to hear it." Sabrina's tone softened slightly. "Try to get some sleep. And knock 'em dead tomorrow, darling."

Scott bid her goodbye and shoved his phone back in his pocket. Sabrina was right. He needed to get a good night's sleep tonight, but the chances of that were pretty much nil. Not when he was this wired. His brain was racing a mile a minute, fixating on all the ways tomorrow could go wrong.

This was his moment of truth. He had one chance to prove he could still do this, and if he fucked it up, no one would ever give him another shot.

Hell, he'd barely even managed to get this shot. Nichole Lincoln had taken a lot more convincing than her husband. Scott had basically had to grovel to win her approval, and that was *after* Robbie had agreed to sign on as an investor in order to foot the bill for Scott's insurance premium.

Scott could feel the doubt starting to creep in, eating away at his self-esteem. He'd spent so much time the last few months trying to convince people he could do this, he'd almost started to believe it himself. But now that he was actually here and facing the imminent reality of his first day on a movie set in four years, all that false confidence he'd been projecting had started to abandon him.

Everybody was worried about him showing up for work, but showing up was the easy part. Scott knew he could do that. It was what came next that sent him into a cold sweat. Because once he was there, he had to actually be *good* at it.

What if he went in tomorrow and sucked?

What if he needed the drugs to fuel his art, and without them he was nothing?

What if his so-called "talent" had been a side effect of the high, and now that he was clean, everyone would realize he'd never been any good at a single fucking thing his entire useless life?

Fuck. He needed to put a stop to this spiral before it got any worse. The trifecta of stress, sleep deprivation, and Sabrina's well-intentioned chiding was doing a real number on him.

This right here was why he needed to start working again. He needed the distraction, needed to keep his mind occupied and his body active to stave off the negative thoughts before they could take control.

So Scott did what he always did when the demons started whispering in his ear: he went to work out. Exercise was the only thing that drowned it out. The focus, repetition, and loud music pushed the unwanted thoughts out of his head, and the physical exhaustion afterward helped keep them away, for a little while at least.

The large, parquet-floored front room of his rental house, which appeared to have originally been designed as a ballroom, had been equipped as a home gym for him. A decent space to work out had been one of the few stipulations Scott had put into his contract—for this very reason. He needed someplace he could blow off steam in the middle of the night when insomnia struck.

He'd already worked out once today, but clearly that hadn't been enough. Maybe the second time would be the charm that would let him get some sleep tonight.

Pulling up his workout mix, Scott cranked the volume on his speakers loud enough to make the windows vibrate and drown out all the noise in his head. Then he grabbed a jump rope and started counting, losing himself in the rhythm.

It took him a minute to realize the off-beat thumping he kept hearing beneath the bass was someone banging on the door. And another few seconds to figure out it wasn't the front door they were banging on, but the one in the living room that connected to the smaller house next door—the one he'd thought was empty.

Shit, and it was after midnight too.

Scott wiped the sweat from his brow as he slid the bolt back, fully prepared to apologize for the loud music.

Except it was *her.*

Grace Speer, the woman who'd unknowingly eviscerated him with an offhand comment in the production office last month, was not only his script supervisor for the next nine weeks, but also apparently his next-door neighbor.

Fucking fantastic.

From her expression, he could tell she was just as surprised and disconcerted by this development as he was. They regarded one another warily as the music continued to blare in the front room.

He'd only seen her one other time since their ill-fated first meeting in the production office: at the table read, during which Scott had successfully avoided speaking to her or making eye contact. But her face was forever emblazoned in his memory. Particularly those stormy blue-gray eyes that seemed to stare right through him.

Those same sharp eyes were staring him down right now, even as her teeth bit down on her lower lip, betraying a hint of uncertainty. Her statuesque figure and graceful features could have been crafted by Michelangelo. She was certainly as cold as a marble sculpture, although at the moment, in an oversized USC sweatshirt, fuzzy pink socks, and flannel pajama pants adorned with what he was pretty sure were hedgehogs, she was slightly less intimidating and probably unaware that her chin-length ash brown hair was sticking up rather hilariously on one side. If they'd never met before, Scott might be tempted to call her cute—or even, if he was feeling generous, beautiful.

Her lips moved, but her words were lost to the boisterous guitar riff emanating from the speakers. "What?" he said, frowning at her.

"The music," she shouted, cupping her hands around her mouth. "Could you turn it down?"

Right, the music. He was the asshole blasting loud music late at night when normal people were trying to sleep.

Fumbling his phone out of his pocket, he tapped the screen and the music shut off. "I didn't know anyone was living next door," he offered as an apology.

Grace's full lips pursed in irritation. "Well, I am."

They stared at one another across the threshold between their respective rental homes. A bead of sweat trickled into Scott's eye, and he reached up to wipe it away with his forearm.

It occurred to him that the next two months would be a lot more pleasant if he could befriend this woman who had such a low opinion of him, and who he'd be working with closely every single day. At the very least, he should apologize for the music at this late hour when they both had an early call time tomorrow.

He just...couldn't bring himself to do it. Apparently he still had some nursing to do on that grudge.

"Thank you," Grace said icily, when it became clear Scott wasn't going to say anything else. "Goodnight."

And she shut the door in his face.

3

Grace was not a natural early riser, but her job frequently required it, so she'd learned to adapt accordingly. Coffee was an absolute must.

When her alarm went off at five in the morning, she could already detect the heavenly scent of French roast wafting upstairs from the coffee maker she'd programmed the night before. She didn't like running late or rushing around, so she always factored in extra time to calmly sit and enjoy her coffee while she psyched herself up for the day ahead. It was a necessary part of her routine, and the balcony off her bedroom made a perfect spot for her pre-dawn meditation and caffeine infusion.

There was a chill in the air that morning, so she pulled her hoodie on before carrying her coffee and laptop out to the black metal cafe table to go over the day's scenes one last time. It was muggier outside than she was used to, but not unpleasantly so, and the air was perfumed with the heady scent of jasmine. The sun wouldn't be up for another hour at least, but the birds were already kicking up a ruckus in the trees of the park, and a few ambitious joggers and dog walkers were making their way around the path below.

Grace was only halfway through her coffee when she heard the door open on the balcony next to hers—the one that belonged to her neighbor, Scott Deacon.

Lucky her.

She still couldn't believe she was stuck living right next door to the spoiled brat actor. When he'd opened the adjoining door last night, she'd nearly had a heart attack. But at least he'd turned down his music without making a scene. The man wasn't entirely bereft of civility. Just *mostly*.

A good neighbor would have apologized and promised not to do it again. Instead, Grace had gotten an annoyed grunt and a cold glare, which seemed to be his default expression.

As Scott stepped out onto the balcony this morning, Grace saw that he was wearing the same athletic shorts he'd been wearing last night and the same nothing else whatsoever, making this the second time in six hours she'd gotten an up-close view of his bare chest. And arms. And abs.

Whatever the man had been doing with himself since dropping out of the public eye certainly seemed to agree with him. He must have put on at least twenty pounds of pure muscle since the last movie Grace had seen him in, and he had this stubble thing happening at the moment that was really working for him. She knew from his bio that he was only thirty-two—two years younger than her—but the last few years seemed to have aged him out of the boyish good looks that had been his hallmark and into a rugged handsomeness that looked even better on him. The whole effect was just very...wow. Talk about a thirst trap.

Except you hate him, remember?

Scott rubbed his hands through his dark hair as he wandered over to the balcony railing to gaze out at the park. He didn't seem to have noticed Grace sitting there on the next balcony over, and she wasn't sure whether she should say something. On the one hand, she didn't want him to think she was lurking in the dark, spying on him like some sort of creeper. On the other, she was entitled to sit on her own balcony—and anyway she'd been here first. Technically, *he* was intruding on *her* solitude.

She was just on the verge of clearing her throat or coughing or something to politely cue him in to her presence, when he stretched both his arms overhead and twisted his torso away from her. The sight of all those muscles flexing and rippling over his back and shoulders rendered Grace momentarily mute.

When Scott twisted back the other direction, he noticed her with a start—right as she was staring at him with her mouth hanging open, *of course*.

"Morning," she said, pulling herself together enough to give him a false, bright smile as she saluted him with her coffee mug.

"Morning," he replied warily.

His expression wasn't exactly friendly, and as the silence stretched out between them, Grace wondered again if he'd even recognized her. They hadn't interacted much at the table read, and he'd been so terse last night when she'd pounded on his door that she hadn't been able to tell whether he remembered their brief meeting in the production office.

It would probably be better if he *didn't* remember their first meeting—not that last night's encounter had gone all that much better. Grace had no idea if this prickliness was just Scott's natural reaction to strangers, or a special treat he reserved for crew members who'd gotten on his bad side.

Regardless, she probably ought to make an effort to be civil. Pissing off the talent wouldn't make her job any easier.

"Nice view," she offered in a lame attempt at small talk, realizing too late that he might think the view she was referring to was his naked torso. "I meant the park," she clarified as her cheeks heated. "It's beautiful up here, isn't it?"

"Sure," Scott agreed without enthusiasm. "Listen, I'm sorry about last night."

Well, that was something. An actual apology. Maybe there was a human being lurking in there after all.

"It's fine," Grace told him, eager to put the incident behind them. "Don't worry about it."

"I have insomnia," he explained, rubbing his thumb and fingertips together at his side. "So I exercise late at night at lot. But I'll wear headphones from now on."

"Does it help?"

His brow furrowed. "What?"

"The exercise. Does it help your insomnia?"

"Sometimes."

"I get insomnia too," Grace said, seizing on this crumb of common ground between them and lurching into nervous babble. "Usually when I'm feeling anxious about something, which is a lot of the time, actually. If I'm not busy doing something then I end up obsessing about everything I need to do, which makes it hard to sleep. I usually just take a Xanax when it gets too bad though."

Scott stared at her without expression. "I'm a recovering drug addict."

"Right." She pinched her lips together with her fingers, desperately wishing she could put that last sentence back in her mouth. "So probably no Xanax for you, then."

"No."

This conversation was turning into a disaster of epic proportions, and Grace still wasn't sure if Scott had even recognized her. So she did what any reasonable person would do under the circumstances: she fled.

"Welp," she said, getting to her feet as she gathered up her laptop and coffee mug, "this has been a super fun chat, but I need to get ready for work." Without waiting for him to respond, she darted inside.

"See you on set," Scott called out as the door closed behind her.

So much for him not recognizing her.

THE FIRST DAY OF SHOOTING ON ANY FILM WAS INEVITABLY chaotic. Everyone was always scrambling around trying to get their bearings and figure out where everything was, what they were supposed to be doing, and who everybody else was. The mood reminded Grace of the first day of school, except that on a film set, unlike the first day of school, they actually had to get work done and not just goof off in homeroom. Which could be a bit of a challenge, what with all the chaos.

One of the things she loved about working with Joe Lincoln was that he set a good example for everyone else in the eye of the storm by being focused, unflappable, and unfailingly polite.

Usually.

Today, he was maybe a little bit flapped.

An alarming percentage of the crew had been late this morning. Apparently this was normal for New Orleans, where people had a more laid-back attitude about everything, including showing up for work on time. On top of that, a key prop was nowhere to be found and two of the sets weren't finished yet, which meant lots of distracting construction noise as they scrambled to get them done.

As if all that wasn't enough, the lead actor was having trouble with his lines. *A lot* of trouble with his lines.

"Cut!" Joe called out, for the fifth time in half as many minutes. "That's the old line, Scott. Grace, can you please give him the new line?" Making everything more difficult was the fact that they'd gotten a new set of revision pages just this morning that included the first of today's scenes.

"*How am I supposed to know what to believe? You change your tune more than Spotify,*" Grace read from the new goldenrod script pages.

"Is that really the line we're going with?" Scott asked, frowning.

"That's the line we're going with," Joe confirmed.

"Am I the only one who thinks that line sucks?"

Grace and Joe exchanged a look.

"Let's just stick to the script for now," Joe said with remarkable patience. "Once we get a printable take of the line as written, we can try some improvising."

They started the scene over, and this time Scott made it halfway through—which was an improvement on the last take—before stumbling over the words and barking out, "Line!"

Grace ground her teeth together and fed him his line. It was part of her job to prompt the actors when they forgot their lines, but she didn't appreciate being barked at. There was a way to ask nicely, and shouting "line" at the top of your lungs wasn't it.

Nice wasn't an adjective that modified the proper noun *Scott Deacon*, however.

"*Goddammit!*" he yelled when a production assistant's cell phone went off in the middle of a take. "Could we get a little fucking professionalism around here?"

"Cut," Joe said, rubbing his hands over the top of his shiny, shaved head. He'd been rubbing it so much it was starting to take on a polish. "Will everyone please double-check that your phones are silent? Thank you." His tone was alarmingly strained. Grace had never once seen Joe lose his temper, but she could feel the tension radiating off him, like it was taking all his effort to hold it in check today.

"And could she possibly stand somewhere other than directly in my eyeline?" Scott snapped, gesturing irritably at Carmen, who was standing off to one side of the soundstage being perfectly unobtrusive.

"Carmen?" Joe said with a pleading look. "Would you mind moving out of Scott's eyeline for me, please?"

"Sure," Carmen replied sweetly before cutting an icy look in Scott's direction. "I'd be happy to."

Grace knew that look, and it meant a certain lead actor's wardrobe was going to be overstarched and itchy tomorrow. Served him right too.

"Let's try that again," Joe said, and the actors moved back into position.

"Quiet on the set," the first assistant director called out. "Roll camera."

"Rolling."

"Marker."

"Twenty-four, A, take nine."

"Action," Joe said.

There was a protracted pause, then Scott growled, "Line."

"Cut," Joe said with a long-suffering sigh.

Two hours. That was how long it had taken to get a single decent take out of Scott and move on to the next setup. Not only could he not seem to get his lines right, but he wasn't hitting his marks consistently, which was going to wreak havoc with the continuity in editing. Grace was actually starting to go hoarse from correcting him so often, and every time she had to point out that he'd screwed up—again—it earned her a stony glare. Like it was *her* fault he couldn't do his job.

So yeah. Fuck Scott Deacon and fuck the private jet he flew in on.

Beside her, Joe leaned forward in his chair and rubbed his temples as the carpenters working on the unfinished set started hammering again. "First days are always tough," he said, sounding like he was trying to convince himself. "We'll get better."

Except *they* weren't the problem. *Scott* was the problem.

Grace knew better than to say that out loud though.

"Give him time," Joe said, cutting a sideways glance at her.

They'd worked together enough that they could usually read each other's minds by now. "He'll find his footing."

Joe seemed like he needed the pep talk more than she did, so Grace gave him her best encouraging smile. "I'm sure he will."

He'd better. Or else the whole production was in serious trouble.

"What a dick," Carmen complained over lunch. "Hundred bucks says he doesn't even remember my name. Can't be bothered to learn his lines, can't be bothered to learn any of the crew's names, but god forbid anyone should stand in His Majesty's precious eyeline."

"He wouldn't let us play music in the makeup trailer this morning," grumbled Tamika, the head of the makeup department. "We always play music in the makeup trailer."

"Seriously, what a dick," Carmen said.

"I guess we should count ourselves lucky he hasn't thrown a chair at anyone," Grace said as she picked the peas out of her chicken pot pie. "Yet."

"He's clean now though, right?" Tamika pushed her salad around on her plate. "I mean, he seems sober, doesn't he?"

He did. Grace had to give him that much. For all that he'd been a pain in the ass, Scott hadn't seemed high—just incompetent and dickish. Based on her encounter with him on the balcony this morning, she assumed he really had cleaned up his act.

He just hadn't bothered to learn his lines.

"Maybe that's why he's so pissy," Grace said. "Maybe he's nicer when he's high."

Tamika frowned as she speared an olive with her fork. "Didn't he get arrested for urinating on a cop once? Only a white boy could get away with shit like that without getting shot."

Carmen nodded. "And let's not forget the time he wandered into his neighbor's house by mistake and passed out in their bedroom buck naked. How out of your head do you have to be to go into the wrong house?"

"You know they put me up in the house right next door to his," Grace said, reaching for her Diet Coke.

Carmen's eyes widened. "Girl. You better double-check that all your doors are locked at night."

"Or not," Tamika added, smirking. "What?" she said off Carmen's raised eyebrow. "He may be a jerk, but he's a hot jerk. I know you've seen those biceps."

"It's one thing to admire from a safe distance," Carmen said, "but I hope we all love ourselves too much to mess with the likes of Scotty Deacon."

"Amen," Grace said. She'd sooner douche with ghost pepper salsa than let that asshole between her legs.

SCOTT PACED AROUND HIS HOUSE LIKE A CAGED TIGER, TOO restless and enraged to sit still.

He'd blown it. Well and truly. Absolutely fucked up his first day back at work.

As worried as he'd been that it would go badly, somehow it had managed to go even *worse* than he'd feared, which was a serious fucking accomplishment.

The most infuriating part was that he'd been so prepared. He'd known the script and his character backward and forward. He'd *learned* that shit.

But then he'd gotten to set this morning, and they'd handed him new pages for his very first scene of the day. Even though he'd had a conversation with Joe about this exact issue, in which he'd made it clear that he didn't want any last-minute script changes because he needed time to absorb and memorize the material before he was expected to perform it.

Joe had been apologetic about it, of course, but it was out of his hands. The production company backing the film had insisted on the changes because they'd just finished negotiating a new marketing partnership and needed to work the sponsoring brand into the script. So that was great. Nice to know artistic integrity was such a priority.

And then there'd been all that fucking construction noise going on while Scott was trying to learn his new lines at the last second. He hadn't been able to get away from it anywhere. They had a goddamn power saw running outside by the trailers, and a whole fucking chorus of hammers that started pounding inside the soundstage whenever Joe said cut.

All the racket had felt like it was drilling directly into Scott's brain, making it impossible to focus. As if he hadn't already had enough stress and anxiety to deal with today, knowing everyone was watching him and judging him. Expecting him to fail.

And he'd done just exactly that.

The guy's never been more than a pretty face. There are dozens of actors more talented and more professional than Scotty Deacon.

Grace's words had dogged him all day. Every time he'd flubbed a line, he felt them hanging over his head like a buzzing neon sign. Whenever Grace corrected him—which was pretty much constantly—he couldn't help thinking about the contempt he knew she was hiding beneath her studiously bland expression and faux-diplomatic tone.

She'd gotten inside his head, dammit. Every time he looked at her, it rattled him, and the harder Scott had tried to pull his shit together, the more he'd screwed up.

Which was too fucking bad, because she was the script supervisor, so she was going to be sitting there watching him every goddamned second.

Scott shoved two pieces of gum into his mouth and dug his phone out of his pocket. He needed someone to talk him down, and there was only one person who could do it.

"Hey, kid," Alfie Crosby said when he answered his phone. "How'd your first day go?"

In Scott's very first feature film role seventeen years ago, he had played Alfie's son. The veteran actor had taken a nervous teenaged Scott under his wing on set, and the two had stayed in touch ever since. Over the intervening years, Alfie had become more of a mentor and father figure than Scott's own distracted father had ever been.

Russell Deacon's career as an Oscar-winning director consumed most of his attention, leaving little time for the offspring of his first, short-lived marriage. When Scott's drug problems got out of hand, his father had been one of the first people to distance himself.

Alfie had been one of a very small group of people who hadn't turned his back on Scott, and he was the only person in Scott's life who truly understood what he was going through, because Alfie was a recovering alcoholic himself.

"Hey, Alfie." Scott squeezed the phone in a sweaty hand as he paced across the kitchen. "Remember how afraid I was that I'd shit the bed and make a fool of myself on my first day?"

"Yeah." There was a murmur in the background on Alfie's end like he had the television on.

"Well, that's exactly what I did."

Alfie made a dismissive noise. "I'll bet it wasn't that bad. We're always harsher judges of ourselves than others."

"Yeah, not in this case. I really blew it."

The television murmur went silent, as if Alfie had muted it or gone into another room. "Tell me what happened."

Scott sighed, closing his eyes as he dredged up the memories. "I couldn't get my lines out. I knew them, but then we got last-minute pages and it threw me. I kept blanking, or mixing the old lines up with new. I couldn't remember my cues, I didn't hit my marks. I was like a complete amateur out there, like I'd never done this before."

"That's just nerves." Alfie's voice was deep and velvety, like an old-time radio host. "You put too much pressure on yourself, and this is what happens. You gave yourself the yips."

Scott pulled the refrigerator door open and stared at neatly stacked rows of dietician-prepared meals designed to maximize his physique. He'd fallen behind on his macros today, which meant he probably needed to eat two more meals before bed, but the thought of eating anything made him queasy. "I'm pretty sure Joe Lincoln thinks I can't act." He grabbed a plastic container without even reading the label and slammed the fridge door shut.

"Lincoln's seen enough cases of first-day nerves to know better."

Scott stared glumly at the meal he'd chosen: "guilt-free" Italian chicken parmesan. "Shit, Alfie, what am I gonna do? How do I go back there tomorrow and face everyone?" He shoved his "guilt-free" dinner in the microwave and angrily jabbed his finger at the keypad.

"You just do," Alfie said. "The same way you stay sober: one day at a time, one hour at a time, one minute at a time. Focus on what's right in front of you that you can control. Prepare for tomorrow's scenes, try to get some sleep, and when you walk back onto that set, don't dwell on past mistakes."

"Right. Like that's possible."

"You're too hard on yourself. No one is expecting perfection from you but you. Everybody fucks up sometimes. What matters is what you do after. So you pick yourself up and you try again. You think everybody's rooting against you, but they're not. For one thing, they don't give two shits about you, because they're all too busy worrying about how they might fuck up. But more importantly, it's not the worst thing in the world to show a little vulnerability. That makes you human, and when people see that you're human, they're more likely to be on your side."

"No one on that set is on my side. I managed to make an enemy of the scripty, the costume department, the makeup department, most of the PAs—"

"All on the first day? That's gotta be a record, even for you."

"I know." Scott watched his dinner rotate inside the microwave, feeling even more dispirited than before.

"Have you tried—I'm just spitballing here—not acting like an asshole?"

"This *was* me trying not to be an asshole," Scott said petulantly.

"Clearly not very hard."

"Has it occurred to you that this is just who I am? That I'm not capable of being anything other than an asshole?"

"Bullshit," Alfie shot back. "I know you, kid, and you're made of better stuff than that. Your problem is that you spend too much time inside your own head. Try focusing all that nervous energy on someone other than yourself for a change. Take two seconds to think about the people around you and what you can do to make their lives a little less miserable. You do that, and not only will you not be obsessing so much about your own mistakes, but people might even start to like you a little."

"I guess." It was good advice that seemed simple enough, but Scott wasn't convinced he could pull it off.

The microwave dinged and Scott took his dinner out of the oven, burning his finger on the escaping steam in the process. *Fucking perfect.*

"What's Step Ten?" Alfie asked as Scott sucked on his injured finger.

Scott sighed. "Continue to take a personal inventory and admit it promptly when we're wrong." It was one of his least favorite of the Twelve Steps, and the one that most consistently seemed to trip him up.

"Did you do that today?" Alfie asked in a reproachful tone.

"No."

"Then you better pull your head out of your ass and do some work on Step Ten, huh?"

Grimacing, Scott carved off a piece of chicken breast coated with a micro-layer of soggy breadcrumbs and stabbed it with his fork. "Yeah."

"Also—and I know you're gonna hate this—you need to start asking for help."

"Alfie—"

"Shut up and listen. People can't help you unless they know you need help. Those people on that set are on your team, whether they like you or not. You've all got the same goal. So when you need their help, tell them. Go sit down with Joe Lincoln tomorrow and talk to him about what's going on and what he can do to help you through it."

"Fine." Scott shoved the bite of chicken parmesan in his mouth. It tasted like his mood.

"I mean it."

"I know."

"So you're really gonna do it? Promise me."

Scott forced himself to swallow the bland, dry chicken in his mouth. "I promise," he answered grudgingly.

"Good. Buck up, kid. Today was just a bump in the road. Hopefully tomorrow will be better. And if not, then the day after probably will."

"Sure." The one bite of chicken parmesan sat in his stomach like a lead ball. Scott dumped the rest of it into the trash, uneaten. His macros could go fuck themselves today.

"Hey. You can do this," Alfie said in a softer voice. "I believe in you. And Joe Lincoln believes in you too, or you wouldn't have this job. Trust us, even if you can't trust yourself."

Before Scott could reply, there was a knock on the door. Not the front door—the one that connected to Grace's house. Because that was just what he needed tonight: more face time with the woman who'd destroyed his confidence.

"Is that your door?" Alfie asked.

"Yeah, I better let you go," Scott said as he strode through the living room. "Thanks, Alfie. Seriously. I mean it."

"That's what I'm here for. Night, kid."

"Night." Scott slid the phone into his pocket, steeling himself before opening the door.

Grace stood on the other side, looking at him like he was the last person in the world she wanted to talk to.

The feeling was one hundred percent mutual.

4

G race was having a spectacularly shitty night.

Thanks to Scott, they hadn't wrapped until ten, after which she'd had to stay to finish her daily reports for the editor, so by the time she finally got home she'd put in a sixteen-hour day. That was on top of the not-so-great sleep she'd gotten last night—also thanks to Scott, and his predilection for blasting death metal after midnight. Basically, everything bad about her day was his fault.

All she wanted to do was curl up on her couch with a glass of wine and decompress in front of the TV for a while before crawling into bed.

There was just one small problem: the power in her stupid house was out.

She could see lights on in the other houses around the park, so it wasn't a neighborhood outage. It was only her house that had lost power. Wonderful.

For a moment, Grace seriously considered saying "screw it" and going straight to bed without dealing with it. But then she'd come home to the same problem tomorrow night, and meanwhile all the food in her refrigerator would spoil, and anyway her phone was almost dead, and she needed to charge it and her laptop for tomorrow and...*crap*.

Instead of going to bed like she wanted, she set off in search of the breaker box. Using her dying phone as a flashlight, she searched the entire house from top to bottom, and when that didn't turn up anything she went out and searched around the outside of the house.

No luck.

The breaker box must be inside Scott's house. His lights were on next door, so whatever was wrong with her power didn't seem to be affecting him. But if the two houses had originally been built together as one, they probably shared a breaker box.

Fucking fantastic.

Because after a long day of dealing with Scott Deacon and his attitude problem, what Grace *really* wanted to do was come home and interact with him even more.

Muttering under her breath, she trudged back inside, unlocked the connecting door, and knocked—a little more politely than last night. After several long moments she heard the bolt on the other side slide back, and Scott opened the door.

He quirked a quizzical eyebrow at her without saying a word, because apparently even a civil hello was too much effort for him.

"Sorry to bother you—again," Grace said, pasting a patently false smile on her face. "But my power's out, and I think we share a breaker box."

His eyes flicked to the pitch blackness behind her, then he stepped back to allow her inside. "Come on. It's in the laundry room."

"Thanks," she said, letting out a breath as she stepped over the threshold into his living room, grateful he hadn't just turned her away.

His house was decorated similarly to hers, but with a little more rock star flair than her humbler cottage. Two huge leather sofas flanked a carved stone coffee table, a baby grand piano sat in front of a set of bay windows, and an enormous painting of a naked woman adorned the wall opposite a giant flat-screen television. *Classy.*

"This way," Scott said, and set off without a backward glance.

Grace followed him through the living room, past a dining table long enough to seat a dozen people, into a spacious kitchen, and to the small laundry room set off to one side.

He opened the ancient-looking metal panel set into the wall and peered at it, his brow furrowing. "Um..."

"Those are fuses," Grace said with a sinking heart. "That's a fuse box instead of a breaker box."

"Yeah." Scott rubbed the back of his neck. "Do you know how to replace a fuse?"

She could Google it, probably, but the real problem was— "I'm pretty sure you have to have a new fuse to replace it with. I don't suppose you've seen any extra fuses lying around?"

"Not that I've noticed."

"Do you mind if I...?" She gestured to the cabinets in the laundry room.

"Knock yourself out." He dug his phone out of his pocket. "I'll call the landlord."

Scott stepped out of the room while Grace rummaged through the cabinets and drawers in search of a fresh fuse. She found laundry detergent, fabric softener—TMZ would probably be thrilled to know that Scott Deacon liked the dryer sheets with the teddy bear on the box—spare light bulbs, a toolbox with an assortment of screwdrivers and wrenches, a toilet plunger...but no extra fuses.

By the time she gave up and wandered into the kitchen, Scott was just getting off the phone.

"Apparently they don't keep spare fuses in the house because they don't want the tenants messing with the panel themselves."

"That's probably wise," Grace said. "Inconvenient for me, but wise."

"He says he'll have an electrician come out first thing in the morning. Sounds like this happens a lot."

"Terrific. So in the meantime..." She glanced toward the yawning blackness waiting for her in her house.

"In the meantime, you're kind of screwed, I guess." He almost managed to sound sympathetic.

Grace rubbed her hands over her face in frustration. "Now I'm really wishing I'd charged my phone and laptop before I left the set."

"You could charge them here," Scott suggested, surprising her. Based on their acquaintance so far, she wouldn't have trusted him to call 911 if she was on fire, and now here he was, calling the landlord for her and inviting her to hang out in his house and share his electricity.

"I don't want to impose," she hedged, cringing at the thought of spending even more time with him. She kind of really did need to charge her laptop tonight though. The alternative was to try to find a coffee shop that was still open, but she was so tired, the thought of it legitimately made her want to cry.

"It's fine," Scott said, flicking a dismissive hand. "Really." And then he smiled at her for the first time ever—a brilliant, beautiful, movie star smile that seemed to transform his whole appearance. "What are neighbors for, right?"

Grace gulped as her stomach did a traitorous somersault. Holy shit, that smile of his was downright lethal—when he bothered to deploy it.

He tilted his head toward the door to her house. "Go get your stuff."

It would only take an hour or so to charge her electronics. One hour of imposing on Scott's hospitality, and then she could collapse into her own bed. She could survive his company for one more hour, surely.

"Thank you. I really appreciate it," Grace said, and went and got her laptop and phone charger out of the bag she'd left by her front door. "Where should I plug in?" she asked when she came back.

"Wherever you want." Scott had settled onto one of the couches and was slouched back against the cushions with his bare feet propped on the coffee table and a copy of the script in his hand. "There's outlets everywhere." He waved vaguely without looking up at her.

After a brief survey of her surroundings, Grace chose an outlet in the dining room, dragging one of the chairs over to the wall to set her devices on while they charged. Once that was accomplished, she straightened, feeling momentarily panicky because *now what?*

Should she go back to her own house and sit in the dark? Or stay here with Scott? And if she stayed here, would they have to, like, *talk* or something? Because *ugh.*

"You're welcome to hang out here while you wait," he said, apparently sensing her hesitation. "There's beer in the fridge if you want something to drink. You can help yourself."

"I didn't think you—" She stopped, snapping her mouth firmly shut, because his addiction wasn't any of her business.

His face was completely devoid of expression as he lifted his eyes to hers. "I keep it on hand for guests. Beer was never my poison of choice, anyway."

Somehow, Grace managed to resist asking him what *was* his poison of choice, because again, not her business. And also, she did not actually want to know the sordid details of his life. It would be easier to work with him if she didn't have to imagine him doing things like snorting coke off a prostitute—which was how he'd reportedly spent his twenty-first birthday, and was a thing she dearly wished she'd never read about him, now that she was standing in his living room beneath a giant watercolor nude.

"Sorry," she said, biting her lip. "I didn't mean to—"

"Don't worry about it." He looked back down at his script. "It's not like my history's a secret."

Grace retreated to the kitchen in search of the offered beer, grateful for something to do with herself. "Wow, you really like chicken," she observed, staring into the fridge. The shelves were lined with plastic containers of custom-prepared meals, almost all of which involved some sort of chicken. Chicken and green beans, chicken stir-fry, chicken salad, chicken chili. It was *a lot* of chicken.

"Like's a strong word," Scott replied ruefully. "I have to consume two hundred grams of protein a day to maintain my current muscle mass, and I don't like fish, so..."

"Sounds unpleasant."

"It's not like I do it for fun," Scott said. "It's literally what they pay me for."

There were two varieties of local craft beer in his refrigerator, and Grace took her time choosing between them. "Bottle opener?" she asked, settling on the one called Canebreak, because she'd never had it before.

"Drawer to the right of the fridge."

Grace popped the top off her beer, then cast her eyes around the kitchen in search of the trash.

"Cabinet to the left of the sink," Scott supplied before she could ask.

She wandered back into the living room and sank down on the couch across from him. "I worked with an actor once who used to drink chicken smoothies every day. He'd throw a whole chicken breast into the blender with a bunch of raw spinach, and walk around the set drinking it like a protein shake."

Scott's hazel-green eyes cut her way. "I tried that once."

"Really?" She scrunched her nose in disgust.

"Made me throw up. Never did it again."

Grace nodded and took a swig of beer. "So when you finish this shoot are you going to pig completely out and eat all the things? Because I totally would."

"Depends if I've got another project lined up after this one."

"Do you?"

"No."

The beer was already working to loosen the knot of tension that had been lodged at the base of Grace's neck all day. "This is good," she said, gesturing at the bottle as she settled back into the couch.

"I wouldn't know. I just bought what the guy at Whole Foods recommended."

"Well the guy at Whole Foods has excellent taste."

Scott watched impassively as she sipped her beer, making Grace wish he'd go back to not looking at her. Though his gaze lacked the animosity he'd exhibited earlier in the day, it still made her uncomfortable to be the focus of his attention.

He sat up, dropping his bare feet to the floor. "Actually, since you're here...there is something you could do for me."

"What?" she asked warily. If he asked her to fetch him a fucking water again, she'd—well, she'd probably go get it for him, because he was doing her a favor and she was a guest in his home. But she'd be silently resentful while she did it.

"Would you mind helping me run lines?" He looked pained, like it embarrassed him to ask. "I haven't quite mastered all the new pages."

"Really?" she replied dryly. "I hadn't noticed."

Instead of the glare she'd expected in response, he blew out a breath, shaking his head. If she didn't know better, she'd almost think he was *amused*.

Running lines after work was the sort of thing that fell firmly into the category of Not Her Job, but since Scott was letting her charge her devices in his house, it seemed like the least she could do. Besides, it was an easy way to pass the time without either of them having to strain themselves attempting to make small talk. Not to mention, Scott actually *knowing* his lines would make everyone's life a hell of a lot easier on set—particularly hers.

Grace held out her hand for the script. "Give it here."

She spent the next hour running lines with him. They went over all the new pages until he had them down cold, and then went back and ran through the whole script from top to bottom. She was surprised to discover he had all the old stuff memorized perfectly. It wasn't that he hadn't prepared at all, it was just the revisions that had given him trouble today, because he hadn't had as much time to learn them.

Between that and the fact that Scott had been perfectly civil to her all night—though still not quite what she'd call friendly—Grace was starting to think maybe she'd judged him a little harshly. Maybe he wasn't a *total* asshole. At least not all the time.

"I think you've got it down," she said, flipping the script closed when they'd finished going through his last scene.

"God, I hope so." He leaned forward, propping his elbows on his knees as he scrubbed his hands over his face. "Today was a disaster."

"I wouldn't call it a *disaster*, exactly," Grace said, trying to be diplomatic.

Scott arched an eyebrow at her. "You sure didn't like me very much."

Her mouth fell open. "I didn't—that's not—I liked you fine," she lied. Badly.

"It's okay." He shook his head, grimacing. "I know I didn't make any friends today."

"Well, you did come off sort of...grouchy."

"I was nervous," he shot back. "It's been awhile since I've done this, and I've got a lot riding on this job."

Grace had a hard time feeling sorry for a guy who drove a Tesla, lived in a mansion, and had made everyone's jobs more difficult by acting like a jerk. "We *all* do," she told him. "And everyone's nervous the first day of shooting, but you were the only one I saw snapping at people."

A muscle ticked in Scott's jaw.

Shit. Why'd she have to go and run her stupid mouth off?

Refusing to let him intimidate her was one thing, but lecturing the lead actor on his attitude problem was going too far.

"I'm sorry," she said, trying to head off the explosion. "I shouldn't have—"

"No, you're right. It's no excuse."

It was the second time that night Scott had surprised her. She'd expected anger, or at the very least defensiveness. Definitely not the contrition she saw in his expression now.

"You know what?" Grace said, deciding it was best to make her exit before she fell through the thin ice she was treading on. "I'll bet my stuff's done charging by now." She went into the dining room and flipped open her laptop. "Yep, ninety-nine percent, which means I can get out of your hair." *Before I wear out my welcome completely.*

"You gonna be okay over there in the dark?" Scott asked, watching as she gathered her things.

"Sure," she said, injecting false perkiness into her voice. "It's not like you can tell the power's out when you're sleeping, right?" Despite her best efforts, the laugh she tacked onto the end had a hollow ring to it.

"Hang on a sec." Scott got up and headed into the kitchen. Grace waited by the door, clutching her laptop to her chest while he dug a flashlight out of one of the drawers. He brought it to her and held it out. "Take this with you."

She accepted it with a smile. *"May it be a light in dark places, when all other lights go out."*

His eyebrows drew together in incomprehension. "What?"

"Galadriel? From *The Lord of the Rings*?" He still looked blank. "Never mind. It's a nerd thing. Thanks for the flashlight."

The corner of his mouth twitched—whether from amusement or irritation, she couldn't tell—and he slipped his phone out of his pocket. "Give me your number. Just in case."

In case what? Grace wondered, but she recited it for him anyway. While he was adding her info to his contacts, she took the opportunity to marvel at how attractive he was when he wasn't being a complete dick. His hazel-green eyes were framed by long lashes, his thick, dark hair begged you to run your fingers through it, and he had a cleft chin most actors would sell their soul for.

Grace's phone vibrated in her hand, startling her out of her ruminations.

"That's me," Scott said. "You can call me if you run into any trouble."

"Thanks." She tipped her phone at him. "And thanks for the use of your electricity."

"Anytime." He gifted her with his movie star smile again, and her knees went a little wobbly.

Stupid, traitorous knees.

"Night," Grace mumbled as she fled to the safety of her dark house with her laptop and her borrowed flashlight.

It wasn't until she crawled into bed twenty minutes later that she bothered to read the text Scott had sent her.

Scott: I'm here if u need anything sleep tight neighbor

5

Day two of shooting went approximately a thousand percent better than day one. The tardy crew members were all on time, the sets were finished, and there were no more missing props. But the biggest improvement was in Scott.

When he strolled onto set that morning, he was like a completely different person: smiling, friendly, addressing all the crew by name. No more Mr. I Don't Have Time for Small Talk. It was as if someone had turned up the charming dial on his personality to eleven.

"Excuse me, Grace?" he said politely after they'd finished rehearsing the first scene.

"Yes?" she answered, looking up from her notebook.

"My second line—does it start with 'but' or 'and'?"

She double-checked the script. "And."

"Thank you."

Scott Deacon, asshole extraordinaire, actually said *thank you*. Grace nearly perished in surprise.

"You good?" Joe asked Scott, eyebrows raised.

"I am now," he replied with a nod.

That was pretty much how the whole day went. Scott was

unfailingly polite and everyone around him was completely shocked—except Joe, who shot Grace a smug *I told you so* look every time Scott said something nice to someone.

"He bought me coffee," Carmen told Grace later as she munched on a baggie of grapes. "And he apologized for yesterday. Can you believe it?"

"He let us listen to music in the makeup trailer this morning," Tamika said. "Anything we wanted. And he was chatty. It was weird."

"I wonder what got into him," Carmen mused as she popped another grape in her mouth.

Grace held out her hand, and Carmen dropped a grape into it. "Maybe he was just having a bad day yesterday," she suggested with a shrug.

Grace wasn't entirely buying the Nice Guy act. The shift in Scott's attitude was a little too extreme. It felt calculated, like a show he was putting on for their benefit. He was an actor after all, capable of turning on his charisma when he needed to. She figured he was simply pretending to be nice in order to ingratiate himself with the crew he'd alienated.

Whatever. Grace didn't care if it was fake. The fact that he was even trying to win them over was a major upgrade. New Improved Scott was focused and professional, which was all she really cared about. He knew all his lines and hit all his marks, which had allowed them to get through the first scene of the day in record time.

"You don't think he's using again?" Tamika whispered as she leaned over to help herself to one of Carmen's grapes. "Maybe that's why he's so happy all of a sudden."

Grace gazed across the soundstage, to where Scott was chatting with a couple of the day players, and thought about the focused determination with which he'd run lines with her the previous night. "No, I don't think it's that. Maybe he just realized he was acting like a jerk."

"Yeah, right," Carmen snorted. "As if."

SCOTT HAD BEEN WORKING HIS ASS OFF ALL DAY TO BUILD better relationships with the crew members he'd pissed off yesterday. He'd brought all the tools in his toolbox to bear: smiles, charm, bribes, even a little careful flirting. So far, it seemed to be working pretty well. He'd detected a lot fewer death glares pointed in his direction today.

His eyes flicked to where Grace sat in front of the monitors, intent on her laptop. He hadn't tried his charm offensive on her yet. Even so, he'd sensed a slight warming in her demeanor. He must have won some brownie points last night. Also, she was probably as relieved as he was that he wasn't screwing up so many takes today.

It was like Alfie had told him last night: she was on Scott's team, even if she didn't like him. They both wanted this shoot to go well, which meant Grace was invested in his success, whether she wanted to be or not.

It was probably time to let go of his grudge against her. Yes, her careless words had hurt him, but it wasn't fair to hold that against her forever. She was entitled to her opinions, and it wasn't like she'd thrown them in his face intentionally.

Besides, at this point he'd definitely pulled ahead in the Acting Like a Jerk Olympics. Continuing hostilities would only make both of them more miserable. Instead, Scott had decided to prove she was wrong about him. She'd judged him based on his past behavior, and now it was up to him to show her he wasn't that man anymore.

Maybe being the bearer of good news would earn him a few more brownie points.

"Got a text from the landlord," Scott said as he approached Grace's chair by the monitors. "He says your power's all fixed."

As she looked up at him, her mask of stony professionalism slipped away and her bee-stung lips spread in a smile. For an exhilarating moment Scott felt like he'd gotten a smile out of a Buckingham Palace guard.

"Whew. Thank god." The smile slid from her face as she focused on him properly. "Thank you again for letting me charge my stuff last night."

Scott swallowed a fleeting sense of disappointment. "You don't have to thank me. It was pretty much the least I could do."

"No, the least you could have done was nothing." Her bluish gray eyes sparked in challenge as they gazed into his. "You did more than that."

He offered her his best, most disarming smile, but instead of returning it, she turned back to her computer, where she was reviewing screenshots of the last scene they'd filmed.

They'd been moving much faster today, due in large part to the fact that Scott wasn't slowing them down as much. Running lines with Grace last night had helped him shake off the yips, and he'd felt his confidence slowly returning throughout the day. His instincts hadn't abandoned him permanently, thank god. They'd just been a little rusty.

Scott helped himself to the chair next to Grace. "It's going a lot better today, don't you think?"

Her attention stayed on her screen. "Yes, it is."

"It's funny how much faster things move along when the actors know their lines, isn't it?" He felt a thrill of triumph when she huffed out an amused breath.

"I wasn't going to say anything, but yeah, it's funny how that works." An almost-smile curved the corners of her lips, exposing a hint of dimple in her cheek.

Emboldened by this tiny victory, Scott leaned in closer, lowering his voice to a murmur. "Aren't you impressed by how nice I'm being to everyone?"

Grace quirked an eyebrow as she turned toward him. "Am I

impressed you're meeting the bare minimum requirements of common politeness? Absolutely."

He felt a small kick in his stomach at the unexpected playfulness of her tone. "Wow," he volleyed, trying not to smile. "Tough room."

"The coffee for Carmen was a nice touch. It's never a good idea to piss off the person in charge of your wardrobe."

"Don't I know it." Scott ran a finger inside the collar of his shirt, which felt like it had been lined with sandpaper. "And I apologized to that PA too."

Grace smirked knowingly, as if she was imagining the layers of itchy starch abrading Scott's skin at that very moment. "His name is Cal."

"I actually knew that."

"I'm sure he appreciates it."

Scott felt his lips pull into a smile as his gaze locked on hers. "Asshole's not my natural state, is what I'm trying to say."

"I guess we'll see, won't we?" The spark had returned to her eyes, daring him.

Challenge accepted.

The first AD called the actors to their places, and Scott pushed himself to his feet. "I guess we will," he threw over his shoulder as he strode away with a smile still lingering on his face.

HALFWAY THROUGH THE DAY ON FRIDAY, GRACE GOT A TEXT from Scott.

Scott: Save me

That was it. Just those two words with no context. She was still squinting at her phone, trying to make sense of the message, when another came through.

Scott: Please

She glanced up and found Scott on the other side of the soundstage, kicked back in his chair. Nate, one of the other cast members, stood in front of him, chattering away while Scott nodded along like he was totally listening instead of surreptitiously texting for rescue.

Grace shook her head as she typed a reply.

Grace: ???

Scott: Nates been talking to me about his juice cleanse for 10 min zzzzzz
Scott: I didn't need to know this much about his bowel movements
Scott: Send help

Grace snorted. Nate had cornered her after lunch yesterday and yammered on about GMOs for a good twenty minutes until she'd finally had to excuse herself and flee to the bathroom. Apparently she'd gotten off easy. He seemed like a nice guy, but man, could he talk, and he did not know how to take a hint.

Grace: So get up and walk away.

Scott: I don't want to b rude
Scott: I'm trying to b nice remember

Grace rolled her eyes. "Hey, Cal," she called out to the passing PA. "Will you please tell Scott that I need to talk to him?"

"Sure thing," he said, and ambled over to where Scott was sitting. She saw Cal pass on the message, and Scott got to his feet and headed her way.

"My hero," he said, smiling at her.

Grace resisted the urge to smile back—barely. "I feel like you could have found a way out of that situation without my intervention."

Scott's smile widened into a heart-melting grin. "Yeah, but this way I get to come over here and pretend to talk to you."

She refused to be charmed by his flirting because she knew it was no more real than his spray tan or his perfect teeth, which were almost certainly veneers. For that matter, his striking green eyes were probably contacts. Pretty much everything about him was fake, including the raw sex appeal he was currently projecting in her direction.

Grace had learned her lesson about pretty-boy actors. Her ex-boyfriend Chris was an actor—as if there weren't already enough hot actors named Chris running around Hollywood. She'd gotten used to women flirting with him wherever they went—sometimes right in front of Grace—because she knew it came with the territory when you were dating someone that attractive. She'd even learned to watch him flirt back without jealousy, because she knew he didn't mean anything by it. It was just a function of his Labrador-like personality, which craved attention and validation anywhere he could get it.

She saw a lot of the same characteristics in Scott, now that he was making an effort to be less of an asshole. It was like the man only had two speeds: arrogant jackass and outrageous flirt.

Grace had foolishly mistaken Chris's neediness for a deeper connection. They'd lived together for a year and she'd helped support him between acting jobs until his career had finally started to take off. They'd even talked about marriage, but agreed they didn't need it because they were both happy with things the way they were. At least that's what Grace had thought, until six months ago, when Chris had left her for his twenty-five-year-old costar.

So, yeah. Grace was done with actors. Never again would she fall prey to their devastating good looks, or their hypnotizing charisma, or their compulsive need to be liked. It was all too exhausting and too crushing to her self-esteem.

Scott could flirt with her all he wanted. She was immune.

BY THE TIME THE END OF THE DAY FRIDAY ROLLED AROUND, Grace was running on fumes, even though it had been a short work week. Adjusting to the intensity and long hours of a shoot always took some time. Thank god she had the next two days off to recharge. Hallelujah. She couldn't wait to go home and do nothing at all.

"Goodnight," Scott said to her as he was leaving the set that night.

"See you Monday," she called out.

"Not if I see you first," he replied with a wink.

As he strolled away, Grace wondered how many women Scotty Deacon had charmed into bed with that wink of his. Probably all of them. It was a really good wink. Good thing she was off actors, or she might be in trouble.

She slept in on Saturday and spent the afternoon vegging out in front of the TV. As she flipped through the channels, Grace paused on a nature documentary, lulled by the narrator's soothing voice and the images from the vast ocean deeps.

"*Attracting a mate in this endless darkness can be even harder than finding food,*" the narrator explained during a segment on angler fish. As he went on to describe how the male fish bit into the female with specially designed teeth, attempting to permanently attach himself to her belly, Grace changed the channel, feeling personally attacked.

She spent the rest of the day watching a *Law & Order: SVU* marathon and didn't leave her house at all. It was heavenly.

On Sunday she dragged herself out of bed to meet Carmen for

brunch. They had mimosas and stuffed French toast, which they walked off with some shopping on Magazine Street.

"What do you think about Dominic?" Carmen asked as they were flipping through the racks in a clothing boutique.

Grace looked up from the stack of sweaters she was pawing through. "Dominic the first AD? That Dominic?"

"Yeah," Carmen said, trying to act nonchalant and totally failing.

"What do *you* think about him?" Grace asked, as if she couldn't already tell by Carmen's expression.

"I think he's kind of cute," Carmen admitted.

"He is cute," Grace agreed. He was a little skinny for her taste, and a little too cheerful, but he seemed like a sweet guy. "And nice too."

Grace wouldn't have pegged him as Carmen's type. She normally went for the beefier, alpha-type guys. The sort that were fun for a roll in the sack, but you'd never want to settle down with.

It also wasn't Carmen's style to be this coy about a crush. Usually when she'd identified a man she was attracted to, she went for it without artifice or bashfulness.

"Do you know if he has a girlfriend?" Carmen asked, still attempting to feign nonchalance as she twisted a lock of hair around her finger. She'd added soft caramel highlights to the ends of her dark hair that looked amazing with her Latina complexion.

"He hasn't mentioned a girlfriend to me." Grace reached up to touch her own too-short locks, which she'd cut off after her breakup in a fit of rebellion she'd regretted every day since. Six months later, they were still barely long enough for a ponytail. Maybe some highlights like Carmen's would liven up their mousy brown color, but with her pale complexion Grace was afraid it would just wash her out even more. "Do you want me to ask him?"

Carmen threw her a warning look. "Definitely not. This isn't middle school. I don't want you passing him a note in history class."

"I can be subtle about it."

Carmen laughed. "No, you can't. Promise me you won't say anything."

"Fine," Grace conceded. "But you should say something to him."

"So tell me," Carmen said, changing the subject, "what's it like being neighbors with Scott Deacon?"

Grace shrugged, turning her attention to a sale rack full of jackets. "He's pretty quiet, actually."

"No raucous sex parties keeping you awake at night?"

"No, thank god."

"That's disappointing."

"He does have really bad taste in music." Grace held up a trench coat for Carmen's opinion. Free fashion advice was one of the perks of being friends with a professional costumer.

Carmen wrinkled her nose. "Grommets? Seriously? It's a raincoat with holes in it. Put it down."

Grace sighed and shoved the trench back onto the rack.

"So how bad are we talking?" Carmen asked. "Like Nickelback bad?"

"Death metal."

"Gross."

"He works out to it, I guess. I had to ask him to turn it down the first night."

Carmen's eyebrows shot up. "You made Scott Deacon turn his music down?" She pressed her palm against her chest, grinning at Grace. "I am so proud of you right now, you don't even know."

Grace rolled her eyes. "I didn't know it was him when I knocked on the door."

Carmen snorted. "That must have been a surprise."

"Yeah, I'll say. He was all sweaty and shirtless too." She felt her chest flush a little at the memory.

"Ah, so you've seen the abs," Carmen said, nodding. "Crazy, right?"

Not only did Carmen get to see all the actors in a state of partial undress during wardrobe fittings, she also got to touch them when she did measurements and alterations. It was almost enough to make Grace wish she'd learned to sew.

"So do they feel as good as they look?" Grace asked. Not that she really cared. She wasn't the least bit interested in Scott Deacon *or* his amazing abs.

"No comment," Carmen replied archly. "I'm a professional."

GRACE WAS BACK AT WORK BRIGHT AND EARLY MONDAY morning for the second week of principal photography. Miraculously, they'd managed to make up the lost time from their rocky first day, so the production was officially back on schedule—much to everyone's relief.

"How was your weekend?" Scott asked, wandering over to Grace's chair while they were setting up for the first shot.

"Good," she said, stifling a yawn. "Quiet. How about you?" She hadn't seen or heard a peep from him all weekend. It had been so quiet next door, she'd wondered if he might have gone out of town. Not that she'd been paying attention or anything. She definitely had not spent her weekend listening for Scott Deacon's comings and goings.

"Same," he said vaguely. "Hey, what's the scene right before this one?" He moved behind Grace's chair and leaned over to peer at her computer screen uninvited. "Is it the one at the restaurant?"

Seriously? Did he really need to press his big, broad chest against her shoulder like that, or put his face right next to hers, close enough that she could smell that cologne he wore? Which smelled really excellent, by the way, even though she wasn't normally a cologne person.

Grace smacked his hand when it started to reach for her trackpad. "Hey! Hands off."

Scott straightened, gazing down at her with an amused look on his face.

"I know actors have no sense of personal space," she said, "but no one touches my computer but me, got it?"

"So noted," he said, fighting a smirk—then losing the fight and full-on smirking at her.

Grace turned to her screen, scrolling to the previous scene in the script. "Yes, it's the restaurant."

"So this is right after I learn my father's secret," Scott said, looking thoughtful. "Don't you think I should say something about it to Nate's character in this scene?"

"That's something you should talk to Joe about." Grace tried not to get involved in the more abstract issues of characterization and motivation. She preferred to stick to facts that could be objectively verified or disproved by the shooting script or her notes.

"I want to know what you think," Scott persisted.

"No, I don't," she said, since he'd insisted. "Your character's not the type to go around sharing family secrets."

"Okay, then," Scott said with that amused smirk on his face again. "We'll do it your way."

"It's not my way," Grace said, looking down to hide the blood traitorously rushing to her cheeks. "It's the writer's."

Scott: Iowa or temple???

Grace: What are you talking about?

Scott: March madness

Grace: I don't like college basketball.

Scott: I'm not sure we can b friends anymore

GRACE REPLIED TO SCOTT WITH THE POOP EMOJI, AND considered the subject closed.

Until he slid into the seat next to her at the commissary at lunch. "Notre Dame or Michigan?" he asked, like he expected her to have an opinion.

She tried not to feel any kind of way about the fact that he'd chosen to sit right next to her, despite there being plenty of empty seats. Or that he'd scooted his chair right up next to hers so his thigh—his extremely large, extremely muscular thigh—was touching hers.

"You can't make me care about your basketball bracket," she replied, keeping her eyes on her phone. Kanye West had gone on another epic Twitter rant last night, and she was trying to get through it before she had to go back to work.

Scott leaned over to peer at her screen. "Are you on Twitter?"

Grace held her phone against her chest so he couldn't read it. "Do we need to have another talk about personal space?"

He smirked at her in that infuriating way he had—that way that said he was perfectly aware of how attractive he was and what it did to the people around him, and that he fully intended to use it to his advantage—before turning his attention back to his own phone.

Grace rolled her eyes and reached for a french fry. Her phone buzzed against her boob, making her start. *Scott Deacon followed you*, the new Twitter notification announced.

She looked over at him and raised her eyebrows. "Seriously?"

"What?"

"Now all your crazy fans are going to start stalking me online for info about you."

He frowned. "I can unfollow you if you want."

"No, it's okay," she said. "I can take it."

"I have no doubt of that," he said, flashing that damned smirk again.

Scott posted a lot of selfies, Grace learned when she followed him back. That wasn't so surprising. He was an actor, and his face was his brand. He was also in the middle of rebuilding his brand, so it was smart to leverage every tool at his disposal.

He didn't just tweet about himself though. He tweeted a lot about the crew, which was pretty sweet, actually.

Wardrobe killing it today and every day making me look good, he'd tweeted along with this morning's selfie, taken in his trailer's bathroom mirror.

He wasn't wrong: Carmen had him dressed in a dark blue denim button-down that fit him so well it should be against the law.

Yesterday he'd tweeted a picture of himself with his arm slung around Dominic, captioned: *My buddy Dom our 1st AD.*

When Grace scrolled back through Scott's feed, she found quite a few pictures of the cast and crew, including one of her from last week that she hadn't noticed him taking. It was a candid, taken from the side as she was scribbling a note in her logbook.

Grateful for our awesome scripty who keeps me in line, he'd tweeted along with it.

Grace smiled to herself as she tapped the heart icon beneath the tweet.

SCOTT TEXTED HER THAT NIGHT AS SHE WAS GETTING READY for bed. At *eleven-freaking-thirty*.

Scott: Boom diggy boom bangy bang

Grace set down her toothbrush and stared at it for a full minute, trying to make sense of it.

Grace: ???

Scott: What songs that from

Grace: Google is your friend.

Scott: I already tried that's y I'm texting u
Scott: Do u know it?

As it happened, she did. But she made him wait while she washed her face and changed into her pajamas. Once she was tucked into bed with the lights off and her night guard in her mouth, she texted him the answer.

Grace: Cobrastyle.

Scott: Thanx

Grace: I could have been asleep, you know.

Scott: I can hear u thumping around over there

Grace was still trying to decide how she felt about the fact that Scott could apparently hear her moving around in her *bedroom* when she heard a tapping on the floorboards next door. It was the familiar, annoying rhythm of "Shave and a Haircut," and she tried to resist, she really did, but she knew that stupid tune was going to be stuck in her head all night if she didn't answer, so she leaned over the side of the bed and rapped the two-note response on the floor.

A second later, her phone vibrated with a new text.

Scott: Sweet dreams

The next morning, Scott texted her another song lyric as she was pulling into her parking space outside the soundstage. Grace recognized it as a line from "Gin and Juice," and replied with a string of emojis: a car, a cigarette, a martini glass, and an orange.

An hour later, Scott texted her a lyric from a Missy Elliott song.

Grace looked up from her phone and spotted him smiling at her from the other side of the soundstage, where he was sitting by himself with his earbuds in.

Grace: What's with all the music?

Scott: Making a new workout mix
Scott: Someone told me u didn't like my old one

Carmen. That traitor.

Grace spent the rest of the week trading random song lyrics with Scott via text. Movie sets were pretty much one long exercise in "hurry up and wait," and it helped pass the downtime between setups.

It didn't mean she liked him though. It was just a silly game to stave off boredom.

"Who's blowing up your phone?" Tamika asked on Thursday when Grace checked her texts for the third time in five minutes.

"No one," Grace said, smiling to herself.

HALFWAY THROUGH THE SHOOTING DAY ON FRIDAY, NATE decided to camp out by Grace's chair in order to tell her all about his workout regimen. In *excruciating* detail. Nate had a slamming bod, so clearly it was working for him, but he'd been talking about bent-over rows for like ten minutes, vastly overestimating Grace's interest in the minutiae of his lifting routine.

When her phone vibrated with a new text message, she snuck a glance at it while Nate continued to ramble on, oblivious to her boredom. It was Scott, texting her a situation-appropriate lyric from "Bust a Move."

He was standing over by the craft services table watching her, and when he caught her eye he lifted his eyebrows suggestively. Grace shook her head slightly and turned her attention back to Nate, who'd moved on from bent-over rows to the benefits of incline benching. A minute later, when she got another text with yet another lyric from "Bust a Move," Grace had to slap her hand over her mouth to keep herself from laughing out loud.

"What's so funny?" Nate asked.

"Nothing," she said as she typed a reply. "It's just my mom."

Grace: STOP

Nate started talking about his protein intake, and Grace smiled and nodded along politely until she got another text.

Scott: Send sos if u need an intervention with poindexter

Grace: Don't be mean. I happen to like Nate.

The next time she snuck a glance at the craft services table, Scott was nowhere to be seen.

"I've been thinking about getting into marathons when I go back to LA," Nate was saying when she tuned back in. "Do you ever do any running?"

"Not unless I'm being chased," Grace told him.

Scott went radio silent for the rest of the day, and he left without saying goodbye after he finished his last scene. Grace told herself it was no big deal. It wasn't like he said goodbye to her every time he headed home for the day.

Except he usually did, now that she thought about it. And today was Friday, which meant they probably wouldn't see each other for the next two days. She couldn't shake the feeling she'd said something wrong.

Saturday night, Grace met up with some of the crew for drinks. Nate and a couple other members of the cast showed up too, but not Scott. Not that Grace was surprised by his absence. As pleasant as he'd been on set lately, he didn't strike her as the pal-around-with-lowly-crewmembers-after-work type. Not to mention the whole recovery thing, which probably made hanging out in bars a nonstarter.

Grace didn't see Scott until Sunday afternoon, when she was sitting on her balcony with a glass of wine and the latest Roxane Gay book. She heard Scott's front door open and close below her, and he jogged down the front walk to meet up with the trail that went around the park.

She couldn't help glancing up from her book every few minutes to track his progress. He made three full circuits before turning off the path and heading home again. As he trudged up the walk to the house, panting and covered in sweat, Grace considered calling out to him, but didn't. She wasn't sure why.

If Scott was aware of her sitting up there watching him, he didn't acknowledge her.

Later that night, after she'd gotten into bed, she reached for her phone and stared at the last texts she'd exchanged with him. It was only ten thirty, and she'd heard his television on downstairs ten minutes ago, so she knew he was still awake.

Grace typed out a lyric from a Salt-N-Pepa song and hit send.

When he replied a few minutes later with the next line in the song, she couldn't articulate why she felt so much better. To avoid thinking about it further, she rolled over and went to sleep.

THE FOLLOWING WEEK, A NEW CAST MEMBER JOINED THE production. His name was Dexter Bell, and he was playing the comic relief sidekick to Scott's brooding action hero. Dex had an improv background and a husband back in LA, and Grace adored him almost immediately for the way his disarming, slightly wacky sense of humor lightened the mood on set.

For the first time since the start of production, they lost takes because the actors were breaking up with laughter. Joe chastised them and cracked the whip to keep things moving, but Grace could tell he was secretly pleased about the energy Dex was bringing to his scenes.

Even Scott looked like he was genuinely enjoying himself for a change and not just pretending. Grace smiled as she watched him struggle to keep a straight face while Dex delivered his lines. The second Joe said cut, Scott dissolved into laughter, clutching his stomach and grinning from ear to ear. It was completely different from the way he usually smiled—artless and spontaneous and just a little bit dorky—and Grace liked it even more than his panty-melting movie star smile.

He should laugh more often, she thought. *He looks good laughing.*

"DO YOU HAVE SNAPCHAT?" SCOTT ASKED THE NEXT DAY, sidling up beside Grace while she was browsing the craft services table.

The craft services on this production were frankly disappointing. Where were the Twix bars? And the Butterfingers? They always had Butterfingers in LA, but here all they had were Hershey's Miniatures. *What a rip.*

"I do not," Grace said as she dug around in the big plastic jar for a Mr. Goodbar. "In case you haven't noticed, I'm not fifteen." She changed her mind and exchanged the Mr. Goodbar for a Krackle.

"Dex got me into it," Scott said. "It's pretty fun."

That explained it. Dex was like an enthusiastic puppy in the body of a six-foot-four-inch black man, and even Scott seemed to have fallen under his spell.

"Check it out." Scott leaned in close and held his phone up in front of her face.

"What the heck is that?" Grace asked, appalled.

"The face swap filter."

"Yikes." She stuck out her tongue, and the image of her face that was superimposed on Scott's head stuck out its tongue back at her. It was funny, but also sort of horrifying.

"And here's one that makes you look like a beauty queen," Scott said, swiping to another filter.

"Double yikes." Grace scrunched up her nose, and the beauty queen version of her on the screen scrunched her nose too.

"How about a flower crown?" As Scott tapped the screen, the image softened and a tiara of flowers appeared on top of her head. It wasn't the worst. He leaned in close again, smiling into the camera, and the image froze for a moment.

"Did you just take a picture of us?" Grace asked as Scott pulled the phone away and tapped the screen some more. "Are you posting that?"

"Yeah." He grinned at her. "It's a great picture of you."

See, this right here was the problem with actors. They basically oozed charisma out of their pores like a plug-in air freshener, so if they were even mildly friendly to you it felt like they were flirting when they weren't. It was easy to mistake the intensity of Scott's smile and all his casual touching for signs of genuine interest, when in reality it was more like the kind of professional flirting that bartenders and salesmen did. Tempting as it might be to play along, it would be pathetic to let yourself believe there was anything real behind it.

But contrary to the appearances Grace worked hard to maintain when she was at work, she was not made of stone. She was a flesh and blood woman possessed of a heart and feelings and stuff, and when a former *People Magazine* "Sexiest Man Alive" smiled at you while saying you looked great, you had to be dead not to feel something.

Which was dangerous. She wasn't allowed to actually start liking Scott Deacon, because liking him led to *liking* him, which led to Trouble with a capital T.

Grace helped herself to a whole handful of Hershey's Miniatures, half-heartedly wishing Scott would go back to acting like an entitled dick instead of being so damned charming.

OKAY, SO MAYBE GRACE DOWNLOADED SNAPCHAT AFTER THAT and created an account for herself—but only because she wanted a better look at that picture Scott had taken of her. And yes, she'd had to start following Scott in order to see the picture, and he'd immediately followed her back.

Sure, fine, she may also have saved a screenshot of it on her phone. It wasn't like she'd set it as her wallpaper or anything.

Not that she hadn't considered it—briefly—before coming to her senses.

It didn't mean anything though. She just liked the picture. It was a flattering filter, okay?

It had nothing at all to do with Scott, or the way his eyes were all soft and crinkly as he grinned into the camera, or how cozy the two of them looked with their faces right up next to each other.

Oh man.

She was so screwed.

THE NEXT DAY, SCOTT POSTED A SHIRTLESS SELFIE TO TWITTER. He was at the gym, drenched in sweat, all bulging biceps and veiny forearms.

One week out from my first fight scene in 4 years. No fear.

Grace stared at it for five solid minutes, because she was shallow and weak.

And then she saved a copy to her phone.

Yep. She was definitely, totally, completely screwed.

6

L ate on Friday, Scott was handed new script pages for Monday's scene. This wasn't just any scene, it was a pivotal moment: the turning point of his character's arc, when he learns the full extent of his best friend's betrayal. The whole film hung on the audience buying into it, and unlike the lighter, more dialogue-heavy scenes they'd shot so far, this one would live or die on the emotional depth of Scott's performance.

He'd already been feeling stressed about it, and that was before he had new lines to learn.

"Did you read them?" Joe asked when Scott tracked him down to complain.

"No, but—"

"Read them. This is a big improvement. It's gonna make the scene even better."

Not if Scott couldn't learn them by Monday.

Memorizing lines had always been a struggle for him. He'd tried all the techniques, every trick in the book, but nothing seemed to help.

It wasn't just the memorizing that was hard for Scott. It was the reading itself. He could *read*—the on-set tutors he'd had growing up had seen to that much at least—but it always felt like a slog. No matter how hard he tried to concentrate, his mind always seemed to lose focus after a few sentences.

His education hadn't exactly been a priority growing up, so it hadn't really mattered. As long as he could read well enough to pass the tests he was given to satisfy the state's requirements, everyone had been satisfied. Beyond that, no one had cared whether he'd excelled at his studies—least of all his mother—so long as his acting career was thriving and he was bringing in a paycheck.

The only way he'd ever been able to learn lines was to have someone else read the script to him aloud. It had never been that much of a problem, because Scott had always had plenty of people around him to help run lines.

Until his career had gone tits up, and Scott had found himself mostly on his own for the first time. The entourage of employees and friends he'd surrounded himself with most of his adult life had disappeared with his employability, leaving him to fend for himself.

In a way, he was grateful. When you were famous it could be hard to separate the real friends from the sycophantic suck-ups trying to worm their way into the inner circle for their own purposes. Now Scott knew with absolute certainty who he could trust when the chips were down, and it was a very small group of people. So few that he could count them all on one hand.

Unfortunately, none of them were in New Orleans with him. He was on his own out here, with ten pages of new dialogue to learn and no one to help him.

"Look," Joe said, "I know this isn't the way you like to work. I get it. Those last revisions were total bullshit, which is what I told the production company. But these—" He shook the rolled-up tube of salmon-colored pages in his hand. "These rewrites are worth the extra effort. They don't just give the scene a polish, they give it more heft. You'll see when you read them."

"Fine," Scott said, rubbing his forehead. There was no point in arguing when Joe felt this strongly. And he trusted Joe's judgment, even if he didn't like it.

"And you've got all weekend," Joe added. "Plenty of time."

For most people, sure. For him? Maybe not.

Scott tried not to let his anxiety about Monday's scene show, but he apparently wasn't successful because Grace texted him a couple hours later.

Grace: Everything okay?

Scott: Fine

He didn't want to talk about it, which was why he'd retreated to his trailer rather than take his bad mood out on everyone else. He just had to get through the rest of today, and then he'd have the whole weekend alone to work on the new pages and brood in private.

Scott stared at the text from Grace, oddly touched that she'd checked on him. That wasn't something she would have done a few weeks ago. Maybe she didn't hate him so much after all. Maybe his plan to win her over was actually working.

She was difficult to read, so until that moment he hadn't really known if she was just tolerating him because she had to, or if she'd actually started to warm up to him a little. But she wouldn't have texted if she was just tolerating him, would she?

The more he thought about it, the more he started to worry his one-word response might seem rude. He didn't want one bad mood to undo all the progress they'd made.

After several more minutes of consideration, he sent Grace another text.

Scott: Thanx for asking tho

When he got home that night, he made himself read the new pages. It took him almost an hour. Joe was right though. They were better.

All day Saturday, Scott worked on the scene. He didn't just have to memorize the new dialogue, he had to rework his performance. The rhythm of the scene was different, the emotional beats falling in new places. He practiced it over and over again, pacing from one room of his house to the next, struggling to read from the script as he experimented with different deliveries.

On Sunday he tried to go off book. It didn't go well. His brain just couldn't seem to hold on to the words when he read them off the page. He needed to hear them spoken aloud.

He tried using one of those apps that let you record yourself saying the dialogue and played it back for you, but he was so distracted by his own labored reading in the recording that he had trouble focusing on the lines he needed to memorize.

After a couple hours of struggling with the app, Scott took a break and went for a run, hoping it would help clear his head. While he made a circuit of the park, he tried to run through the scene in his head, but he still couldn't get all the way through it. He kept hitting a big blank space where the words should have been but weren't. Every time he started the scene over, he hit the wall in a different place. He could feel the words dangling just beyond his reach, but he couldn't make them appear on command.

In the shower after his run, he tried going through the scene some more, but had no better luck. At eight o'clock, when he'd been at it for almost forty-eight hours and still couldn't get through the whole scene without fucking it up, Scott threw his script across the room in frustration. The more he messed up, the more it made him mess up.

He'd gotten too far into his own head. He was giving himself the yips again.

As he stooped to retrieve his crumpled script from the floor, he heard the sound of Grace's television next door. She was watching nature documentaries again. The sonorous murmur of the narrator's voice had a calming effect that drew Scott nearer. He leaned against the wall, clutching his script in his hand as he listened.

Grace was just on the other side, probably only a few feet away from him at this very moment. He contemplated the door, picturing her sitting on her couch as she watched television.

They saw very little of each other outside work, for all that they were neighbors. It was rare that he managed to catch a glimpse of her coming or going. He could hear her TV sometimes, the opening and shutting of her front door, and her footsteps creaking on the wood floor upstairs, but the life she lived right next door to him remained mostly a mystery, just as his life must be to her.

She could help him work on tomorrow's scene. But that would require admitting he needed help.

His fist clenched around the script. They'd been getting along better, but he still wasn't sure she actually *liked* him.

The last time they'd run lines together it had been an enormous help. Working with her one-on-one had helped him get over some of his nervousness. It was almost like it had created a conditioned response, so when he'd looked at her the next day on set, instead of feeling like a failure, he'd felt more confident, remembering the work they'd done together.

That was what he needed now.

Before he had a chance to change his mind, Scott knocked on the door.

GRACE STARTLED AT THE KNOCK ON THE DOOR THAT connected to Scott's house. Despite all their texting, he'd never knocked on her door before.

Tossing aside the blanket wrapped around her legs, she brushed the cookie crumbs off her T-shirt and ran a nervous hand through her hair before opening the door.

Scott stood on the other side, one hand propped on the door-frame like he was posing for a photo shoot. That was where the pin-up look ended, however. His hair was sticking up haphazardly, his T-shirt was misshapen and stretched out at the neck, and there were circles darkening the skin around his eyes.

Grace blinked at him. "Hi."

"Hi." The smile he gave her didn't quite reach his eyes. "Are you busy?"

"No." She stepped back, gesturing him inside.

He walked past her, his eyes skimming around the room, taking in the box of cookies on the coffee table and the nest she'd made for herself on the couch. "Nice place."

She shut the door and swept the blanket and extra pillow off the couch, tossing them onto the chair by the window to make a place for him to sit down. "What's up?"

He glanced at the couch but continued to stand, shoving his hands in the back pockets of his jeans. "I was hoping I could get you to do me a favor." The corner of his mouth curled in a famil-iar, flirty smirk, but it only had half its usual wattage.

"Okay," she said without hesitation. Two weeks ago, she would have been surly and resentful at the idea of lifting a finger to help Scott outside work. But that was two weeks ago. Now she was volunteering to help him without even knowing what he wanted from her. Things really had changed between them.

His eyes locked on hers, his expression unreadable, then lowered to the floor. She saw the muscles in his jaw clench before he spoke. "Would you mind running lines with me?"

They'd gotten new pages on Friday for one of the scenes they were shooting tomorrow—and also, it suddenly occurred to Grace, Scott had seemed sort of tetchy and distant toward the end of the day. She hadn't put the two together before, but now it crossed her mind that the one might have been the reason for the other.

"You were upset about the new pages Friday, weren't you?" she said. "About having to memorize them over the weekend."

A muscle ticked in his jaw and he looked away, which was all the confirmation she needed. She thought back to the way he'd behaved on the first day of shooting, and a light bulb went off.

"Wait—is that why you were so pissy on the first day? Because we'd gotten new pages at the last minute?"

Scott paced over to the window and ran a hand through his hair before answering. "Yes."

She studied his profile: the stern jut of his chin, the hard line of his mouth, the apprehension creasing his brow. He was genuinely upset, and she was having trouble understanding why. Script changes were an annoyance, but they were also a fact of life. It wasn't like they'd had all that many compared to some projects she'd been on. "You know, there are techniques you can use to help with memorization if—"

"I've tried them. All of them." He sounded angry. "You don't understand."

"You're right," she shot back, his tone making her defensive. "Why don't you try explaining it to me instead of getting snippy?" If he was going to knock on her door asking for a favor, the least he could do was not act like an ass.

He didn't look at her as he spoke. "I have a hard time memorizing lines off the page. The only thing that seems to work is for someone else to read them aloud with me. If you don't want to—"

"I didn't say that."

Scott turned, and when his eyes finally met hers, Grace realized he wasn't angry at all—he was ashamed.

She felt a guilty pang in the pit of her stomach. "Sit down."

He hesitated before stalking over to the couch. Dropping down on it, he bent his head and ran both his hands through his hair. No wonder it was so messy.

Grace dug her script out of her bag and sat down at the opposite end of the couch, pulling her legs up under her and twisting her body to face him.

There was something she wanted to ask him, but she wasn't sure how he'd take it. Actually, no, she had a pretty good idea how he'd take it: badly.

His eyes slid her way warily. "Go ahead and say it."

"What?"

"Whatever you're thinking."

"Do you have dyslexia?" She'd worked with a few actors with dyslexia, and she knew they sometimes had more trouble with their lines.

He looked surprised. "No." His forehead creased. "That's where you mix up letters right? I don't have that. It's more like..." He shook his head again, frowning. "Anything more than a few sentences and I can't seem to hold on to the words—it's like they disappear from my brain as soon as I read them."

Grace nodded slowly. "Have you ever been tested for a learning disability?"

He snorted. "No."

"Maybe you should be. I'm no expert, but I think it's possible you might have one."

For a second he looked like he wanted to protest, but then he pressed his lips together, frowning. "Maybe."

"You could have told me, you know."

When he lifted his eyes to her, his expression was so wary and mistrustful it made her chest feel tight. "I'm telling you now."

"But you could have told me sooner, instead of spending the whole weekend trying to do this by yourself and getting all stressed out."

"I don't like to talk about it. I don't like people to know."

"I can see that."

His entire body was rigid with tension, like he was bracing himself for an attack. "When people look at me, all they see is the strung-out asshole I used to be. Everyone's already expecting me to fail. I don't need to give anyone another reason to think I'm going to screw up."

Guilt twisted in the pit of Grace's stomach, because that was exactly how she'd seen him at first, and he must have known it.

He shrugged like it didn't matter. "Only my sister and a few close friends know. When I'm in LA, I can usually get one of them to help me learn my lines. But now I'm here, and I don't know anyone, and we keep getting new fucking pages every other week..." He trailed off, scowling.

"You know me," Grace said.

"I didn't want to be a burden." Scott's lips pressed together in a thin line, his expression heartbreakingly haunted.

It was her first real glimpse of the scars that had been left behind by the things he'd had to overcome. "It's not being a burden to admit you're struggling," she said, starting to understand why he spent so much time hiding behind a false persona. "If you let people know you need help, they're usually happy to give it."

He barked out a bitter laugh. "That...hasn't been my experience."

"I'm sorry if that's true." She wanted to reach out to him, to take his hand or...something, but uncertainty held her back. She didn't know him that well, and she wasn't sure he would welcome it.

Scott looked away, and she saw his Adam's apple bob as he swallowed. "I've burned a lot of bridges, and this job is basically my last shot. I had to call in the only favors I had left to get it, and if I screw this up, that's it for me, my career's over. I'm just— I'm terrified I'm going to blow it."

"That's not going to happen," Grace said, trying to project confidence. She opened her script and flipped to the salmon pages that had come in on Friday. "I'll help you."

"Grace," he said quietly. She glanced up and their eyes met.

"Thank you."

She held his gaze for a few seconds, then nodded and looked down at the script again. "Come on," she said. "Let's do this."

Grace started at the beginning of the scene, reading both characters' dialogue aloud. After a few minutes, Scott leaned back and tucked his hands behind his head, listening. The next time she looked at him, he had his eyes closed. His brow was wrinkled in concentration, but most of the tension in his body language was gone.

They spent two hours working on it together. Scott wanted to go over the scene again and again, long after it was clear that he knew it backward and forward. But Grace understood his nervousness better now, so she didn't mind keeping at it until he felt comfortable.

By the time they finally called it quits and she walked him to the door, it was coming up on eleven. His body brushed against hers as he moved past her to pause in the doorway. Unexpectedly, he leaned down and kissed her on the cheek.

"Thank you," he murmured against her cheek. His stubble felt prickly against her skin, and she had to suppress a shiver.

"You're welcome," she replied in an unsteady voice as her stomach gave a little lurch.

His eyes slid over her face with a new kind of intensity, their green depths even more vivid than usual. For a second they dipped lower, seeming to catch on her chest before his throat constricted in a swallow and he stepped backward over the threshold and into his own house. "Goodnight," he said, offering a tenuous smile.

"Goodnight." Grace pulled the door closed before he could see the color pinking her cheeks.

Monday, the day of Scott's big scene, also happened to

be the start of a week of location shoots. First stop: an empty office building in the Central Business District.

Scott wasn't in the first scene of the day, so his call time wasn't until ten. Miraculously, he actually managed to sleep in a little, and got up feeling more rested than he had in a while. Working on his lines with Grace last night had done wonders for his confidence.

He went for a short run, followed by a shower, and was able to recite the entire scene in his head flawlessly.

Unfortunately, by the time he made it to base camp, his nerves were jangling again. As soon as he was done with hair and makeup, he stuck his earbuds in and holed himself up in an empty office next to the one they'd be shooting in. Clutching his script sides in a white-knuckled grip, he paced around the small space, trying to get into character and push everything out of his mind except the scene ahead. It helped a little, but he still felt edgy and unbalanced. Apprehension dogged his every breath, settling in his limbs and making them feel heavy.

Remembering how working with Grace had helped calm him down last night, he tracked her down to ask if they could go over his lines one last time. Something about her efficient profession- alism grounded him, and the quiet monotone in which she recited his cues helped him focus and shut out some of the negative voices in his head.

"You've got this," Grace said after they'd run through the scene twice.

He shook his head. "I need to be in the moment. I can't be thinking about the next line, I have to *know* it."

"You do."

Scott shook his head again, frowning in uncertainty. "I don't know."

"I do," Grace said. "I believe in you."

He searched for the lie in her expression, but couldn't find one. Maybe she did believe in him. Had he really won her over to his side? From antagonists to...he wanted to say *friends*, but he wasn't sure they were quite there. He wanted to be there though, to an extent that surprised him.

If he could win Grace over, after the low opinion she'd had of him, maybe he could win everyone else over too. Maybe he could really come back from all the mistakes he'd made.

"You're not in this alone," she told him. "Every single person on this set is in your corner. We're all rooting for you."

Scott opened his mouth to tell her...something. How much he appreciated her help, how much her faith in him meant. He wasn't sure what he wanted to say or how to say it, he just knew he needed to say something.

Before he could get the words out, Joe's hand landed on his shoulder. "Ready to rehearse?"

Reluctantly, Scott tore his eyes away from Grace to give Joe a nod.

"You nailed this scene in pre-production rehearsals," Joe said, giving Scott's shoulder a reassuring squeeze. "So I only want you to play it halfway for now. Save the good stuff for the camera, okay?"

"Okay." Scott cast one last look at Grace, taking strength from the unhesitating confidence he saw in her expression before making his way over to the set where Nate was waiting for him.

GRACE WATCHED ON THE MONITORS AS THE ACTORS WALKED through the scene. Scott's delivery was word-perfect but strained, his nervousness showing through in the stiffness of his movements. As soon as they were done, he put his earbuds in and retreated to an empty office while they tweaked the lighting with the stand-ins.

Twenty minutes later, Dominic called for final checks. They were doing Scott's coverage first, and he stood rigidly on his mark while Tamika did a last-second touch-up, blotting the shine on his forehead.

"He's sweating," Carmen whispered beside Grace.

"He'll be okay," Grace murmured. She was almost as tense as Scott, gripping the arms of her chair so hard her fingers were tingling.

"Picture is up," Dominic called out. "Quiet, please. Roll camera."

"Rolling."

Scott shook out his arms and closed his eyes, tilting his head from side to side.

"Marker."

When the camera assistant holding the slate stepped out of frame, Scott's gaze was fixed on the floor.

Joe called action, and Grace held her breath.

Scott looked up at Nate, and he wasn't Scott anymore—he'd transformed completely into character. On the first few lines, his delivery was light and effortless, in stark contrast to his edginess before the camera started rolling. But as the scene progressed and he started to react to what Nate's character was saying, a spectrum of emotions played out in his expression. It was understated at first, simmering just beneath the surface, but when he finally erupted in an outpouring of rage and grief and regret, it was breathtaking in its vulnerability.

Every single person watching was transfixed by Scott's performance. When Joe called cut at the end of the scene, there was a pregnant moment in which the only sound was Scott's ragged breathing. Then the entire crew burst into spontaneous applause.

"That's it, that's gonna be the take," Joe told Grace, grinning.

Scott looked around him, blinking in surprise, and slowly broke into a smile. Nate clapped him on the back, and Joe yanked off his headset, jumping up from his chair to shake Scott's hand.

Grace swiped at her eyes as she made a note in her log to let the editor know the first take was the director's favorite. She could count on two hands the number of times an actor's perfor-mance had brought her to tears on set, and Scott Deacon had just made the list.

They did three more takes for good measure, all of them solid, but none could match the magic of that first one, so they moved on to the wide shot. Scott continued to give it everything he had on every take, even when they were shooting Nate's coverage, which was generous of him, and more than a lot of actors would do. By the time they wrapped the scene, Scott was visibly drained, and he disappeared immediately to change out of his wardrobe. He wasn't in the other scene they were shooting at the location that day, so Grace didn't get a chance to talk to him before he headed out.

When she finally got home that night it was nearly ten, but the downstairs lights were on in Scott's house, and she could see the flicker of his television through the curtains. She went into her own house and changed out of her work clothes and into yoga pants and a T-shirt. Then she went back downstairs and stood in front of the door to Scott's place.

She was torn between wanting to congratulate him and being afraid to disturb him after an exhausting day. In the end, she took a chance that he'd appreciate the congratulations more than being left alone, and knocked on the door.

"It's open," Scott called out.

Grace slid the bolt on her side and pushed the door open, wondering when he'd stopped locking it. Had he been expecting her to drop by tonight?

He was lounging on his couch watching a basketball game with his bare feet propped on the coffee table, and he sat up a little, smiling as he tilted his head in greeting.

"You must be feeling pretty pleased with yourself," she said, one hand still on the doorknob.

He shrugged. "I did okay."

She would have written it off as false modesty if she hadn't seen all the self-doubt eating him up last night and today. It was a paradigm shift to realize that underneath the slick, confident exterior, Scott didn't actually think very highly of himself.

"That was better than okay, Scott. That was amazing."

His smile turned wry. "Careful how much you stroke my ego. You don't want it going to my head." It was supposed to be a joke, but the tone wasn't quite right.

Grace leaned against the doorframe and crossed her arms. "When you get your Oscar nomination, I'll be able to say I was in the room where it happened."

He blew out a scoffing breath. "Yeah, right."

She hadn't expected him to be so uncomfortable accepting a compliment. How could someone who appeared so cocky be so uncertain of himself? "I'm serious. I think that scene might earn you a nomination."

"That's sweet, but…it's never going to happen." His shoulders sagged a little, in a way that broke her heart. "Honestly? I'll be happy just to avoid getting panned by the critics for once."

Grace shook her head at him, feeling a sharp stab of affection. "You really know how to talk yourself out of a victory, don't you?"

He cracked a smile for her. "It's a gift."

"All right, I'm going to stop bothering you now," she said, turning to go.

"Hey, Grace," he called out just before she closed the door.

"Hmm?" She paused, raising her eyebrows at him expectantly.

He hesitated like he had something important he wanted to tell her, but when he finally spoke all he said was, "Thanks for all your help."

"That's what neighbors are for, right?"

After she crawled into bed that night, Grace curled up with her phone and scrolled through her Twitter timeline. When she got to Scott's latest tweet she couldn't help smiling.

Great day on set today. Couldn't have done it w/o the support of this amazing crew. Love u all!

7

Tuesday they were shooting on location in Jackson Square all day. The call time was two hours before dawn, so they could wring every second of sunlight out of the day, and Grace could not stop yawning on the transport van to the location.

"Wakey, wakey," Scott said, leaning over the back of his seat to shake a plastic tumbler filled with something thick and green and disgusting-looking in front of her face.

"Ugh," Grace grumbled. "Get that away from me." She couldn't help but smile a little though, even through her sleep-deprived crankiness.

An hour later, as the first streaks of light were glimmering in the sky above the river, Scott showed up at the pop-up tent where video village had been set up, and presented Grace with a white paper bag and a tall styrofoam cup from Café du Monde.

"For me?" she asked, perking up considerably. "Did you seriously walk over there and buy me coffee?" He didn't seem to have gotten anything for anyone else. Just her. Her brain filed this information away to obsess over and analyze later, when he wasn't standing two feet away grinning at her.

"Café au lait," Scott said smugly. "And beignets."

Grace narrowed her eyes at him in suspicion. "Did you make one of the PAs do it?"

"As a matter of fact, I did it all by myself. And I had to take a picture with the employees, so I hope you appreciate it."

"I do!" she said, beaming at him. "You're officially my favorite person today."

He blinked at her, his smirk fading into something else entirely. Whatever that expression on his face was, it sent Grace's stomach tumbling into a free fall. Rather than examine it more closely, she focused her attention on the bag in her hand. Inside was a mountain of powdered sugar, and buried beneath it were three pillowy squares of fried dough.

"Don't inhale while you're eating those," Scott warned her.

"Not my first rodeo," Grace told him, excavating a beignet. "Want one?"

"Noooo." He held up his hands in a warding gesture. "I'm doing a water cut for that fight scene on Thursday."

Right. He'd be shirtless, which meant the Abs of Glory would be on full display. Grace found herself looking forward to Thursday with a little more enthusiasm.

"Sucks for you," she said, giving him a taunting grin as she bit into a beignet.

His eyes homed in on her mouth with laser beam focus. "That's fine. I'll just enjoy them vicariously by watching you eat."

"Does this get you off?" she asked archly and took another bite.

Scott licked his lips. "Not gonna lie, it kind of does."

Grace couldn't help laughing at his retriever-staring-down-a-dog-treat expression, which led her to make the fatal mistake of inhaling with the beignet in front of her mouth. Coughing sugar out of her lungs, she clapped a hand over her mouth as a cloud of fine white powder billowed out in front of her.

Scott sidestepped the powdered sugar typhoon and patted her on the back, chuckling. "Told you not to inhale."

"Grace Speer, if you are eating powdered sugar anywhere near my wardrobe I will *kill you!*" Carmen shouted from across the set.

THE GULF COAST WAS HAVING AN UNSEASONABLY COOL SPRING, and it turned out to be a beautiful day for shooting outside. The humidity was down to a crisp—for New Orleans—fifty percent, there was a pleasant breeze blowing off the Mississippi River, and the sky was a brilliant blue behind the white towers of St. Louis Cathedral at the far end of the square. The production had hired some local musicians to play in the background of the scene for color, and they improvised in between takes, filling the air with cheerful music.

"Are they going to do that all day?" grumbled Ed Dudley, the perpetually grumpy director of photography. "I can't hear myself think over that infernal racket."

There were a few pages of dialogue between Scott and Dex to cover in the morning, and then later a foot chase across the square with some stuntmen. A crowd of tourists lined up along the barricades to watch them shoot, and during lunch Scott gamely went over to sign autographs and pose for selfies.

In the afternoon, when they were getting ready to shoot the chase, Scott announced that he wanted to do all of his own running.

"No need," Joe said, shaking his head. "Ben can double you for the long shots." Ben was Scott's stunt double, and he looked enough like him that the two could be related, although Ben was more than a few years younger than Scott.

"I can do it," Scott insisted.

"I'm sure you can," Joe said, "but I'm not sure you should."

Grace glanced up in time to catch the flash of irritation that crossed Scott's face. She had no doubt he could do the running, based on the circuits she'd seen him doing around the park, but she also understood why Joe was reluctant to take any unnecessary risks with his lead actor.

Scott rested his fists on his hips and peered out across the square, striking a very Superman-esque pose, except in this case he looked like he was counting in his head to quell his frustration. "You'll be able to shoot my face if I do it myself. It'll look better."

"He's not wrong about that," Ed Dudley interjected.

Joe was still skeptical. "You twist an ankle, it'll shut down production for days."

Scott rolled his eyes. "Come on, man. I'm not gonna twist an ankle running across a park."

Joe looked over at Ben, and then at Stephen Choi, the stunt coordinator.

Stephen shrugged. "Let him do it if he wants."

Scott got his way, and ended up sprinting the length of the square at least thirty times before they were through getting all the shots they needed.

"Having any regrets yet?" Grace asked while Scott was chugging water between takes.

He wiped his mouth and grinned like a kid who'd won a prize goldfish at the school carnival. "I could do this all day."

They finished their last shot a half hour before they lost the light. The musicians must have played "When the Saints Go Marching In" a hundred times that day, and Grace was pretty sure she was going to have that stupid song stuck in her head until she died.

Scott took the seat next to her in the transpo van and blatantly read over her shoulder while she checked her Twitter feed. She didn't bother chastising him this time, and ten minutes later he was fast asleep with his head resting on her shoulder. He looked so peaceful, she let him stay there the rest of the ride.

WEDNESDAY THEY WERE SHOOTING OUTSIDE AGAIN, ON THE
south shore of Lake Pontchartrain, and once again the call time
was at the asscrack of *OMG it's still dark outside* o'clock.

The lake was immense: so big it was apparently impossible to
see the opposite shore even on a clear day—and today the sky was
about as clear as the sludge-filled Mississippi River. The predawn
sky was heavy with clouds, and a sharp, steady wind was blowing
off the water. Between that and the spray kicked up by the
choppy waves beating against the sea wall, Grace was shivering
inside her North Face windbreaker.

"Cold?" Scott asked as she stomped her feet to keep warm.

She shook her head. "I'll be fine once the sun comes up."

He pulled off his knit cap and put it on her head. "Here," he
said, tugging it down over her ears.

"You don't have to give me your hat," she protested. Although
it was soft and warm, and it smelled like him and whatever excel-
lent-smelling hair products he used. It made Grace want to pull it
down over her face and breathe in a lungful of the sensual Scott-
scent, but she managed to strangle the impulse—barely.

He shrugged. "I'm heading to hair and makeup. I won't be
able to wear it anyway."

"Thank you," she said, already starting to feel warmer.

"Take good care of it," he called out as he trudged off to the
makeup trailer. "That's my lucky hat."

At 6:56 the sun came up, and at 7:15 it started to drizzle.

Grace huddled inside the tent set up for the monitors, while
PAs followed the talent around with umbrellas. Until the cameras
started rolling, and then the actors were stuck out in the
elements, trying to deliver their lines without looking like they
were getting a face full of rain. Carmen and Tamika had their
hands full keeping the actors looking dry, and Ed Dudley was so

busy worrying about how the rain was affecting his shots that he didn't even have time to complain about it.

When they broke for lunch, Scott showed solidarity with the crew by eating his unsalted chicken breast and raw kale in the damp, drafty catering tent instead of warm and dry in his trailer.

"How many more setups do we have left to get through?" Tamika asked wearily.

"Twelve," Dominic said. He was sitting next to Carmen, Grace couldn't help noticing, even though Carmen kept insisting there was nothing going on between them. Of course, Grace was sitting next to Scott, and it wasn't like that meant anything at all.

"Hey!" she protested when Scott sneaked a Swedish meatball off her plate. "You'll endanger the six-pack."

"Yeah," Dex said, pointing his fork at Scott. "Some of us have residuals riding on those abs."

"You're making me regret not staying in my trailer," Scott grumbled genially.

Dex leaned over to Grace conspiratorially. "You're doing god's work. Keep it up."

The rain slowed everything down, but they just barely managed to get all their shots in before they lost the last of the day's light. Grace had never been so glad to climb into the transpo van at the end of a location day.

"You want your hat back?" she asked Scott when he slid into the seat next to hers.

"You keep it," he said, smiling at her in a way that made her stomach flip. "It looks better on you anyway."

She was certain he'd been kidding earlier about it being his lucky hat. He probably had a million knit hats just like it.

That was what Grace told herself, anyway.

———

"I love my job," Tamika sighed as she watched Scott and Nate rehearse.

"Me too," Grace agreed.

It was Thursday, and they were shooting at a boxing gym in Metairie. It was...not a nice location, although Grace was sure the rustic brick walls and vintage light fixtures would look lovely on camera. But otherwise, the building was dank and grubby, and it smelled like old rubber and stale testosterone, a fragrance that was not at all improved by yesterday's rain.

However, they were shooting a scene where Scott and Nate sparred in the ring, all shirtless and sweaty. So the view went a long way toward making up for the stench.

In addition to foreshadowing the big conflict between Scott and Nate later in the film, this boxing scene was meant to be *Sunset Limited*'s version of the *Top Gun* beach volleyball scene. It wasn't quite Val Kilmer in the sand, but Grace would definitely buy a ticket to it, if she wasn't already getting to watch for free.

Sometimes her job could be pretty great.

Even though it was ostensibly just a friendly sparring match, it was supposed to highlight the increasing tension between the two characters, and the fight choreography was elaborate. Every motion had to be carefully planned and executed so the actors and stuntmen didn't get injured by a stray punch or elbow. Both Scott and Nate had wanted to do as much of the fight as they could themselves, so they were doing a last-minute run-through with Stephen and their stunt doubles to make sure they had it down before the camera started rolling.

Dex wandered over to where Tamika and Grace were sitting, twisting the cap off a bottle of coconut water. "What are you guys"—he followed their gazes and stopped—"doing," he finished distractedly.

"Talking about how much we love our jobs," Tamika said with another sigh.

"Mmmm, I heard that." Dex sank down next to Grace, his

attention riveted by the action in the ring. "Who do y'all think is hotter—Scott or Nate?"

"Scott," Tamika said without hesitation.

Grace swiveled to look at her, eyebrows raised, and Tamika shrugged.

"What about you?" Dex asked, elbowing Grace.

"They're both nice to look at," she said noncommittally.

"Hmmm," Dex said, twisting his mouth to one side. "After a thorough scientific analysis and much consideration, I think I'm going to have to go with Nate."

"Really?" Grace said. "Nate?"

Dex arched a speculative eyebrow at her. "I thought they were both nice to look at."

"Scott smells really good," Tamika interjected, her gaze still locked on the men in the ring. "Have you noticed that?"

Grace definitely had, but she chose not to comment.

"True," Dex agreed with enthusiasm—apparently everyone had been going around sniffing Scott. "But Nate's taller, which is important when you're my height. And Scott's got that tiny bootie."

Grace tilted her head as she watched Scott dodge one of Nate's punches. "You think it's tiny?"

She wouldn't call Scott's ass small—it filled out the boxing shorts he was wearing quite nicely—but she supposed it was smaller than Nate's, which looked like two bowling balls in a hammock. Scott was leaner than Nate overall, but Grace preferred that. Nate was so muscular he was verging into body-builder territory, which had never been much to her taste.

Not much about Nate was to her taste, to be honest. He was objectively gorgeous and perfectly nice, but whenever she was talking to him she couldn't help wishing she was talking to someone else.

Dex shrugged. "I'm an ass man, what can I say?"

"I like Scott's scruff," Tamika said. Her eyes shifted to the side of the ring where Scott's stunt double was watching the action, and her smile got wider. "I like it on Ben too."

"Scruff's good," Grace agreed.

"All that friction," Tamika said. "Totally adds to the sensation."

Dex swung his head around, eyes widening. "Are you talking about what I think you're talking about?"

"What?" Tamika said innocently.

"Y'all are nasty!" Dex cackled. "I love it."

There was a cry of pain from the ring where the actors were rehearsing, and Grace's head snapped around.

Scott was on the floor, curled up on his side. When he rolled onto his back, there was blood all over his face.

"Fuck," Scott groaned as he rolled onto his back. "Ow. Dammit." He reached up to touch his nose experimentally. It didn't seem to be broken, but his fingers came away covered with blood.

It was Scott's own damn fault he'd gotten hurt. He'd made the fatal mistake of letting himself get distracted—well, not fatal, just excruciatingly painful.

He'd known Grace was watching him rehearse and he'd wanted to impress her, like some kind of fucking schoolboy showing off at recess. Instead of paying attention to what he was doing, he'd been paying attention to how he looked while he was doing it.

And that was how you got a stray fist in the nose.

"Aww, jeez. I'm so sorry, man." Nate stared down at Scott in horror as Stephen and Joe rushed up.

"I'm okay," Scott assured them before they could say anything. "It was just a love tap."

"We'll let the set medic be the judge of that." Joe's gruff tone meant his budget was probably flashing before his eyes.

They helped Scott sit up, and the medic came over to examine Scott.

"I'm fine," Scott grumbled while she checked him for signs of a concussion. "He didn't hit me that hard." His pride had taken the brunt of the injury. Here he'd been trying to look cool for Grace, and he'd ended up looking like an idiot instead.

Schoolboy pretty perfectly summed up how Grace made him feel. He couldn't seem to keep his eyes off her—and when she wasn't around he couldn't stop thinking about her.

Even now, with blood running down his face and his nose throbbing with pain, he was keenly aware of her watching him from the edge of the crowd that had formed around the ring.

"Hard enough to make you bleed like a stuck pig," the medic said as she felt along the ridge of his nose.

Scott was pretty sure her name was Janel, and he winced when she hit a tender spot. "I'm a bleeder. It'll stop on its own in a few minutes." He tried to hold still as maybe-Janel stuffed cotton in his nose to absorb the blood, and cleaned up his face with an alcohol wipe.

When she was done, she handed him a cold pack and announced that nothing was broken and he'd be fine.

"Thank god for small favors," Joe said, and he and Stephen helped Scott out of the ring. "Let's get a wheelchair over here to get him back to his trailer," he ordered Cal, who was hovering nearby.

"No need," Scott mumbled from underneath his cold pack. "Just give me five minutes and I'll be ready to get back in the ring."

"Don't be a hero," Joe said. "Ben can stand in for you today and we'll make up the close-ups another day."

"We don't have the location another day." Scott knew what a

delay like that would cost the production, and he'd be damned if he'd be the cause of it.

"That's my problem," Joe said.

Scott shook his head. "I'm telling you I'm fine, and I'm going to do this scene myself. Today. Just let me sit here for a minute until my damn nose stops bleeding, and I'll be good to go."

"You are one stubborn motherfucker," Joe grumbled, but he was grinning when he said it.

Scott sank down on one of the folding chairs set up outside the ring and leaned his head back to help stanch the bleeding.

"Everybody disperse and give the man some peace," Joe told the nervous crowd that had gathered around. He clapped Scott on the shoulder. "I'll check back with you in ten," he said before dragging the location manager off to confer about the possibility of getting the gym for a little longer.

Almost everyone managed to find somewhere else to be except Nate, who hovered over Scott, wringing his hands and apologizing profusely.

"It's fine, man," Scott told him, letting his eyes fall closed as he held the ice pack in place. "It happens. It wasn't even your fault, it was mine."

Nate continued to hang around, monologuing about the nervous nosebleeds he used to get as a kid, and Scott was about five seconds from snapping at him to get lost—because he did *not* have the patience for Nate's yammering right this moment—when he heard Grace's voice like an angel swooping in to save him.

"Hey Nate, I think Dominic was looking for you."

Her nearness caused the strangest sort of ache in Scott's chest. It was simultaneously too full and too tight. Half hopeful but also half painful, because what did he have to be hopeful about?

GRACE FELT A LITTLE BAD FOR THROWING DOMINIC UNDER THE bus, but it was for a good cause. Desperate times, etcetera.

"You sure you're all right?" Nate asked Scott, obviously reluctant to leave him.

"It's fine. Go," Scott told him, barely biting back a growl.

"Last I saw, he was out by the trailers in the parking lot," Grace offered helpfully. She was fairly sure Dominic was actually in the locker room they were using as a holding area for the extras, so that should keep Nate busy for at least five minutes.

Nate wandered off, and Scott opened one eye to peer up at her. "Thank you for that."

"Are you okay?"

His eye closed again. "I'll live. Believe it or not, this is not the first time I've been punched in the face."

"Shocking."

He smiled faintly. "You weren't worried about me, were you?"

"No."

Scott opened both eyes this time.

"Maybe a little," Grace admitted.

His smile got wider and he closed his eyes again. A bead of perspiration dripped off his chin and traveled down the valley between his pecs. Grace was close enough to him that she could smell the musky tang of his sweat, mingled with the woodsy scent of his cologne and the sharper, coppery odor of blood.

"Does it hurt?" she asked.

One of Scott's shoulders lifted in a shrug. "Not as much as some things."

Grace wondered what he meant by that, what could have hurt him more than being punched in the nose, but she didn't dare ask. "Can I get you anything?" she asked instead.

"I'm good, thanks."

She started to move away, but Scott lifted his head and caught her by the wrist. "Keep me company?"

"Okay." She sat down beside him. "Put your head back."

He did, and closed his eyes again. He was bare-chested and his abs were on display in all their magnificent water-cut glory, but Grace couldn't take her eyes off his hand—the one that had been wrapped around her wrist a few seconds ago. It was resting on his thigh, in easy reach, and she thought about how it would feel to hold it in hers. He was injured, and he'd asked her to sit with him. She wondered if it would be okay to hold his hand under the circumstances.

She thought she might like to. A little too much, maybe.

"Hey, man," Cal said, coming up behind her with Scott's gray hoodie. "Figured you might want your hoodie."

"Thanks, buddy." Scott sat up and let Cal help him into it.

"Your phone's in the pocket," Cal said. "You need anything else?"

"No, I'm all set." Scott zipped the hoodie up and settled back with his ice pack again.

"Give a shout if you change your mind." Cal gave Grace a nod before shuffling off.

"Take a picture of me," Scott said, slipping his phone out of his pocket and nudging Grace with it.

"What?"

"I want to post a picture of my busted face."

Grace couldn't imagine why, but she took the phone from him.

His lock screen was a picture of him with his arm around a beautiful young woman in a crop top. It looked like maybe they were in a bar or a nightclub, but it was hard to tell.

"The passcode's 1234," Scott told her.

Grace shook her head as she keyed in the numbers. "I can't believe you. You know how stupid that is, right?"

"Yeah, but I'm too lazy to memorize anything else."

When the phone unlocked, it opened to a thread of text messages with someone named Robbie. She assumed it was

Robbie Scarborough, and exited out of the messaging app before she could accidentally read any of them.

Scott's wallpaper was set to the same photo as his lock screen.

"Who's the girl?" Grace asked, trying to sound casual as she searched for his camera among all the apps.

"My sister, Paige."

"Ah." Grace hated herself for being so relieved to hear that.

"She's at NYU film school. I told her not to get into the business, but..." He shrugged. "She never listens to me."

"That's little sisters for you, I guess. Or so I've heard. I wouldn't know myself, being an only child." Grace held up the phone, focusing on Scott's face. "Ready?"

He sat up and lowered the ice pack. His nose was bright red and there was a bloody cotton ball hanging out of one of his nostrils. It looked like his right eye might be starting to bruise too. "Get in nice and tight," he told her.

"If you say so." Grace snapped the picture and held it up for his approval.

Scott grinned in delight. "Awesome. Instagram it for me?"

She navigated to his Instagram app and opened up the photo. "Filter preference?"

"No filter."

"Caption?"

Scott chewed on his lower lip while he thought about it. "There's no good way to get punched in the face."

Grace nodded as she typed it in.

"Make sure you cross-post it to Twitter too."

"Done." She passed his phone back to him.

When he took it, his hand closed over hers, and his thumb lightly stroked across her knuckles. "Thanks."

"Bleeding stop yet?" Tamika asked, appearing out of nowhere with her makeup kit, and Grace jerked her hand away from Scott's.

He pulled the bloody cotton out of his nostril and carefully scrunched his nose. "I think so."

"Let's see the damage," Tamika said, tipping his chin up for a better look.

"How bad is it?" he asked.

Tamika smiled. "It's fine."

"That bad, huh?"

"Don't worry, I've got you covered," she said, twisting open a pot of concealer.

Grace left them alone so Tamika could work her magic.

8

F riday's shoot was on a street in the Irish Channel with Nate and some of the supporting cast. Scott wasn't on the call sheet at all, which meant the lucky bastard was getting a three-day weekend. It was probably for the best, since he'd begun developing a nice shiner by the end of the day yesterday from his run-in with Nate's fist. They'd gotten the boxing scene in the can though, and Scott had managed to do all the close-ups himself, just like he'd said he would. Hopefully by Monday the bruising would have faded.

Based on the running commentary Scott was texting Grace on the trashy daytime television he was watching, it sounded like he was really making the most of his day off.

The weather was gorgeous for shooting outdoors, but the day seemed to drag without Scott on set. Which was a feeling that Grace refused to interrogate too closely. It was Tamika's birthday though, so there was cake at lunch. And they'd made plans to take her out for drinks after work.

One of the locals on the makeup crew suggested a bar in the Bywater, and it turned out to be a great little place with a patio out back and a low-key jazz trio playing original music. A bunch of the cast and crew turned up, and they took over two long tables out on the patio.

Grace had texted Scott the details earlier in the day, just in case he wanted to drop by and wish Tamika a happy birthday. Not that she actually expected him to or anything. Even so, she couldn't help looking toward the door every few minutes.

"I know what you're doing," Carmen said, leaning over and elbowing Grace in the ribs.

"Ow! Your elbows are like pointy sticks," Grace complained. "And I'm not doing anything."

"You're watching for Scott."

"I am not watching for Scott, because he's not coming."

"How do you know?"

"Because he never comes out for drinks with the crew."

"Is that so?" Carmen said smugly. "Then how come he just walked in?"

Grace swiveled her head around so fast she almost pulled a muscle.

Scott was indeed standing over by the door in conversation with Cal. A murmur went through the other tables on the patio as people craned their necks to gawk at the celebrity amongst them. While he might have been a has-been to Hollywood insiders, outside of LA celebrities were still celebrities, and Scott was one of the more recognizable ones. He was also one of the more attractive, particularly in the body-hugging leather jacket and jeans he'd worn tonight.

As he talked to Cal, Scott's eyes drifted around the space until they found Grace, and he casually nodded a greeting. She waved, then turned back to Carmen as she felt her face go bright pink.

"What were you saying?" Carmen asked with a smirk.

"Shut up," Grace said, reaching for her beer.

Carmen turned her attention back to Scott, looking him up and down in undisguised appreciation. "He is a fine-looking man, I'll give him that."

"Don't stare at him like that," Grace hissed. "He's not a piece of meat."

Carmen snorted. "You can't tell me you don't want to lick those abs. I mean, *I* want to lick those abs."

"Maybe a little," Grace admitted. "Purely as a scientific exercise."

"Hey," Scott said behind her.

Grace choked on her beer and narrowly managed to avoid spitting it all over Carmen.

"Scott!" Carmen said in an overly perkily voice. "How's your nose?"

"Still a little tender, but it's better."

"I didn't think we'd see you tonight."

"I couldn't miss Tamika's birthday," he said. "I owe her a birthday drink. Speaking of which...I need to go talk to the bartender." His hand fell on Grace's shoulder and squeezed briefly before he moved off.

"That was super smooth," Carmen told Grace, "the way you turned bright red and didn't say anything to him at all."

"My beer went down the wrong way. I was busy trying not to asphyxiate, okay?"

Carmen sipped her own beer, studying Grace over the rim of her glass. "Oh, shit. You're not just in lust, you actually like him."

"I—what? No. Absolutely not. Do I look delusional to you?"

Carmen's forehead wrinkled. "Is this a trick question?"

"I'm done dating actors," Grace said firmly. "Actors are like toddlers, only with bulging biceps and winning smiles and abs you can grate cheese on. But still: toddlers. They are not relationship material."

"Uh huh," Carmen said, not buying it. "You better watch yourself, girl. That is a minefield you're thinking of plowing into."

"I'm not plowing anything—and yes, I heard it," she said, rolling her eyes as Carmen snorted with laughter. "I promise you,

I have no feelings for Scott Deacon, other than a healthy appreciation for a well-sculpted body."

"That's why you two are always texting each other like a couple of high-schoolers, I guess."

Grace shrugged. "We live next door to each other. We're friendly. But that's it. Our relationship is completely professional and platonic."

"Oh, sweetie." Carmen took Grace's hand in hers and squeezed it sympathetically. "I had no idea you had it this bad."

Grace pulled her hand out of Carmen's grasp. "Don't be ridiculous."

"Just promise me you'll be careful," Carmen said, growing serious. "Because that man is dangerously hot, and as much as he's been flirting with you—"

"He has not been flirting with me," Grace insisted.

Carmen let out an exasperated sigh. "You can't possibly be this obtuse. Bringing you beignets, loaning you his hat—"

"Okay, fine, he's flirty, but that's just how he is with everyone. It doesn't mean anything."

"Grace!"

"It doesn't! I'm telling you, I am not interested in Scott Deacon and he is definitely not interested in me."

Grace knew full well that as soon as this shoot was over, she and Scott would go their separate ways and probably never see or talk to each other again, unless they happened to end up working on another project together one day. That was just how on-set relationships went. Whatever friendship they might have right now was only temporary—a relationship of convenience. Real, lasting friendships, like the one she had with Carmen, were the exception, not the rule.

Carmen rolled her eyes. "Just because you refuse to let yourself see it doesn't mean it's not there. Look, don't get me wrong, the man is sex on two legs, and given the chance I would definitely rock that like a hurricane. But you are not me, my friend."

"What's that supposed to mean?"

"It means you can't separate sex from emotion, and you know I'm right about that."

It was true that Grace had never once been in a non-serious relationship with a guy. She always got attached to the men she slept with. It wasn't that she was opposed to casual sex on principle, but in actual practice, she didn't get the appeal. She liked the middle part of relationships better than the beginning. The comfortable part, when you could relax and enjoy being together. All that stuff at the beginning—the getting to know each other part, the making someone like you part—it was an awful lot of work. And she didn't see the point of doing all that work for someone she wasn't interested in keeping around.

But maybe she was missing out. Maybe there was something to be said for casual. For not getting attached.

"Hey, that's not a criticism," Carmen said off Grace's frown. "It's one of the things that makes you the precious unicorn I love and would die to protect. But look at what happened with Chris: you turned a bangable moment into a two-year relationship with a freeloader who traded you in for a newer model as soon as he started earning a little money on his own."

"Wow. Harsh, Carm." Although admittedly an accurate description of what had happened. Grace had gotten comfortable with Chris way too fast. She'd been so busy settling in for the long haul that she'd never really stopped to ask herself if they were right for each other—or if he felt as strongly about her as she did about him.

"I'm sorry sweetie, but I'm not here to baby you. I'm here to make sure you don't get hurt like that again. And Scotty Deacon has trouble written all over him."

Grace rolled her eyes. "You need to chill, because no one's having sex with anyone."

"Speak for yourself," Carmen said, her gaze moving to Dominic.

"Fine," Grace grumbled. "*I'm* not having sex with anyone."

Carmen linked her arm with Grace's and dragged her out of her seat. "Come on, let's go get shots."

Half an hour and two rounds of shots later, Carmen was boldly flirting with Dominic, Tamika was getting seriously cozy with Ben, Scott seemed to have chatted up half the women at the bar, and Grace was trapped in a conversation with Nate. Story of her life, really.

Nate was being super tactile and flirty tonight—far flirtier even than Scott in extra-charming mode—which was weird, because he wasn't usually a touchy person in general. Not only was he punctuating every point he made by touching her arm or her hand or her shoulder, but in the middle of telling her a story about the last film he worked on, one of his hands landed on her knee and just sort of stayed there, lightly squeezing her thigh.

When it became clear he wasn't going to remove it on his own, Grace lifted his hand off her leg and dropped it back into his lap. He was so engrossed in the story he was telling he didn't seem to notice, but he steered clear of resting his hands on her thighs after that—although he kept doing the above-the-waist casual touches.

He'd had a few drinks, which she assumed was a contributing factor in this new, flirtier Nate, but she hadn't noticed him doing it with anyone else tonight. In fact, he'd spent most of his time at the bar with his attention focused on her.

Grace was not always an expert at social cues, but she wasn't stupid. She knew that she could probably go home with Nate tonight if she reciprocated his flirting.

If she wanted to try casual sex, this would be a perfect opportunity. He was gorgeous, and more importantly he seemed sweet. The actor part was not a selling point, but if it was just for one night, she supposed she could make an exception.

The problem was that when Grace tried to visualize herself having sex with Nate she came up blank. Literally couldn't imagine it. Every time she tried, her brain went somewhere else, like he was so boring he couldn't even hold her attention in her imagination.

This was why she didn't do casual sex. She just couldn't be bothered to make the effort most of the time.

Mercifully, after another ten minutes, the drinks finally caught up with him, and Nate excused himself to go to the men's room. Grace breathed a sigh of relief when Dex took his seat.

Carmen, who was her ride tonight, was deep in flirt with Dominic at the other end of the table, so Grace caught the waitress's attention and ordered herself another beer.

When she brought it a few minutes later, she handed Grace back her credit card.

"Oh, I'm not ready to close out my tab yet."

"It's taken care of," the waitress said.

"By who?"

"Scott Deacon had me transfer all the tabs in your party onto his card." The waitress leaned in close and lowered her voice. "He's like, crazy hot in person, isn't he?"

"Yeah," Grace agreed, watching Scott flirt with one of the women in the hair department. "He's dreamy."

By midnight, Tamika and Ben had left together, Nate had shifted his attentions to one of the makeup assistants, and Grace was beyond ready to go home. But Carmen and Dominic were still gazing into each other's eyes like a couple of lovestruck idiots, and Grace was actually really happy for them, so she guessed she could stick it out a while longer for Carmen's sake.

"Hey," Scott said, sliding into the chair next to her.

"Hey," Grace said back. It was the first time she'd talked to him since he got there, when she'd almost choked to death and hadn't managed to get any words out.

"Want another drink?" he asked with a nod at her mostly empty pint glass.

"Nooo," she said, pushing her glass away. "I've had enough."

She'd already had like four beers tonight. Or maybe five. Plus all those shots.

He tilted his head sideways, smiling at her. "You okay there?"

"Yep." She nodded to show him just how okay she was. "I'm great." Yikes, that was too much nodding, because now the room was starting to spin a little. Only they weren't in a room, they were outside, so it was like the whole world was doing the spinning. Yeah, not great.

"Have you had any water tonight?" Scott asked.

"Nope, just beer. And whatever's in a buttery nipple. That's a gross name for a drink, isn't it? Buttery nipple. What do you think's in it?"

"Too much sugar, that's what. Here." He put his drink in her hand. "Drink this."

Grace squinted suspiciously at the clear liquid. "What is it?"

"Club soda with lime."

She gave it a tentative sip and scrunched up her nose. Definitely club soda with lime. *Blech.* She hated club soda.

When she tried to hand it back to him he shook his head. "Finish it."

Grace reluctantly took another sip of Scott's yucky club soda while he flagged down the waitress to order a glass of water. It was super funny how, even though she was covering half the tables on the patio, their waitress just happened to be hovering nearby, ready to leap into action the second Scott looked like he might need something. She called him "honey," too, and touched his shoulder briefly before she left to get the water. *Gross.*

Scott turned back to Grace, and his knee bumped against her leg. "Are you having a good time?"

She nodded, more carefully this time. "Thanks for picking up the tab, by the way. That was nice."

He shrugged like it was nothing. Grace was a little too tipsy to do the math, but four hours worth of drinks for twenty people was definitely not nothing. Not to her, anyway, but she supposed maybe to someone like Scott it was nothing.

His leg was still resting against hers, all solid and warm and muscular inside his expensive designer jeans. She could feel the heat radiating off him through her own jeans, and it set her stomach fluttering in a way that didn't have anything at all to do with being drunk. Scott's thigh was *right there*, just begging her to rest her hand on it.

But then Grace remembered Nate and his thigh-touching and how unwelcome it had been.

No touching the platonic coworkers.

She cleared her throat. "I was surprised you came out tonight."

Scott's eyebrows jumped up slightly. "Why?"

"You didn't answer my text." She shrugged. "I wasn't sure if you'd want to hang out in a bar."

"I wasn't sure either," he admitted. "But I'm glad I did."

They were sitting really close, and Grace wasn't sure how that had happened. Had he leaned into her or had she leaned into him? They were close enough that she could count his eyelashes, and all the different shades of purple in the bruise under his eye. She wasn't used to being quite this close to him, and it made her feel dizzy.

"I'm glad too," she said, a little more loudly than she'd intended. "I mean, I'm glad you're glad. I'm glad you're having a good time. I mean, you seem to be having a good time, anyway. Are you having a good time?"

Ugh. What am I doing?

"I am," Scott said, his eyes crinkling with amusement.

Great. Grace was so glad he found her amusing. That was perfect. Exactly what she was going for.

His gaze lingered on her, and the amusement shifted into something else entirely—something unexpectedly intense. Grace felt herself starting to flush again under the weight of it, but then

Scott's attention shifted to the other end of the table, where the rest of their party was sitting.

"I missed this." There was something wistful and a little sad in his voice.

"What?"

"The sense of community you get from working on a set. The way it bonds you. The connection with other people." He looked down at his lap, and she saw his jaw tighten. "My life has been pretty lonely the last few years."

"I'm sorry." She reached for his hand without thinking. By the time she realized she'd done it, it was too late to take it back because his fingers had tightened around hers, trapping them.

He looked down at their intertwined hands and shook his head. "You don't have to be sorry. I'm just glad to have it again. And I wouldn't be here if it wasn't for you."

Grace's forehead furrowed in confusion. "What do you mean?"

"You're the one who encouraged me to stop pushing people away."

"If by encouraged you mean I yelled at you, then yes, I definitely did do that."

He smiled at her, wide enough to show off his dimples. "Whatever you did, it was exactly what I needed."

The way he was looking at her was really a lot. It was probably just the alcohol, making everything feel more intense, but it was like this concentrated beam of mega-hotness directed straight at her.

The waitress came back with the water, and Grace slipped her hand out of Scott's. She gulped down half of it in one go, trying to cool herself off.

"Easy," Scott warned, watching her with one eyebrow slightly raised.

"I'm fine," Grace said, then winced, pressing the heel of her hand against her forehead. "Ow, brain freeze."

"Hey." Carmen tapped her on the shoulder.

Grace opened her eyes and twisted around to look at Carmen, who had taken the chair on her other side. "Yep?"

"You okay?" Carmen asked, frowning.

"Yep," Grace said again, popping the P for extra emphasis. "Just a little brain freeze." She held up her glass of ice water for illustrative purposes.

"So...I'm going to take Dom home," Carmen said, hooking a thumb over her shoulder at Dominic. He was standing a few feet away with his hands shoved in his pockets and a sheepish look on his face, like he was trying to pretend he wasn't totally about to go have sex with Carmen. "But I'll drop you off first, okay?"

"No, no, no," Grace said, shaking her head. "You don't have to do that, I'll just call a cab."

Carmen rolled her eyes. "You're not calling a cab. I'm your ride, and I'm taking you home."

"Carmen," Grace hissed, wrapping her hand around her friend's wrist and tugging her closer. "I am not getting in the way of you and Dominic. That's not what friends do."

"Grace," Carmen hissed back. "I am not abandoning you at a bar. That's not what friends do."

"How about if I take her home?" Scott interjected.

Grace spun around, eyes widening. "Oh, no! You don't have to—"

"You literally live next door to me," he said. "It couldn't be less out of my way."

"I don't know," Carmen said, frowning at Scott.

"I promise to be a perfect gentleman," he said without a trace of mockery. When that didn't seem to be enough to satisfy Carmen, he held up three fingers. "Scout's honor."

Carmen looked at Grace. "Are you okay with this, sweetie? Because if you're not—"

"It's fine," Grace assured her. "As long as Scott doesn't mind, I don't mind."

Carmen turned back to Scott, and her eyes narrowed dangerously. "You know I will kill you if anything happens to her, right? Like, I will literally murder you."

"Noted," Scott said, drawing back a little.

Carmen leaned in to hug Grace. "Don't do anything stupid, okay?" she whispered.

"I won't," Grace whispered back. "Now go. Have fun with Dominic."

She watched Carmen walk over to Dominic and take his hand. They were positively beaming at each other, and it was pretty much the cutest thing she'd ever seen.

"Do you want to stay?" Scott asked. "Or are you ready to take off?"

"I'm fine with whatever," Grace said, turning back to him and stifling a yawn.

He smiled. "Just let me pay the tab and we'll go."

SCOTT'S RENTED AUDI HAD REALLY COMFORTABLE SEATS. THEY were much more comfortable than the Hyundai Accent the production had rented for Grace.

His Audi was so comfortable that she accidentally fell asleep on the ride home. One minute Grace was looking out the window at the beautiful old houses they were driving past, and the next Scott had opened her door and was gently shaking her awake. "We're here. Think you can walk?"

"Yeah, of course," Grace insisted, jumping out of the car a little too quickly, because as soon as she stood up she felt light-headed and her vision started to tunnel.

Scott reached out to steady her. "I've got you," he said, wrapping an arm around her.

Grace let herself lean into him until her vision had cleared. And then she kept leaning into him and let him guide her to the house, because he was warm and comfy and it was a chilly night.

His body was crazy firm, but also somehow snuggly, which didn't seem like it should be possible, but there he was, being snuggly and firm at the same time.

As soon as they got to Grace's front door, Scott let go of her and took a step back. The sudden loss of contact left her chilled.

"Do you have your key?" he asked, shoving his hands in his pockets.

She dug in her purse for it and unlocked the door. When she turned back to him, it felt like he was standing even farther away than before, like he wanted to make sure she didn't get any wrong ideas about his intentions.

Message received. Loud and clear.

"Thanks for the ride," Grace said, being careful not to close the distance between them.

"Drink some water before bed, okay?"

"Sure."

"I'm serious," Scott said.

She offered him a smile. "I can tell. You know how I can tell? Because you're making your serious face, which is totally different from your just joking around face."

"Promise me."

God, he was *extra* hot when he was acting like a mother hen. It was so unfair.

"I promise," Grace said.

Unexpectedly, he stepped forward and wrapped her up in a cushy hug. "Goodnight, Grace," he said against her hair before letting go of her and stepping decisively away from her again.

"Goodnight," she mumbled and fled inside her house.

We're just friends, she told herself firmly as she stood in the kitchen drinking the promised glass of water. He'd made that pretty abundantly clear tonight. *Friends and nothing more.*

Maybe if she repeated it to herself enough times, she'd actually accept it.

Ten minutes later, as she was crawling into bed, Scott sent her a text.

Scott: Did u drink water?

Grace rolled her eyes as she typed her answer.

Grace: Yes, mom.

Scott: Good girl now go to bed

She did.

9

Poppy Carpenter was playing Scott's love interest, and Monday was her first day on set. Even though she was the female lead, she was only needed for the second half of the shoot, because she wasn't actually in that many scenes.

The first time Grace had read the script, she'd noted that not only did it not even come close to passing the Bechdel Test, but aside from some bit parts there were a grand total of two whole women in the cast: Poppy and another actress named Sareh Davani, who was playing a sexy assassin. Not so incidentally, the screenwriter of *Sunset Limited* was male. Shocking.

Poppy's casting was a little weird, because Poppy happened to be the ex-fiancée of Scott's friend Robbie Scarborough. Robbie and Poppy had been one of Hollywood's favorite couples until about five years ago, when they'd gone through a very public, very messy breakup. There had been speculation that Scott was responsible for the breakup, inspired by his subsequent falling out with Robbie and downward spiral into increasingly out of control behavior.

And now Poppy was playing Scott's love interest in a film

partially funded by Robbie, and they had a fairly explicit sex scene to shoot later in the week. So, yeah. A little weird.

Hollywood could be incestuous like that. It was like a small town where everyone knew everyone else, so that kind of thing happened more often than you might think. Actors ended up doing love scenes with their ex-girlfriend—or their best friend's girlfriend, or their girlfriend's best friend, or some equally awkward matchup—all the time.

The first time Grace met her, Poppy was in her underwear. It was her wardrobe for the scene she was filming that morning—because the screenwriter was a man, so of course it was—and holy moly, talk about abs you could grate cheese on.

Usually, when the wardrobe was that revealing, the actors covered up with a robe between takes, but Poppy didn't seem to feel the need. Not that Grace could blame her. Poppy's body was insane. If Grace had a body like that, she'd walk around naked all the time, like even to the grocery store probably.

In addition to having the body of a fitness model, Poppy had long, lush brown hair, stunning blue eyes, and an adorable dimpled smile. She made a point of introducing herself to Grace right away and telling her how much she was looking forward to working together. Then she very ungracefully adjusted her boobs in the beautiful lace bra she was wearing and said, "Jesus, this thing feels like it's lined with nails. Why can't anyone design sexy-looking tittyholders that don't feel like you're strapping yourself into a goddamn Iron Maiden?"

Grace liked her right away.

Poppy went out of her way to make friends with the rest of the crew too—even the extras, which she definitely did not have to do. Poppy Carpenter's star was on the rise, and she'd been working a lot more regularly than Scott, even if she didn't have quite his level of name recognition yet. Given his insurance situation, it was likely she was being paid more than he was for this film. But despite the fact that she was on track to be the next

Jennifer Lawrence, Poppy was unpretentious, down-to-earth, and nice to everyone.

Even Scott, when he finally showed up to set.

Grace had been a little worried, frankly, about how the two of them were going to get along. She wasn't sure how Scott would react to having someone from one of the more unsavory chapters of his past around. If there was any lingering tension from whatever interpersonal drama had gone down between Poppy and Robbie and Scott in the past, it could make for some uncomfortableness on set. But not only was there no evidence of any strain between the two of them, they seemed as chummy as best friends. Or more than best friends, even.

"Am I crazy, or is he flirting with her?" Tamika asked, watching Scott and Poppy on the other side of the soundstage.

Poppy had changed into actual clothes for her second scene of the day, and she and Scott were sitting next to each other with their heads bent together, laughing about something on Poppy's phone. Scott had draped his arm across the back of Poppy's chair with his hand resting comfortably on her shoulder.

"He's definitely flirting with her," Carmen said, pursing her lips in disapproval.

"They're flirting with each other," Grace said when Poppy reached over and squeezed Scott's thigh. She wanted to look away, but she couldn't seem to make herself stop watching them.

Scott was smiling, like *really* smiling instead of fake smiling, and he looked more relaxed than Grace had ever seen him. He leaned in close to whisper something in Poppy's ear, and whatever it was must have been hilarious, because she threw her head back and let out a peal of laughter. "Scotty!" she shrieked, punching him in the arm. "You're terrible!"

She called him Scotty. And he didn't seem to mind in the slightest.

Tamika wrinkled her nose in distaste. "She was engaged to his best friend. Isn't that kind of...skeevy?"

"Super skeevy," Carmen agreed. She shot a sympathetic look at Grace. "Sorry. I guess I was wrong."

"I'm not," Grace said, determined to ignore the knot in the pit of her stomach. "I told you it was nothing."

"I'm still sorry," Carmen said.

———

POPPY HAD TO EAT A DONUT IN THE SCENE SHE WAS SHOOTING with Scott in the afternoon.

Because women who look like fitness models definitely eat donuts all the time, Grace thought with disgust.

Scenes with food were always a nightmare for continuity, because the food kept getting eaten, and Grace had to make sure it was eaten the exact same amount in every take, from every angle. Which meant props needed to have a lot of identical donuts on hand, and Poppy had to keep taking bites out of them.

On the third take of the two-shot, Poppy got a smear of chocolate on her face when she bit into the donut.

"You've got a little something—" Scott said while they were still rolling. He pointed at Poppy's cheek, playing it off in character. "Right there."

"That's not in the script," Grace whispered. Beside her, Joe nodded absently, but he let it play out.

Without breaking character, Poppy ducked her head shyly and made a moue. "Where?"

Scott tipped her chin up, the barest hint of a smile playing across his lips, and swiped his thumb across her cheek.

"*So* not in the script," Grace muttered to herself.

"Did you get it?" Poppy asked, blinking up at Scott through her lashes.

Without breaking eye contact, he slowly brought his thumb to his lips and licked the chocolate off. "Got it."

It was pretty much the most sensual thing Grace had ever

seen. Their chemistry on-screen was incendiary, and Joe was grinning like he'd just gotten the best Christmas present ever. "Print that," he said excitedly. "Did you get the new dialogue?"

Grace nodded as she made a note in her script.

She got it, all right.

TUESDAY MORNING, JOE STALKED ONTO SET LOOKING LIKE someone had peed in his oatmeal.

"What's wrong?" Grace asked, eying him warily. It must be something pretty bad to have affected his mood this much.

He sighed, lowering himself heavily into his chair. "We're getting new pages today."

"Okay." It was late in the game to be tweaking the script, but it wasn't completely unheard of. Based on the way Joe was frowning, Grace assumed there was more to it.

He leaned forward and set his coffee cup on the floor while he dug around in his messenger bag. "For tomorrow morning's scene."

"I thought you were happy with that scene as is," Grace said, frowning.

Joe popped two ibuprofen and swallowed them down with a mouthful of coffee. "I am. This is coming from the backers."

Which meant there'd been a fight over it. And Joe lost. No wonder he was pissed. "Does Scott know?"

"He will soon enough."

Grace chewed on the inside of her lip. "He's not going to like it."

"*I* don't like it," Joe said. "He can take a number."

When Scott came in a couple hours later, Grace intercepted him on his way to his trailer. "Did you hear about the new pages?"

He nodded. "Joe texted me this morning." He didn't seem that pissed about it, which was good. Non-pissed Scott was much easier to work with than pissed Scott.

"I'll have to stay a little late tonight to update my breakdown for the morning," Grace said, "but I can come over and help you learn the new lines when I get home."

He laid his hand on her shoulder, and the heavy warmth of his touch burned straight through her clothes to heat her skin. His strong fingers squeezed gently as his eyes gazed directly into hers. "Thank you. I appreciate that, but you don't have to."

"I don't mind."

He let go of her. "No, I mean—Poppy's going to come over and work with me."

"Oh," Grace said. "That's great."

Poppy must be one of the close friends who knew about his trouble with memorization. Which totally made sense. They went back years. And since she had to learn the new dialogue too, they might as well kill two birds with one stone. It was a great plan. The best plan.

Scott ran his hand through his hair, making it stand up all spiky on top. "Thank you though. I really do appreciate the offer."

Grace shrugged. "I'm glad you've got someone else to help."

"Sorry," he said, hooking a thumb over his shoulder. "I've gotta run and get changed into wardrobe. I'll talk to you later though?"

"Sure," she said to his back as he walked away.

It wasn't that Grace was jealous. Jealousy was about someone else taking what you had, and it wasn't like she'd ever *had* Scott. Far from it.

If anything, she was happy for him. It was great that all of Scott and Poppy's scenes together sizzled with sexual tension. And it was great that they got along so well off camera too. Grace was glad he had someone on set he felt comfortable with. She was. Truly.

It was just...she'd gotten kind of used to being the person Scott was comfortable with on set.

But now Poppy was helping him learn his lines, and she was calling him *Scotty*, and he hadn't texted Grace in two days.

It was fine. It was whatever. It wasn't like she had a claim on him anyway. She'd always known their friendship wasn't meant to last.

Just because Scott was good at making you feel special, it didn't mean you were.

<hr />

"THIS NEW DIALOGUE'S KIND OF CHEESY, ISN'T IT?" POPPY SAID as she flopped down on Scott's couch with her fifth beer of the night. Not that Scott was counting. Except he was definitely counting.

"Just be glad they're not making us pimp mattresses or tennis shoes or something." Scott slumped back into the couch across from her and riffled the edges of his script, watching the rainbow of pages flip past.

"You didn't *really* have to do that?" Poppy asked, appalled.

"No, not really." He had a little, but if it helped get the movie made, he was in no position to complain. "Listen, thank you again for doing this. You have no idea—"

"Quit thanking me. It's nothing."

It wasn't nothing. She was more in demand than ever, and the window during which an actress could pick and choose her projects was terrifyingly narrow. For Poppy to give up even a few weeks of her schedule to take a role that was, quite frankly, beneath her at this point in her career, was far from nothing. That she'd done it for Scott, after everything he'd put her through already, meant more to him than he was capable of expressing.

He also knew Poppy didn't like talking about things like that any more than he did.

More than he *used* to, he corrected himself. Emotional honesty was one of the many things he was trying to get better at—with only limited success so far. Like everything else about him, it was a work in progress.

"It's not really that bad," Poppy said, laying the flat of her hand on the script sitting next to her on the couch. "There's some good stuff later on that I'm looking forward to sinking my teeth into. It's just this one scene. They're really going all in on the clichés."

"I try to think of it as an homage." Scott frowned as Poppy knocked back a third of her beer in one long swig, and he bit down the urge to say something about it. "Joe tried like hell to fight them on it, but I guess the backers were nervous there wouldn't be enough sexual tension unless they literally hit the audience over the head with it."

Poppy snorted. "Between us? I don't think it's gonna be a problem."

"No," Scott agreed, smiling faintly. "Definitely not."

He and Poppy had always had plenty of chemistry. A little too much. Even now, years after their physical relationship had ended and they'd settled into a comfortable friendship, the air between them still felt energized.

This would be their first time working together, and Scott was relishing the opportunity to put all that excess chemistry to work on-screen. They had a great rapport, and there was honestly no one he'd rather share scenes with in his big comeback. Just having Poppy here was a huge boost to his confidence. He'd never be able to thank her enough for attaching herself to the project on the condition that he was the lead. Scott hadn't even had to ask— she'd volunteered to do it. The producers hadn't been able to turn down a chance to get Poppy Carpenter on board, even if meant bringing Scott along as baggage.

He loved Poppy, even if he recognized now that they'd made a disastrous couple. Their brief, reckless flirtation with a romantic relationship had been as tempestuous as it was toxic, born as much from a mutual desire for self-destruction as anything else.

Poppy understood him better than anyone, but only because they were so much alike. The two of them were like competitive siblings who had a tendency to bring out the worst in one another. Their similarities made a great foundation for a friendship, but a terrible one for a romantic partnership.

Poppy took another long swig of beer and rubbed her nose with the back of her hand. "I think the way we're playing it is good. Giving it an ironic edge helps counteract the cheese factor. And based on yesterday's scene, I don't think we'll be short on sex appeal." She smirked at him. "By the time we get to the actual love scene, they're gonna have to spray us down with a fire extinguisher."

"Mmmm," Scott murmured in unenthusiastic agreement. The thought of Thursday's love scene filled him with gut-churning dread. Not because it was with Poppy—he was far more comfortable doing it with someone he knew than a near stranger—but because he always hated doing love scenes. Pretty much every actor he knew loathed them, but for Scott it was a particular kind of hell. It wasn't the nudity so much as the rawness and intimacy. He could generate tears at the drop of a hat and dredge up deep wells of emotion with no problem, but ask him to simulate lovemaking and it triggered the kind of stage fright and self-consciousness he rarely experienced as a performer anymore.

"Don't be such a baby," Poppy said, well aware of his dislike of love scenes. "It's not like it's anything we haven't done before."

Scott glared at her. "You know that doesn't make it any less awkward, right?"

His discomfort was compounded exponentially by the fact that Grace would be there. Taking fucking notes, no less. He didn't even mind so much that she'd see him naked. Hell, he'd be happy to strip for her, provided *she* was the one he was taking to bed. He hated with every atom of his being that the first time

Grace saw what he looked like having sex, it would be with another woman.

He wondered again if he should have kissed her Saturday night after the bar, even though he knew the answer. That wasn't how he wanted things to happen between them—even if she had been giving off some serious *please kiss me* vibes.

It was the first time Scott had felt like maybe Grace was actually interested in him. Attracted to him, even, on more than just a superficial level.

Christ, he'd wanted to kiss her. *So much*. But he knew he'd done the right thing by waiting. Just because he hadn't looked half bad to her through beer goggles in the moment didn't mean she actually *liked* him. The absolute last thing he wanted was to be a mistake she regretted the morning after.

He'd finally gotten to a place where he could believe Grace cared about him, but he still couldn't help feeling like it was rooted in pity. Her interest in him felt more like the sort of support you'd offer to a struggling coworker than a potential love interest.

Scott wanted to be able to believe Grace liked him—*really* liked him—for who he was, but he wasn't sure that was possible.

Poppy drained the last of her beer and went into the kitchen, chucking the empty in the recycling bin before pulling open the fridge.

"You're hitting those beers pretty hard," Scott said when she opened another one.

She gave him a withering look. "It's not like anyone else is gonna be drinking them, is it?"

"That's your sixth one." Poppy was maybe a hundred and ten pounds soaking wet. Six beers was a lot for someone that size. Also, how the hell was she maintaining that weight while consuming so much beer? Scott was afraid to even think about it.

She glared at him as she raised the bottle to her lips. "Lay off, Mom."

"Maybe you should slow down a little."

"I don't need a sanity check from a guy who once tried to get high off a can of Sterno," she shot back at him.

Poppy had always boasted that she was a functional alcoholic —as opposed to Scott, the dysfunctional drug addict. But he could remember a time when he'd been able to function with his addiction too. He'd gotten by just fine for years before it started to become a noticeable problem.

Just because the problem hadn't been noticeable didn't mean it hadn't been a problem. If he'd only recognized the signs *before* it got out of hand, he could have saved himself a lot of pain and misery.

He'd tried to talk to Poppy about her drinking before, but she always got defensive with him. She wasn't ready to hear it yet. He just hoped she didn't have to hit rock bottom like he had before she was ready to admit she had a problem.

Scott held up his hands in surrender. "Fine, but you're not driving anywhere after all those."

"You're not gonna make me take a fucking Uber?"

"No." Scott sighed. "You can crash here tonight."

At least that way he'd be able to keep an eye on her.

GRACE WAS RUSHING TO CHOKE DOWN A BAGEL BEFORE WORK when there was a knock on Scott's side of the adjoining door. She swallowed down the bite in her mouth and did a quick check of her reflection in the toaster to make sure there was no cream cheese in her teeth before opening it.

It wasn't Scott—it was Poppy. Wearing one of Scott's T-shirts and nothing else. Nothing else that Grace could see, anyway. Scott's T-shirt hung down halfway to Poppy's knees, so it was impossible to tell if she was wearing underwear.

God, please let her be wearing underwear. If she wasn't, Grace did not want to know.

"Hey!" Poppy said in a voice that was far too perky for six in the morning. Somehow, even with bed head and no makeup, she still managed to look stunning, because of course she did.

Grace snapped her mouth closed and tried to smile, like it was nothing to her that Poppy was at Scott's house first thing in the morning. That Poppy was wearing his clothes. That they had obviously spent the night together.

"Um, hi," she managed in what she hoped was a normal, friendly voice.

"Scotty doesn't have any milk," Poppy said.

Grace stared at her blankly. Her brain was still struggling to process this new information that Poppy and Scott were sleeping together, and it was functioning on a bit of a delay.

"He doesn't do dairy," Poppy went on, "and I don't do coffee without cream." She paused, tilting her head to the side. "But he said you might have some," she added hopefully when Grace didn't say anything.

That was when Grace finally noticed the steaming coffee mug in Poppy's hand. "Right, sure, of course. Come in." She stepped back and waved Poppy inside. "Sorry, I'm not quite awake yet."

"Your place is cute," Poppy said, peering around as she followed Grace into the kitchen. "It kinda matches Scotty's."

"Yeah, I guess they were built at the same time or something." Grace leaned into the fridge for the half-and-half and handed it to Poppy.

"Thanks." Poppy poured a generous dollop into her coffee and offered it back.

"Keep it," Grace said. "I've got another one."

That was a lie, but she couldn't face the thought of Poppy stopping by to borrow cream every time she had a sleepover at Scott's. Grace didn't want to know that much about Scott's sex life—or Poppy's, for that matter. She didn't even want to know as much as she already knew about it.

Poppy's eyebrows lifted. "You sure?"

"Yeah," Grace said, smiling. "Keep it in Scott's fridge. You know, for the next time."

"Okay, well, thanks." Poppy shrugged and took her coffee creamer and her attractive bed head back over to Scott's.

Grace locked the door behind her, then went into the kitchen and tossed her bagel in the trash. For some reason she didn't have much of an appetite anymore.

10

Today was not turning out to be Grace's day.

She'd forgotten to gas up her car last night, so she had to stop on the way in to work. Then she ended up dripping gasoline on her shoes, which stank up the inside of her car, which in turn brought on a raging headache. On top of that, she managed to spill her travel mug of coffee down the front of her shirt, so by the time she arrived at work she was late, under-caffeinated, covered in coffee, rocking a nauseous headache, and in no mood for anyone's shit.

Which was when she discovered she'd left her laptop cord at home.

"Aaarrrgh!" Grace wailed, holding her empty laptop bag upside down and shaking it over the desk in her corner of the cramped production office.

"What the hell?" Cal said, eying her warily from the doorway.

Grace sighed and dumped her laptop bag on the floor, shoulders slumping in defeat. "I forgot my laptop cable."

Cal pointed at her chest. "There's coffee on your shirt."

"Really?" Grace snapped. "I hadn't noticed that I'd poured hot coffee all over myself. Thanks so much for pointing it out."

Cal took a step back. "Jeez, someone's touchy today."

"Sorry, sorry, sorry." Grace sank into her chair and buried her face in her hands. "It's just been a real Monday, you know?"

"It's Wednesday," Cal pointed out helpfully.

"Yeah, but between the gasoline and the headache and the coffee and the power adapter, it's feeling a lot more like a Monday." She pushed herself upright and flipped open her laptop. "I've got maybe six hours of battery life on this thing, if I'm lucky."

Cal regarded her silently for a moment, one eyebrow slightly raised. "I think I know where I can scrounge up a power cord for you."

"That would be...so great," Grace said, giving him a watery smile. "Thank you, Cal. You're my hero."

"Yeah, whatever," he mumbled, wandering off.

Grace dug through her purse for a bottle of ibuprofen and swallowed two pills down with the dregs of her now-cold coffee. Then she used up some of her precious battery life to get the script pages and logs ready for the day's shooting. Once she'd gotten all her prep work out of the way, she went downstairs and hit up craft services for a fresh cup of coffee before heading out back to the wardrobe trailer.

Carmen took one look at her and started digging through the racks for a clean shirt while Grace regaled her with the saga of her morning—leaving out the part about Poppy and Scott, because she didn't want to spread gossip, but also because she didn't want Carmen feeling any sorrier for her than she did already.

Grace's shitty morning didn't have anything to do with Scott and Poppy anyway. They were both free to sleep with whoever they wanted. It was no skin off her nose.

By the time they were ready to start shooting, Grace had acquired a clean shirt and a borrowed laptop cable that Cal had found for her, bless him. Unfortunately, they were shooting on the bar set today, which meant lots of background extras and lots of drinks. Which meant a lot of continuity details to keep track of, and because she'd only gotten the script pages yesterday, she wasn't as prepared as she liked to be.

"That guy in the red shirt should be standing at the bar," Grace told Dominic on the second setup.

"But I wasn't at the bar in any of the other takes," Red Shirt said.

"Sorry, did I say red? I meant blue," Grace amended.

"Which blue shirt?" Dominic asked helplessly. "There are like three."

"Blue polo. Right there." Grace pointed at the offending extra, who quickly scooted over to the bar.

"Are we good now?" Joe asked.

Grace nodded. "Yes."

"All right," Dominic called out. "Settle in."

"Wait!" Grace said. "Sorry! That shaker needs to be on Poppy's right side, not her left."

The prop guy started forward to remedy the mistake, but before he could get there, Poppy moved the shaker herself. "I got it," she said. "We cool now?"

Grace gave the set another once-over to make sure there was nothing else she'd missed before giving the all clear. Dominic called for quiet again, sound and cameras started rolling, and Joe called action.

It was the scene where Scott and Poppy first meet, and it was pretty straightforward on paper—Scott walks into the bar where Poppy's bartending, orders a drink from her, and questions her about one of the bar's regular patrons. But because it was Scott and Poppy, the entire interaction was shimmering with sexual tension.

Scott really played it up, pausing when he first caught sight of Poppy and letting his gaze grow heated before he made his way over to her. When she saw him approaching, Poppy made a purring sound in the back of her throat and arched her back, showing off her boobs. She had spectacular boobs. Natural too, by all appearances. Everything about Poppy was perfect, basically. No wonder Scott had slept with her.

Grace found it unreasonably difficult to watch Scott and Poppy acting together now that she knew they were actually *together* together. Watching them canoodle and flirt for the camera felt weirdly intimate and intrusive, like she was peeping through their bedroom window. It was dumb and irrational, but she couldn't help it, and she also couldn't look away, because she had to watch them in order to do her job.

She was not loving her job today.

When they finally broke for lunch, it felt like she'd been at work for sixteen hours instead of six. And because nothing was going her way, catering was serving up corned beef and cabbage, which would be unappealing on a good day, but today, when she was still feeling nauseous and vaguely headachy, was a big fat nope. So Grace skipped the noise and cabbage smell of the commissary in favor of a little alone time at her desk.

She felt like karma owed her one at this point, but apparently not, because on her way to the office she rounded a corner and ran smack into Scott. Like, literally crashed face-first into his massive, rock-hard chest.

She let out an embarrassing shriek, more from surprise than pain, and stumbled backward.

"Whoa," he said, grasping her upper arms to keep her from falling.

"Sorry!" Grace's hands flailed out and wound up on his chest for lack of anywhere else to go.

"Are you hurt?"

She shook her head. "Nope, just a klutz."

He was still holding on to her, and they were so close they were practically chest to chest, and she felt paralyzed by the overwhelming nearness of him. Scott's hands slid up her arms to her shoulders, and his eyes roamed over her face like he was searching for evidence of injury or head trauma.

Grace swallowed, suppressing the urge to shiver. "I should really pay more attention to where I'm going," she said with a nervous laugh. Then she realized she was basically caressing his chest, and jerked her hands back. "Sorry."

Scott let go of her and she took a big step back, exhaling.

"You sure you're okay?" he asked, frowning.

"Yep, still in one piece." Another nervous laugh slipped out.

He nodded, shoving his hands in his pockets. "Hey, I hope it's okay that Poppy knocked on your door this morning. I didn't think you'd mind."

"I didn't. Why would I mind?"

"I don't know. I just wanted to check."

"Poppy's great! I love Poppy! And I happened to have cream for her coffee, so really, it was perfect for everyone." All of which was true, although she might be overplaying the enthusiasm a tad.

"Okay," Scott said, like he wasn't quite buying it.

"Okay," Grace echoed. "Well, I'm just gonna..." She tilted her head in the direction of her office. "I'm gonna go."

He nodded, and she practically sprinted away from him.

Grace muddled her way through the rest of the day, keeping her distance from Scott as much as possible. And he did her the favor of keeping his distance from her, which was just great. Fantastic, even. It was nice to know her company wasn't wanted anymore now that Poppy was here.

But then Thursday rolled around. The day they were filming the love scene.

Shooting sex scenes was always uncomfortable even under the best circumstances. Being naked and simulating sex in front of a room full of people was generally terrifying and humiliating for the actors, and not nearly as much fun to watch as you might think.

Even though they were shooting on a closed set with only minimal crew, there were still a dozen-ish people present, so it was a weirdly public activity. The whole thing was highly choreographed, every little movement blocked out in advance, so it wound up being very mechanical and not sexy at all. But at the same time, there was actual skin-to-skin contact happening, and they were pretending to do something that was supposed to be intimate, only with a sweaty guy holding a boom mic over their heads, sending every little sound to a group of people watching with headphones on.

Joe had already spent a lot of time working with Scott and Poppy, prepping for the scene, so they only did a quick run-through for lighting and sound before the actors went to change into wardrobe.

The first half of the day involved a lot of kissing and removing of clothing, which required a lot of intervention from the wardrobe and makeup departments. At the end of every take, they had to get Scott and Poppy re-dressed and reapply all the makeup they'd basically just licked off each other's faces.

Gross.

There were a few lines of dialogue at the beginning of the scene before they started kissing. Then Scott took Poppy's shirt off, revealing her very pretty, very uncomfortable-looking bra. Then more kissing. Then Poppy took Scott's shirt off so everyone could see the six-pack he'd done another water cut for. More kissing. He picked her up and carried her to the bed. Kissing. He laid her down and crawled on top of her. Kissing.

There was just a whole lot of kissing.

Complicating matters was the number of angles they had to shoot from: close-ups, mediums, low angles, over-the-shoulders. It was a lot of setups and a lot of takes. And in between every one, Joe was giving them direction on their technique: more intensity, less tongue, gasp louder.

Honestly, the sounds were maybe the worst part of all of it. Grace could almost kind of separate herself from what was happening a few feet away when she was watching on the monitors. Keeping her attention focused on the screen made it easier to look at the shot clinically and only think about the relevant technical details. But all the gasping and moaning and slurping and smacking sounds coming through her headset and going directly into her brain were a lot harder to ignore.

Plus, there was the mortifying fact that she had to actually correct the actors from time to time on the mechanics of their lovemaking.

"Um, Scott," she said at the end of a take. "Remember, you need to pull Poppy's bra strap off her shoulder before you start kissing her breast."

Good thing that wasn't awkward or anything. Especially now that she knew they were actually sleeping together offscreen. Grace was going to have to anesthetize herself with an entire bottle of wine when she got home tonight.

Scott nodded, like this was all a totally normal day at work. "Bra strap, then boob. Got it."

Poppy, who currently had a makeup artist cleaning Scott's saliva off the boob in question, poked Scott in the shoulder and rolled her eyes. "Get it right, sheesh. What are you, an amateur?"

Poppy was amazingly unselfconscious about her body, even when it came time for Scott to peel off her bra. They were shooting her tastefully from behind, so all you saw on-screen was her upper back as he unhooked her bra and took it off. But she was sitting in Scott's lap at that point with her legs wrapped around his waist, and his face was basically right in her breasts. She was wearing nipple covers, but he was still getting an eyeful. Not that it was anything he hadn't seen before, apparently. He wasn't the only one who could see her though. There was a sound guy standing like two feet away, and a camera operator right behind her, and the rest of the skeleton crew off to the side.

Grace couldn't even imagine being brave or confident enough to do something like that, but Poppy seemed utterly unfazed by it all. After every take, a wardrobe assistant scooped Poppy's bra off the floor and helped her put it back on in front of everyone. And the whole time, Poppy was just sitting there in Scott's lap with her chest in his face, cracking jokes like it was no big deal.

By the time they broke for lunch, they'd only made it to the halfway mark. Which meant when they came back, they'd be at the part where both actors were completely naked. Well, mostly naked. There wasn't going to be any frontal nudity, thank god, so Poppy would still be wearing her nipple covers, along with a flesh-colored G-string.

Scott, on the other hand, had a rather prominent butt shot, so he'd be wearing something called a modesty pouch. Which was a total misnomer, because it did nothing whatsoever to protect anyone's modesty or dignity or anything else. It was basically just a cloth bag with a drawstring—indelicately referred to as a "cock sock"—that the actor stuffed his genitals into to cover them up.

Grace wasn't sure how it had been decided that Scott would do nudity and Poppy wouldn't. Whether that had been Joe's artistic vision or what the backers wanted. Whether Poppy's management had put their foot down or Scott had volunteered. She wasn't privy to those kinds of conversations, and it wasn't the sort of thing she was going to ask anyone about.

When she'd first gotten the script, she'd been a little excited at the prospect of getting an eyeful of Scotty Deacon's ass. Not anymore. Now that she actually knew him, it was more uncomfortable than anything else. Not that she wouldn't be perfectly happy to see him naked—just not under the current, extremely awkward circumstances. The fact that Grace was sitting beside Joe and Ed Dudley with Poppy strutting around looking like a sex goddess took a lot of the fun out of it.

Grace tried really hard to avert her eyes when Scott shrugged out of his robe, but she couldn't help sneaking a small peek at him. He was...yep. *Really* naked. The modesty sock did not leave much to the imagination. His body was outrageous—all muscly and hard and *wow*, that water cut was no joke because his abs were popping way out—but it felt really wrong to be enjoying the view, so Grace fixed her gaze on her laptop screen and didn't look up again until the actors were in position.

Their position, by the way, was extremely provocative at this point in the scene. Scott was on top of Poppy, grinding away with his bare ass in the air, while she writhed around beneath him and made sex noises. Even though all their NC-17 bits were technically covered, there was still a whole lot of intimate contact happening. Grace was deeply uncomfortable, but then so was everyone else in the room, although they were all trying hard not to act like it.

Scott's backside was just *really* front and center in the frame. It was impossible not to look at it. And when you were looking at it, it was impossible not to admire the firm roundness of his glutes, and the perfect curve of his lower back muscles as they met his hips, which were gyrating in a way that couldn't help but make Grace feel certain things.

Then there was the matter of his skin, which was smooth and unblemished, with no trace of a tan line, which naturally led the mind to wonder things like whether he'd had to get his butt waxed or if he was naturally hairless back there, and whether they used bronzer to get that sun-kissed glow or if he tanned nude—which were not the sorts of things Grace had any business wondering about one of her coworkers.

Every time they finished a take and Scott climbed out from between Poppy's legs, Grace had to forcibly tear her gaze away from him before she embarrassed herself gaping at the perfect V of his Adonis belt and that one vein in his lower abdomen that snaked down toward—

Yeah. Better just to look away when he was walking around all distractingly beautiful and so very mostly naked.

"Let's try it a little faster this time," Joe told them. "Give me more desperation."

They did it again, and this time Scott ground his hips faster and Poppy's sex noises sounded more desperate. It was...intense.

But Joe still wasn't happy. "Poppy, maybe try moving your hands lower. Like you're urging him on."

Grace honestly didn't know how Joe was maintaining his stoic facade through all of this, because she was positive her face must be three different shades of red right now.

"When you say lower, you mean on his ass, right?" Poppy asked wryly. "You want my hands on his ass?"

"That's what I want," Joe said, cracking the barest hint of a smile.

Poppy cupped Scott's butt cheeks with both hands, curling her fingernails into his skin, and Scott let out an undignified yelp that would have made an excellent addition to the blooper reel if the camera had been rolling. "Hey! Careful back there!"

"Too much ass grab?" Poppy said, smirking at him.

Scott shook his head at her good-naturedly. "If you leave scratches, they're going to have to put more makeup on my butt cheeks, and no one here wants that."

They did it a few more times, until Joe was finally satisfied with their grinding and sex noises and butt-grabbing. Scott and Poppy kept the mood light, teasing each other and laughing between takes, but they both looked relieved when they'd finished with the wide shots. There was still the medium and the close-ups to do, but they could at least put on pants for most of those, since their lower halves wouldn't be in the frame.

"Are my hands in this shot?" Scott asked when they were about to start the next setup.

Ed frowned at the monitor, then at Scott. "Yes. Both of them."

"What are they supposed to be doing again?"

There was a pregnant moment of silence before Grace realized that *she* was the person who was supposed to answer that. "Uhhhh, hang on," she said, scrolling back through her screenshots of Scott naked on top of Poppy having pretend sex. Yeah, this was totally not weird at all, no siree. "Um, your right hand"—her voice cracked a little and she cleared her throat—"is propped on the pillow next to her head. And the other..." Grace squinted at the screen. "Looks like it's underneath her?"

"Like this?" Scott asked, wedging his palm under Poppy's back and looking over at Grace.

"Lower," Grace said, praying for a lightning bolt to strike her and put an end to this uncomfortable moment.

Scott moved his hand down and looked at her expectantly.

"Little more. Like on her hip."

"How's that?"

Grace swallowed. "Yeah, right there."

God. How is this my life?

She was literally instructing the man she had a crush on where to put his hands on the woman he was actually sleeping with, while they simulated sex in front of her and a group of her coworkers. There was not enough wine in the world to wash this day away.

By the time they finally wrapped that night, Scott and Poppy had been simulating sex for close to twelve hours, and they both looked drawn and exhausted as they pulled on their robes and slipped back to their trailers. Even good sex would be excruciating after twelve hours, and Grace couldn't even imagine what it must be like to do *this* for an entire day. It had been hard enough just having to watch it.

When she got home that night, the lights were on downstairs in Scott's house. Grace couldn't tell if Poppy had come home with him again or not, but she tried not to let herself think about it. As soon as she got inside her own house, she switched on the TV and cranked the volume. If Poppy was next door, Grace did not want to know. And she certainly didn't want to hear them together.

She'd heard enough of Poppy and Scott's sex noises to last her a lifetime.

11

First up on the call sheet Friday was the "morning after" scene that followed the love scene they'd shot yesterday. Fortunately for everyone, it was pretty tame. Scott and Poppy would be in bed, but they'd mostly just be talking and they'd get to be partially covered by the sheets. Even with Scott shirtless and Poppy flashing copious sideboob, it felt like a cakewalk compared to yesterday.

About halfway through the morning, Grace got a text from Scott.

Scott: What did 0 say to 8?

It was the first text she'd gotten from him since Sunday, when he'd sent her a picture of a bell pepper he'd claimed looked like Nate.

The answer arrived before she had a chance to reply.

Scott: Nice belt

Grace glanced over at Scott's chair, but it was empty.

"My sister loves that joke," he said behind her, making her jump. "And you looked like you could use a smile."

"It's funny," she said.

He came around to stand in front of her and raised a quizzical eyebrow. "You didn't laugh." He was wearing flip flops and athletic shorts and an unzipped hoodie with no shirt because he was going to have to go crawl back under the covers with Poppy in a few minutes.

Grace tried to avoid staring at his abs and wound up just looking shifty. "Well, it's not funny *ha ha*. It's more like clever funny."

"Are you all right?" Scott asked, frowning slightly.

She forced a smile and tried to make her voice sound perky. "Yeah, fine. Why?"

"You've just seemed sort of distant all week, like maybe you were avoiding me. I didn't do anything to piss you off, did I?"

"No, definitely not. I've just been distracted with..." She waved her hand vaguely. "Stuff." *Ugh. Why aren't I better at lying?*

"Do you want to talk about it?"

"Not really."

Scott sat in Joe's chair and bumped his arm against hers. "I feel like we haven't talked in days."

"We literally talk all day long at work," Grace said instead of admitting the truth—that she'd been feeling the exact same way. Because as much as she liked Scott, she didn't entirely trust either his intentions or her own feelings where he was concerned. Not to mention the whole Poppy situation, which made things even more confusing.

"That's work talk," he said. "I mean talk like this." He nudged her arm again. "Like friends."

Grace's chest clenched, and she looked away. "It's just been one of those weeks, I guess."

"Tell me about it." Scott sighed, sagging back in his chair. "I guess I've been pretty distracted too."

She looked over at him—really *looked* at him—and noticed the lines of tension around his eyes, and the fact that he wasn't smiling as much as he usually did. "Are *you* okay?"

He nodded, and his jaw moved like he was grinding his teeth. "I'm just glad yesterday's finally in the rearview mirror. It's been hanging over my head all week."

"Yeah, that must have been"—Grace only barely managed to stop herself from using the word *hard*—"awkward."

Scott snorted and reached up to scratch his shoulder. "Try mortifying. Being naked in front of your coworkers is pretty much everyone's worst nightmare, isn't it?"

Grace hadn't realized it had bothered him that much. Not that she thought he'd enjoyed it particularly, but he'd seemed to take it in stride. "You didn't seem bothered when you were doing it. You seemed really confident."

He shrugged. "I'm used to pretending in front of an audience, I guess. But it's hard to look people in the eye when you know you're going to have to do something that embarrassing in front of them, so I've been keeping my head down all week. Thank god for Poppy. It's so much easier to do a scene like that with someone you're comfortable with, and she's a real pro."

"Yeah. Thank god for Poppy," Grace echoed, trying not to sound bitter.

Scott shifted to one side and dug around in his pocket. "You want some gum?"

When Grace shook her head, he unwrapped a stick of Trident and shoved it in his mouth. He'd been chewing a lot more gum this week. She'd assumed it was for Poppy's benefit, because of all the kissing, but now Grace wondered if maybe it was a nervous habit—something he did when he was stressed.

"I think I've finally got another job lined up after this," he said, rolling the wadded-up gum wrapper between his thumb and index finger.

Grace turned in her chair to face him, smiling. "Scott! That's great!"

He shrugged without meeting her eye.

"Isn't it?"

His jaw worked as he chewed his gum. "It's not what I was hoping for. But as my agent keeps reminding me, it's better than nothing." He sounded bitter, and a little defeated.

Grace started to put her hand on his arm to comfort him, but stopped herself. He was in a relationship—or something—with someone else. She had no business putting her hand on him, even if it was meant in friendship. "Things will get better," she said. "Pretty soon people will be beating down your door."

Scott glanced at her without acknowledging the compliment, which she knew he was mentally talking himself out of. "What about you?"

"What about me?"

"Do you know what your next job's going to be?"

She sat back in her chair and stretched her legs out in front of her, pointing her toes. "Not yet. I was thinking it might be nice to take a few weeks off before jumping into the next one. Location shoots always leave me feeling off-kilter."

Scott nodded and snapped his gum, looking unhappy. "Yeah, me too."

GRACE WAS JUST TRYING TO FIND CARMEN.

That was the only reason she was out back by the trailers in the first place. She needed to ask Carmen if she was bringing Dominic to brunch tomorrow, so she'd know whether to make the reservation for two people or three. Grace could have just texted, but she'd been cooped up inside the soundstage all day, so she'd thought it would be nice to take a walk out to the wardrobe trailer and get some fresh air.

Except Carmen wasn't in the wardrobe trailer. When Grace came out, she heard what sounded like footsteps behind it, so she peeked around the side to see if it was Carmen.

It wasn't Carmen.

It was Poppy and Sareh, the other actress in the cast.

And they were kissing.

Like, a lot.

Grace backed away quietly and hurried back inside the soundstage.

Shit.

Shit, shit, shit.

Why hadn't she just texted Carmen?

———

ONCE SHE'D RECOVERED FROM THE INITIAL SHOCK, GRACE couldn't decide whether or not to tell Scott. On the one hand, telling him seemed like the right thing to do. The thing a friend would do. But on the other, it was really none of her business. She didn't actually know anything about Scott and Poppy's relationship, or what sort of ground rules they'd set. For all she knew, they weren't exclusive. Maybe he wouldn't care. Maybe he even knew already.

On the *other* other hand—and this was the thing that stopped Grace cold—if he *didn't* know, and he *did* care, it would hurt him. As much as she didn't want him to be hurt, she also didn't want to be the one to deliver news that would cause him pain.

So she waited.

She could always tell him later, at a more appropriate moment. When he didn't have to walk onto set a few minutes later and film a scene with Poppy.

Yeah, waiting was good.

"Big plans for the weekend?" Scott asked at the end of the day when Grace was packing up to go home.

"Uh, not really," she said, turning away from him to wind up her laptop cord—but really so she didn't have to look him in the eye. "Brunch with Dominic and Carmen, but that's about it."

Scott leaned over the back of Joe's chair, watching her. "So are they dating now?"

"Yeah, I guess."

"Good for them. Is it serious?"

"I don't know. Maybe."

Now would be a really good time to tell him, if she was going to do it. The work day was over and he'd have the whole weekend to hash things out with Poppy if he needed to.

She should definitely tell him now.

"What about you?" she asked, trying to sound casual. "Any plans this weekend?"

He stared down at his fingernails, picking at a cuticle. "I don't know, actually. Poppy said something about getting together, but she can be kind of flaky."

"Ah."

Tell him. Tell him tell him tell him.

"All right, I'm going to head out," Scott said, straightening. "Enjoy your weekend."

She didn't tell him. Because she was a coward.

———

No one had warned Grace about the cockroaches in New Orleans, and she felt like this was a grievous oversight. They were not like normal cockroaches. They were super roaches. Like, the size of small rodents. Apparently they lived in the trees and dropped down on unsuspecting passersby occasionally. Horrifying. This was why she hated nature.

Grace had grown up in the desert, where they didn't have roaches like that—and also they didn't really have trees. Yes, okay, they had scorpions, but scorpions were different. She was used to scorpions, and they didn't fly. Oh yeah, the cockroaches in New Orleans could fly. What kind of bullshit was that?

She'd seen a few of them outside, dive-bombing the front porch light. On more than one occasion, she'd had to hold her bag over her head and run past them in order to get into her house at night.

Horrifying.

But as long as they stayed outside, she could deal with it. Inside, however, was a whole other matter.

Unfortunately, the giant disgusting tree roaches had a habit of crawling in through the plumbing. There had been one in the bathroom at work last week, and she'd had to beg Cal to kill it for her so she could pee.

Grace did not like bugs in her house. Her house was supposed to be a sanctuary from creepy crawly things and, you know, nature in general. That was the whole point of houses, was to keep nature out.

Someone needed to tell that to the roach in her kitchen.

Not only could she swear that it was at least four inches long, but it had the nerve to hide under her sink, and *then* it had to go and fly at her face when she'd opened the cabinet to get out the dish detergent.

Anyone would have screamed under the circumstances.

SCOTT HAD JUST FINISHED HEATING UP ONE OF HIS DEPRESSING high-protein meals in the microwave—tonight's culinary punishment was "spicy" BBQ chicken with brown rice and equally brown broccoli—and was about to force himself to eat it when he heard Grace scream.

The sound pierced the wall between their houses, striking cold fear into his heart and sending a spike of adrenaline through his system that propelled him across the room as the scream was followed by the sound of shattering glass.

"Grace!" he shouted, trying the door and finding it locked on her side. "Grace, are you okay? Open the door!" He rattled the handle in frustration, trying to decide how long he should give her to answer before he broke down the damn door.

Fortunately for the door, the door's owner, and Scott's shoulder, Grace responded right away. "I'm okay," she called out, and Scott sagged against the door in relief.

As soon as he heard the lock slide back, he jerked it open. "What happened?" he asked, grasping Grace roughly by the arms. Her lungs were heaving, her face was blotchy, and her eyes were tearing up. "Are you crying?"

She shook her head as she reached up to touch her cheek, seemingly surprised by the wetness there. "It's nothing," she wheezed, struggling to catch her breath.

"It's not nothing, Grace, you're shaking." He was holding her so tightly he was in danger of leaving bruises on her arms, but he couldn't make himself let go until he knew she was okay.

"No..." She began to shake even harder, and it took him a second to realize it was with semi-hysterical laughter. "It's just...there was a roach," she managed to get out in between gasping breaths.

Scott stared at her in disbelief. "A roach?"

"It flew at my face, Scott! *At my face!*"

He pressed his lips together, trying not to smile and failing at it pretty hard.

"I really hate roaches, okay?" Her voice quavered as it rose in pitch. "Especially when they jump out at you suddenly from inside a dark cabinet and go straight for your face."

"Okay," Scott said soothingly, and pulled her to his chest, wrapping his arms around her trembling body.

Grace sank into him, her fists clutching at his T-shirt as her face nuzzled against his neck. He breathed in slowly through his nose, inhaling the warm, slightly sweet undertone of her skin, and the herbal scent of her shampoo. The nearness of her was like a drug. Now that he'd had a taste of it, he was afraid one hit wouldn't be enough.

She pulled away after a moment, and it was with an overwhelming sense of reluctance that he let her go. Their eyes met, and something passed between them that was intense and terrifying and a little too *real*, before they both found something else to look at as they shuffled farther apart.

"So where's this villainous attack roach?" Scott asked, starting for the kitchen before he lost his senses completely.

"Wait." Grace grabbed his arm to stop him. "I broke some dishes."

"Yeah, I heard." He looked down at her hand where it was touching him, and she let go of him. "I'll be careful," he said, swallowing the lump in his throat. "Where's your broom?"

"Next to the washing machine."

He stooped to grab one of her shoes off the floor on his way into the kitchen, arming himself for the battle ahead. Stepping carefully around the broken glass, Scott peered under the sink, looking for this nefarious roach.

"Do you see it?" Grace asked.

"Ummm..." There it was, lurking beneath the disposal. He aimed the shoe at it with a vicious smack—that totally missed its target. "Dammit."

He tried again.

And again.

"He's a crafty son of a bitch," Scott muttered. "I'll give him that."

"Scott?"

"Don't worry, I'm not going to be defeated by a goddamn roach."

He took another swipe at the offending bug and knocked over several bottles of cleaning fluid. The commotion scared the infernal thing out into the open, and when it scampered across the floor Scott brought the shoe down on it with a satisfying crunch.

"Ha!" he shouted triumphantly.

"Is it dead?"

"Yeah. Don't come in here though."

"What happened?"

"Nothing, I just don't want you to have to see it." He set about cleaning up the mess, disposing of the squashed carcass in the garbage, cleaning all traces of it from the bottom of Grace's shoe, and sweeping up the broken glass, which he unfortunately did not manage to do without cutting himself.

"Okay," he said a few minutes later, when he'd finished straightening up and wrapped a paper towel around his bleeding finger. "It's safe."

Grace ventured back into the kitchen, her face lighting up when she saw that he'd cleaned, putting everything back to its pre-roach attack state. "Oh my god, you're the best! Totally my hero." For a second she looked like she might hug him, but stopped herself.

He put on a smirk to hide his disappointment. "Any other vermin in need of executing while I'm here?"

Grace shuddered. "I hope not." Her eyes widened as they fell on the bloody paper towel he was holding. "What happened?"

"It's nothing," he said, shrugging. "I cut myself cleaning up the glass."

"Oh, no! I'm so sorry. Here, let me get you a Band-Aid."

"It's not bad. Don't worry about it."

"Did you wash it?" She dug around in a drawer, coming up with antiseptic spray and bandages.

"Yeah," he said, not wanting her to go to any more trouble for him. "It's fine, really."

"Let me see." She took his hand and peeled off the paper towel, squinting at his injured index finger.

Scott blinked and looked away, his eyes watering at the warm tenderness of her touch. It had been an embarrassingly long time since anyone had touched him with that kind of gentleness, and he didn't want her to see how much it affected him. "What's the verdict?" he asked, struggling to keep his voice light.

"I think we'll probably be able to save the finger," she said with a teasing smile. "As long as we can stave off gangrene." She sprayed antiseptic on the cut and carefully wrapped it in a Band-Aid.

"Thanks," he said, flexing it experimentally when she was done. "You've got the magic touch." He flashed a grateful smile at her, and was surprised to see a cloud pass across her face.

"Scott, I have to tell you something," she said, wringing her hands.

The smile slid from his face. "What?"

"It's about Poppy."

He went still, bracing himself for bad news. "What about Poppy?" Had her drinking gotten so bad Grace had noticed it on set? Had she done something?

Grace bit her lip, obviously dreading whatever she needed to tell him, which did nothing to ease his apprehension.

"Grace?" he prompted.

"I saw Poppy and Sareh together...they were kissing."

"Oh," he said, relieved it wasn't something bad. "Okay." He hadn't known about Sareh, but he couldn't say he was surprised. She was definitely Poppy's type.

Grace took a half step toward him before hesitating, her hand hovering in the air like she wanted to reach for him. "I'm so sorry, Scott."

"It's fine. Really."

"It is? You're not upset?"

"Poppy's allowed to do whatever she wants—or whoever, for that matter."

"Oh." Grace looked confused. "Okay."

"Did you think we were together?"

"Well, I mean...kind of? Because——"

"Because she spent the night," he finished for her, grimacing. "We're just old friends. That's it."

Her brows slanted in disbelief. "Sleepover friends?"

Scott looked down at the floor, not quite sure how to explain. "Poppy and I, we're—it's complicated."

"Apparently."

"There's a lot of history between us." He reached up to rub the back of his neck. "Look, I'm not going to pretend nothing's ever happened there, but that's all in the past. *Way* in the past."

"It's really none of my business." Grace's eyes skated away, but not before Scott caught a glimpse of the judgment in them. He couldn't blame her. He'd slept with his best friend's ex-fiancée; even though it was after they'd split up, it was still a crappy thing to do.

"Poppy and me, we're a lot alike," Scott said, feeling like he owed Grace some sort of explanation. He closed his eyes and grimaced. "A little too much. We've seen each other through some shit and I owe her for—" The words died in his mouth. He couldn't bring himself to tell Grace about the times Poppy had nursed him through a bad comedown or tried to get him clean, searching his house and throwing out his pills. How she'd been the first person to drag him kicking and screaming to a rehab stint that didn't take. "I care about her," he went on, "but I've accepted that we're not very good for each other long-term, which is just as well, because Poppy's not big on commitment."

"And you are?" Grace asked, her keen gray eyes seeming to stare right through him.

Scott looked down at the floor. "Statistically? Not so much, no."

Commitment hadn't been something he'd ever wanted, back when the option had been open to him. He'd been too busy having a good time to tie himself down. It was only later, when he'd torpedoed most of the relationships in his life, that he'd started to see the value of deeper connections. Only when he'd proved himself undeserving of that kind of trust and companionship had he begun to long for it.

Who would want him now, after he'd shown the world just how low he could sink?

"Anyway," he said, shoving his hands deep in his pockets, "when Poppy came over to run lines the other night, we got caught up talking, and by the time we were done it was late and she'd had a lot to drink, so she stayed the night. In my guest room."

"Well, good," Grace said, looking like she was ready for the conversation to be over. "I mean, not good that you're not together, just good that she's not cheating—" She shook her head, wincing. "I'm glad you're not hurt. That's all."

"I'm not hurt," Scott said, touched that she'd been worried about him. "But it's nice to know you care."

Grace's eyes met his as she threaded a nervous hand through her hair, which fell around her face in loose waves the color of a sunlit beach. Everything about her was so fucking beautiful. Her long, graceful fingers, her eyes like the color of the ocean at dawn, those lips that always looked like they'd just been kissed, all soft and slick and swollen. Jesus, how he wanted to taste those lips.

Something inscrutable flashed in her expression that made Scott's heart beat faster, but before he could get a proper read on it, it was gone. "Right, so anyway, thanks for taking care of my roach situation," she said, moving toward the door.

Scott followed her, taking the hint. On his way out, he paused with his hand on the doorknob. "I make house calls twenty-four seven," he said, offering her his most charming smile. "Should the need ever arise."

Grace smiled a little too brightly. "Okay, well, goodnight!"

"Goodnight," Scott said, thumping the doorframe with his palm on the way out.

He was going to need to take the coldest fucking shower of his life tonight.

———

GRACE STARED AT HER PHONE, SMILING AT THE TEXT SHE'D JUST gotten.

Scott: Knock knock

Jokes were his new thing, apparently. He'd texted her a new one every day since Friday. They were always these really awful, punny kid jokes that shouldn't be funny at all. And yet she found them completely adorable.

Grace: Who's there?

Scott: A broken pencil

Grace: A broken pencil who?

Scott: Never mind its pointless

Grace was not supposed to be having these sort of feelings about her actor coworkers. She had a very firm rule in place. It was a good rule.

She didn't even like actors. They were needy. And self-centered. And shallow. And unreliable. And based on her most recent experience, ragingly mediocre in bed. She did not want to date another actor.

But then there was Scott.

She *liked* him. She couldn't help herself.

Yes, he had an unsavory past, and under ordinary circumstances he was the sort of man she wouldn't touch with a ten-foot pole. But she had to admire the way he owned up to his mistakes without making excuses for them. It was obvious he'd worked hard to change. Now that she knew him, she had a better understanding of just how much he'd overcome to rebuild his life.

But more than that, he was kind, and generous, and loyal. Sure, sometimes he got his head stuck up his ass and acted like a bit of a jerk, but now that she understood what was going on when he got like that, it was easier to forgive. And he was pretty good about making up for it once he got over himself and realized he was doing it.

Not many people could say that—especially not people who'd spent most of their life being catered to and indulged at every turn.

She just...she *liked* him. God help her.

Scott: What's blue and smells like red paint?

Grace: What?

Scott: Blue paint

Grace: That's terrible.

Scott: Made u smile tho

"Let's see what today's new Snapchat filters are," Scott said, plopping down next to Grace as she was finishing her lunch on Wednesday.

"Do they still have the one with the butterflies?" she asked around a mouthful of french fries. "I liked the butterflies."

He reached over and snagged a fry off her plate as he was thumbing through the filters. "No more butterflies. How do you feel about vomiting rainbows?"

"Thumbs down."

"Oh, here we go." He held his phone out and snapped a selfie. "What do you think?" he asked, showing it to her.

The filter had given him a glittery lion face that was oddly sexy. "Nice. You look just like Simba."

"I'm posting it," Scott said, smiling as he typed with his thumbs. "You know, when I was a kid I wanted to marry Nala. I think she was my first crush." He paused and looked up at her. "Is that weird?"

"You mean because she's a lion?"

"Yeah."

Grace shrugged. "I wanted to marry Simba. If you're weird, I'm weird too."

Scott grinned at her. "Match made in heaven."

See, the problem was that the flirtier he acted, the harder Grace crushed on him. It was impossible not to find the attention thrilling when it was coming from someone as attractive and charismatic as Scott. But it was also a little bit heart-wrenching, because she knew he wasn't actually flirting with her. It was just how he was. His way of being friendly.

This was Scott Deacon: he'd slept with hundreds of women, probably. The man had no shortage of game. If he'd actually been interested in her, he would have done something about it by now. It wasn't like he hadn't had plenty of chances.

But he hadn't done anything about it, which meant he didn't *want* to do anything about it.

Grace was trying to be fine with that, with just being friends, but it was getting harder every day.

12

They were being graced with a VIP visitor to the set: Robbie Scarborough, who was flying in for the weekend to hang with Scott.

Robbie wasn't due to get in until Friday at lunchtime, and the whole morning Scott was as antsy as a kid on Christmas Eve. At the end of almost every take, Grace saw him pull his phone out to check the time.

Scott wasn't the only one excited about their expected visitor either. Every straight woman and gay man with badge access to the soundstage seemed to have found a reason to hang around the set this morning.

When Robbie finally strolled in, escorted by a starstruck intern, Scott transformed before Grace's eyes. There were a lot of bro-y hugs and hearty backslaps and throaty laughter, and so many 'sups and dudes and mans she felt like she'd wandered into a frat party. It was strange to see Scott so animated, and she couldn't help wondering if this was what he'd been like all the time when he was younger and less sober. Before he became so intense and so damaged.

Robbie Scarborough was as glossy as his headshot, with the

same floppy blond hair and boyish grin that made an entire generation of Millennials swoon during their formative years. Grace had never been that into him growing up, but she couldn't help being a little dazzled when Scott introduced him, and Robbie projected that dreamy smile directly at her.

"Nice to meet you, Grace Speer," he said, holding her hand for just a little longer than necessary.

He did that with all the women Scott introduced him to, Grace couldn't help noticing. Looked them in the eyes, flashed that smile, and repeated their full names, all while holding their hands meaningfully in his. It was like a hypnotist's trick, and it worked like a charm. Every single woman in the room was left starry-eyed and dazed when Robbie Scarborough was through with her.

Movie stars. It really was like a superpower.

The only woman Robbie didn't try to charm was Poppy. When she showed up on set a little later, she went straight over to give him a hug, but something about it struck Grace as strained. It wasn't that it was an unaffectionate hug, exactly, it was just that it was unaffectionate for Poppy. Robbie's smile lost a little of its luster too. Not that Grace could blame them. She wasn't sure she'd be half so civil if her ex showed up on set.

"How've you been?" Poppy asked Robbie, fidgeting with the hem of her shirt.

"Good." Robbie shot a sideways glance at Scott, who was staring determinedly at his shoes. "I'm good."

They were standing close enough that Grace couldn't help overhearing, but she didn't feel right eavesdropping on their awkward reunion, so she got up and headed over to the craft services table until they were ready to start shooting again.

There was an extra chair set out by the monitors for Robbie, with a headset so he could listen to the scene they were shooting. When Dominic called the actors to their places, Robbie took his seat, giving Grace a wink as he settled in. After watching exactly one take, he pulled out his phone and concentrated his attention on that instead. Five minutes later, he got up, grabbed a bottle of Vitamin Water from the craft services table, and disappeared outside.

Grace didn't see him again for the rest of the day.

"What happened to Robbie?" she asked Scott later.

He stole an M&M out of her palm and popped it in his mouth. "I gave him the key to my place so he could crash. Jet lag."

The time difference between Los Angeles and New Orleans was only two hours, but okay. It must be exhausting, flying through two whole time zones on a fancy private jet.

"Hey, so I'm having a party tomorrow night," Scott said, helping himself to another M&M. Now that he'd finished all his shirtless scenes, he was being less rigorous about his diet. "Nothing too wild, just a few people."

Grace leaned toward her laptop to skim the email that had just come in from the editor. "I promise not to call in a noise complaint on you," she said distractedly.

Scott tilted his head to catch her eye. "I was actually hoping you'd come."

"Oh," Grace said, forgetting about the email. "Sure. Definitely."

"Great." Scott stole another M&M. "Eight o'clock."

She nodded. "I'll be there."

Shit.

AT EIGHT THIRTY, GRACE STOOD IN FRONT OF THE DOOR TO Scott's house with her stomach twisting. She could hear voices next door, and music. She'd been hearing the music for the last half hour—some kind of electronic dance music with a monotonous beat so you couldn't tell where one song started and the next one began.

Scott had said eight, but Grace knew better than to show up on time to a party, even though it was basically killing her to be intentionally late. She was really not very good at parties.

Grace stared at the adjoining door and wondered if she should go around to the front instead. No, that was dumb. She should just knock on this door, like she always did. But what if they didn't hear her over the music? Maybe his side was still unlocked, and he was expecting her to let herself in? Unless that would be too forward, just barging in uninvited. Except she was invited, and there were already other people there. She could hear them.

God, her palms were sweating. Why was she so nervous? It was just a stupid party.

A party at the home of a gorgeous movie star she happened to be attracted to. No big deal.

Get it together. You can't stand here all night.

Grace reached out and tried the door. It was unlocked, so she pushed it open.

Scott's house was bright and warm and full of people. Well, not full. There were like ten or twelve people there, mostly from the cast or the stunt team. All of them beautiful people with perfect bodies and gorgeous hair and great clothes.

This was fine.

"Grace!" Dex shouted, detaching himself from a clump of people in order to greet her with his arms thrown wide. He pulled her into a friendly, sloppy hug, and she instantly felt a thousand percent more comfortable. She knew Dex. Dex was great. This would all be fine.

Grace felt even better when Dex dragged her off to the kitchen to procure her a glass of wine.

The kitchen was where Scott was, making food. Some kind of canapés with goat cheese and prosciutto. There was a cheese plate already sitting out, and a charcuterie board, and a platter covered with vegetable crudités.

"Hey," Scott said, looking up at her and smiling. His brown

button-down brought out the green of his eyes even more than usual, and Grace's breath caught when that piercing gaze met hers. "I'm glad you made it." He stopped assembling canapés long enough to give her a kiss on the cheek.

"Can you believe this guy can cook?" Dex said, thrusting a glass of rosé into Grace's hand. "If I wasn't already married and he wasn't straight..." He shook his head sadly.

"Can I do anything to help?" Grace asked Scott.

"Yeah, taste this for me." He held a canapé in front of her face.

Grace opened her mouth, and he placed it on her tongue.

"What do you think?" he asked earnestly, like her opinion was deeply important to him.

"It's delicious," she assured him, and her heart gave a little lurch at the way his whole face lit up.

"Scotty, what'd you do with the olives, man?" Robbie shouted from the pantry, and Scott abandoned Grace and the canapés to go help him look.

She followed Dex back to the living room with her wine, and squeezed onto one of the couches between him and Stephen Choi, the stunt coordinator. She knew most of the people there, but some of them she knew better than others, since she didn't have all that much to do with the stunt crew. Nate was there, along with Sareh and Poppy, and Ben and Tamika—who were apparently an item now—and some of the other supporting cast members. There weren't many people from the rest of the crew though, other than Grace and Tamika.

Stephen introduced Grace to his wife, Jeannie, who worked as a stuntwoman too, and she and Grace talked across him until he finally gave up and switched seats. Another dozen or so people showed up over the next hour, and Scott made the rounds of the room, playing the good host and doling out lots of cheek kisses and handshakes. He checked in with everyone intermittently to make sure they were taken care of and having a good time, like he felt personally responsible for all his guests. It was sweet, but it meant Grace didn't really get to talk to him, because he was always passing by on his way to talk to someone else.

She watched him drift from group to group: laughing, smiling, making small talk, and reflexively touching everyone he engaged with. He was even more outgoing than usual, a whirlwind of shoulder squeezes, backslaps, and hugs, punctuating every laugh with a friendly touch of some kind. His attentiveness seemed magnanimous rather than manipulative, but it was impossible to tell how genuine it was. Was this party person who Scott really was, or just another act he was putting on? He wore so many masks that Grace honestly couldn't make heads or tails of him sometimes.

By eleven o'clock the party had thinned out a little and gotten more relaxed. Someone had changed the music, and Poppy was lip-synching to Britney Spears while Sareh egged her on, laughing. When the song switched to NSYNC, Grace was surprised to see Robbie join Poppy for a duet, and even more surprised when they dragged a reluctant Scott up there with them. He was a little self-conscious at first, but he knew all the words and dance moves by heart, and Grace gathered this wasn't the first time they'd sung this song together.

Not long after that, someone suggested charades, and everyone started organizing themselves into teams. Grace was by herself in the kitchen at that point, grazing on what was left of the crudités, and no one noticed when she slipped into the empty front room.

It was an actual, honest-to-god ballroom, with a crystal chandelier hanging above a parquet wood floor, and floor-to-ceiling windows looking out on the park. But it had been converted to a workout room and equipped with a treadmill and rower and a rack of dumbbells. The room was dark, lit only by the moonlight filtering in through the leaded antique glass, and Grace stood by the window and looked out at the night, comforted for a few minutes by the knowledge that no one could see her.

She'd go back to the party in a few minutes. She just needed a break. She was tired, but she wasn't ready to go home yet. She wasn't ready for tonight to be over. To give up a chance to be close to Scott for a while longer.

She liked him *so much*.

There was a lot of excited shouting coming from the game of charades in the next room. It sounded like they were really getting into it. Actors. They did love their charades.

Maybe she would just go home. Sneak back into her house while they were all distracted and crawl into bed. No one would miss her, probably.

"Grace?" Scott said behind her.

Her heart gave a little kick, and she turned toward him the way a flower turns toward the sun: instinctively.

"There you are," he said, stopping in front of her. "I was afraid you'd left."

She looked up at him and forced a smile. "Still here."

His forehead creased. "Are you having a good time? I'm worried you're not having a good time."

"I am." Now that he was here with her, she was. She was addicted to the way she felt around him, even though it hurt whenever he shined his light on someone else.

His frown deepened, like he didn't believe her. "Really? Then why'd you sneak off on your own?"

She shrugged. "I'm not really a charades person."

"What's wrong with charades?"

"Nothing. It just triggers all my childhood insecurities about performing in front of an audience."

He pursed his lips. "You're not having a good time."

"I am," she insisted. "This is me having a good time."

"Standing alone in a dark room?"

"Please don't feel responsible for my emotional well-being.

You should go back to your party." She didn't want him to be unhappy on her account. It wasn't his fault she was having all these feelings, or that she found parties exhausting, or that she hated charades with every atom of her being.

"I don't care about the party. I'd rather be here with you." Scott reached for her—just a simple, soft brush of his fingers down her arm, but it was enough to make her heart lurch, even though it was the same touch she'd seen him give a dozen other people tonight.

It made Grace feel even more tired. She was exhausted from playing this game with him. Trying to figure out what was genuine and who she was supposed to be in response to all of his breathtaking Scott-ness.

"Of course you care about the party," she said with a sigh. "You worked hard on the party."

"I did work pretty hard on the canapés. Did you like the canapés?"

"I loved the canapés."

"Good." He gifted her with one of his devastating winks. "I was hoping to impress you."

She pulled back a little. "You don't have to keep doing that."

"What?"

"Pretend to flirt with me."

His smile slipped. "Who said I'm pretending?"

"I already like you, okay?" she blurted out before she could stop herself. "You don't have to keep trying to win me over. And we both know you're not actually interested in me, so really it's all just kind of—"

"How do you know I'm not interested in you?" he interrupted.

"Because I'm me and you're you and I'm definitely not your type."

Scott raised an eyebrow, his expression equal parts curious and offended. "What do you think my type is?"

Grace knew exactly, because one of them was sitting in the next room. "Leggy actresses with thigh gaps and perfect hair."

He shook his head. "That used to be my type, like ten years ago. Not anymore. Not for a long time."

"Okay, then what's your type?"

His mouth twisted into the barest hint of a smirk. "Snarky script supervisors who refuse to put up with any of my shit."

Her throat went dry. "Scott." It was supposed to be a warning, but it came out as a whisper.

"Grace." The soft, slightly breathy way he said her name made her legs tremble. His eyes dropped to her mouth, and he leaned into her. His hands found their way to her waist, and then—

He was kissing her.

She was being kissed by Scott Deacon.

"Scott-EEE!" Robbie bellowed from the next room. "Where'd you go, man? Your team needs you."

Grace jerked back, but Scott held on to her, keeping her from moving too far away.

"Yeah, okay!" he called back over his shoulder. "Be right there." His forehead pressed against hers. "Sorry," he muttered.

She nodded, barely able to remember how to breathe, much less form words.

"Come back to the party with me?" He took her hand in his and squeezed. "Please?"

Grace nodded again and let Scott lead her back to the party. When they reached the doorway of the living room, his hand released hers and moved to the small of her back. He guided her to one of the couches and cocked his head at Robbie to scoot over. Then he nudged her into the empty space and perched on the arm of the couch next to her.

"Hey! Why do y'all get Grace on your team?" Dex asked accusingly.

"Yeah, you guys are already a man up on us," Poppy protested. "If she's playing, it's on our team."

"She's not playing," Scott said. "She's just watching." He gave Grace's shoulder a reassuring squeeze, and she leaned into him gratefully.

Everyone went back to playing charades, and Grace tried to look like she was paying attention.

She'd kissed Scott. *Kissed* him.

Sort of.

She'd been so surprised it was happening that she hadn't had time to respond properly. And then Robbie had interrupted them —*damn him*—and Scott had stopped kissing her before she'd even had a chance to kiss him back.

He probably thought she hadn't liked it. Or worse: he thought she was a terrible kisser.

Oh, god. Scott Deacon had kissed her and now he thought she was a terrible kisser.

She could do better. She just needed another chance to get it right. A do-over. Next time she wouldn't be so unprepared.

Unless...unless when Scott had said he was sorry, he'd meant for kissing her? Maybe he wished he could take it back. Maybe he didn't want a do-over.

She couldn't even remember what it felt like to kiss him. She'd been so stunned, she'd kind of blacked out for a second. Scott's lips had been on hers and she couldn't remember how they'd felt. How was that fair?

The game of charades dragged on for another hour, and then the lip-synching started up again. Every time Scott caught her eye, he smiled, but then this little crease appeared in his forehead that Grace couldn't decipher. Other than that, he acted like nothing had happened at all.

She stuck it out for a while, hoping for a chance to get Scott alone again. But Robbie always seemed to be close by and didn't show any signs of slowing down anytime soon. And he was staying at Scott's place, so it wasn't like he was going to be leaving anytime tonight. It would be pointless to try and wait him out.

"I'm going to head home," Grace said finally, pushing herself to her feet just after one a.m.

"Hang on, I'll walk you out," Scott said.

He followed her to the door and reached out to open it for her.

"Sorry," he said again, leaning against the doorjamb.

She wanted to ask him what for, but this wasn't the time to talk about it with all of his friends a few feet away singing a rousing chorus of "Africa" by Toto. "Goodnight," she said instead.

He bent down and kissed her cheek. "I'll talk to you tomorrow, okay?"

Grace nodded and went back to her house, feeling a little like she'd just been hit by a train.

13

For the millionth time in the last three hours, Scott stared at his phone's screen with his thumbs hovering uncertainly over the keyboard. He wanted to text Grace, but he couldn't figure out what to say.

He'd finally worked up the nerve to kiss her, but it hadn't exactly gone like he'd hoped. In retrospect, doing it when he had a houseful of guests in the next room hadn't been ideal timing on his part. But the moment had presented itself, and he hadn't wanted to let it slip away again. He didn't want to regret not kissing her when he had the chance—twice.

If only Robbie hadn't interrupted. If only Scott hadn't panicked at Grace's deer-in-the-headlights expression. If only he'd told Robbie to fuck off and had stayed with Grace long enough to talk to her. And maybe kiss her a little more, assuming she was okay with it.

That was the question though, wasn't it? *Was* she okay with it? Jesus, he hoped she was a little more than just *okay* with it.

It had been hard to tell, in the dark room, in that too-short moment they'd shared. It had all happened in the space of two heartbeats. Barely enough time for Grace to react, much less for Scott to gauge her reaction. Had he imagined it, or had her lips started to soften just before Robbie's untimely interjection had brought an abrupt end to their kiss?

At least she hadn't tried to leave immediately after, which he took as a good sign. She hadn't pulled away from him either. She'd let him hold her hand, and she'd leaned against him when they were sitting on the couch. She wouldn't have done that if she hadn't wanted to be there, right? If she hadn't wanted to be near him?

He should definitely text her.

Fuck, he had no idea what to say.

He was terrible at composing words. He could improvise a million charming off-the-cuff retorts when he was talking to someone in person, but put him in front of a keyboard and he froze up completely. His mind just went blank. And his usual tactic of quoting song lyrics and corny jokes wasn't going to fly in this situation. He highly doubted Grace would appreciate a knock-knock joke as his first communication in the aftermath of their interrupted kiss.

Just type something. Anything.

Hi.

Decent start. Now what?

Sorry about last night

No. Gah. That sounded like he was trying to take it back. Delete.

The tone needed to be happy. Enthusiastic, even. Like he was excited about the future and looking forward to taking the next step. Assuming Grace *wanted* to take the next step. He should probably check in with her on that to make sure she was actually on board and not horrified it had ever happened in the first place.

How the fuck was he supposed to translate all that into a text message?

"Yo, you ready to eat our way through this town?" Robbie asked, coming downstairs with his shoes in his hand.

Scott looked up from his phone. "Huh?"

"Culinary tour of New Orleans? You psyched?" Robbie set his bespoke Italian oxfords on the floor in front of the couch and went into the kitchen.

"Oh, yeah. Definitely." Scott shoved his phone back into his pocket as he leaned forward to snag his cup off the coffee table.

"What is with you, man?" Robbie shot a quizzical look at Scott as he poured himself a cup of coffee. "You've been all kinds of distracted since I got here. You okay?"

"Yeah," Scott said. "Yeah, I'm good."

"You sure?" Robbie brought his coffee into the living room and sat down across from Scott. "It'd be understandable if it was a tough adjustment for you, getting back to work for the first time, on an out-of-town shoot. New Orleans is pretty much party central, and you're out here on your own."

"I'm fine, Robbie." Scott met his gaze levelly. "Really."

He didn't want Robbie worrying about him or thinking he was in danger of relapsing. Not after everything he'd already put his best friend through. Sure, Robbie's relationship with Poppy had already ended before anything happened between Scott and Poppy, but that didn't excuse it. Sleeping with your best friend's *ex*-fiancée was still a betrayal. And that had been far from the first or the last shitty thing Scott had done as the drugs had taken over his life. It was just one more dump in the bucket of shit that had driven a wedge between them.

And yet, despite all that, when Scott had gotten out of rehab that last time—the time it finally took—Robbie had been there waiting for him. He'd been there for him ever since, supporting him through every step of his recovery. Robbie and Poppy had been the only two friends from the old days who hadn't abandoned Scott after he'd bottomed out. He owed everything to them. His sobriety, his sanity, this second chance at a career. Robbie had pulled strings to get Scott an agent, and had invested a chunk of his savings just to get him this job.

There was no fucking way Scott was going to let him down.

"Okay." Robbie nodded. "I just want to make sure you know that you can talk to me if you need to."

"I appreciate that," Scott said. And he did, but he didn't feel like he could take Robbie up on his offer. Not when his friend had so much money riding on this project. Scott wasn't going to admit how much he'd struggled when he first got here, or how fucking terrified he'd been. How he hadn't been sure he could do this. Robbie didn't need to know any of that, because it would only make him doubt Scott. And Scott could generate enough doubt for the two of them on his own.

Robbie's eyes dropped to his coffee mug. "Poppy told me last night that it was going well. That you seemed happier than she'd seen you in a long time."

"Yeah," Scott said, surprised how true it was. "I am. It feels good to be working again. The whole crew's been great. Really supportive."

Robbie nodded, tracing the rim of his mug with his thumb. He cleared his throat. "So...Poppy and this Sareh chick...is it serious?"

Scott winced. "I dunno, man. You know Poppy."

Robbie and Poppy had negotiated a peaceful armistice a few years ago. Their shared mission to support Scott through his recovery had facilitated the forging of a tentative friendship on the ashes of their broken engagement. But it wasn't an easy friendship. Scott could detect an undercurrent of strain whenever they were together, and he wasn't entirely convinced Robbie wasn't still hung up on her.

Robbie smiled ruefully. "Yes, I do."

"I hope it turns into something serious," Scott said. "I think Poppy could use a little stability right now." He hadn't shared his concerns about Poppy's drinking with Robbie, because it didn't seem fair to burden him with it. But Robbie had two eyes, and he could see the warning signs as well as Scott could. Better, maybe.

Robbie pushed himself to his feet. "So you ready to go or what?" He went into the kitchen and dumped the rest of his coffee in the sink. "This chef buddy of mine I was telling you about, he's set up a whole tour for us. Private tasting menus at four of the hottest New Orleans restaurants. I think the first one we're going to was on *Top Chef* or something."

"Sounds great," Scott said, getting to his feet. "Let's do it."

Texting Grace would have to wait until later.

Or maybe he'd just hold off until he could talk to her in person. The odds of him fucking up and saying something stupid via text were scarily high.

Robbie was flying out first thing in the morning, and Scott could talk to Grace after that. He'd find a good time to pull her aside so they could talk about that kiss.

And whether or not there was going to be a second one.

GRACE WAS A SLEEP-DEPRIVED, CRANKY WRECK WHEN SHE GOT to work Monday morning. She'd hung around the house all day yesterday obsessively checking her phone and waiting to hear from Scott, but hadn't heard a peep. Although she knew from all the clomping around and muffled voices coming through the walls that Scott and Robbie had slept until past noon, gone out shortly after that, and hadn't gotten home until nearly midnight. So maybe Scott was just busy? It was Robbie's last day in town, so she supposed she could understand if he wanted to spend it with his friend.

Now that she was back at work and under imminent threat of seeing Scott face-to-face, Grace's anxiety levels were nearing an all-time high. He wasn't on the call sheet until eleven, so she spent the whole morning trying to ignore the knots in the pit of her stomach and focus on work—with only limited success.

"You okay?" Joe asked when she messed up a line prompt.

"Yeah, sorry," she muttered, grimacing. "I'll get my head in the game."

"You're doing fine." He gave her a reassuring smile that only succeeded in making her feel guiltier.

When Grace finally saw Scott, a ball of nervous dread leapt into her throat. He was all the way on the other side of the lot, rushing off to hair and makeup because he was running late, and he didn't even see her, but for a second her heart forgot how to beat.

Once he finally came on set, he barely even had time to nod in her direction before they started rehearsal. And then he was busy talking to Joe and the other actors about the scene. And then hair and makeup needed to do a touch-up. And then it was time for the first take.

When they broke for a camera change, Grace saw Scott start to head in her direction, but Nate got there first and started telling her about this new restaurant he'd found that was great for clean eating. Scott met her eye with a look that she couldn't interpret, then went and sat down by Poppy.

Goddamn Nate.

By the time he'd finished describing the lentil and veggie omelet he'd had for breakfast yesterday, they were ready to roll again.

Finally, almost an hour later, they took another break to set up for the next shot. Grace was in the middle of talking to Dominic about the next scene when Scott came and found her. "Can I have Grace for a minute?" he asked, interrupting.

"Sure," Dominic said, and Grace swallowed down a spike of nerves as he walked away, leaving her and Scott alone.

"Can we talk?" Scott asked her.

She nodded. "Yeah, of course."

"Not here," he said. "My trailer?"

She nodded again, and Scott's hand settled in the small of her back, guiding her outside.

His trailer was the nicest on the lot, and the closest one to the stages. He held the door open for her, and she climbed up the steps and inside.

The interior was spartan and utilitarian, without any personal effects on display to make it seem homey. A tub of protein powder sat on the kitchenette counter, some resistance bands and dumbbells lay scattered around, and a few stacks of scripts covered various surfaces, but otherwise it was uncluttered.

Grace wasn't sure if this was a sit-down conversation or a stand-up conversation, so she hovered nervously by the dining table. She was vibrating with tension and didn't know what to do with her hands, so she wound up twisting them in front of her.

Scott pulled the door shut and turned to face her. "Sorry we didn't get a chance to talk yesterday. I was out with Robbie all day."

"It's okay," she said. Then, before she could stop it, the tsunami of word vomit she'd been holding in for a day and a half came tumbling out: "We don't have to talk about it. I mean, we can, but if you'd rather not, that's fine too. We can just pretend it didn't happen if that's what you want. Talking's way overrated, I mean, what's even—"

"Grace." Scott's hands settled on her shoulders, and she snapped her mouth shut as his eyes bored into hers. "I don't want to pretend it never happened."

She exhaled, dropping her head forward in relief. "Oh, thank god."

He laughed, and she felt his fingers brush against her cheek.

They settled under her chin and tipped her face up to his. He was such a pleasure to look at this close, she almost forgot to be nervous.

"I'm not sorry I kissed you. In fact..." He paused, his eyes going beautifully soft and crinkly. "I'm really hoping you'll let me do it again."

"Oh," she breathed, feeling her cheeks warm as she remembered how to be nervous again.

Scott bent his head until his lips were just a breath away from hers. "Is that okay?"

Grace didn't let herself think as she surged up and pressed her mouth against his.

It was *so* much better this time.

She was an active participant in the kiss, for one thing, instead of just standing there dazed and frozen. And she was fully aware of what was happening. She had the presence of mind to appreciate how soft his lips were—*so* soft, softer than she'd ever imagined—and how his mouth tasted—like spearmint and sweet relief. His stubble prickled, but it was the good kind of prickle. The contrast between the softness and the prickliness sent a jolt of happiness down her spine.

She didn't want it to ever end, but of course it had to eventually.

When Scott pulled away, Grace curled her arms around his neck and ran her fingers through his hair—both because she wanted to and because she needed to keep him close. She didn't want him getting away this time, not even an inch.

He didn't seem interested in getting away. His broad hands roamed over her back as his hips pressed into her, pinning her up against the table. "Grace," he whispered, pushing his forehead against hers.

"Scott," she breathed on a long exhale. There wasn't enough oxygen in his trailer. She felt like she'd just hiked up Pike's Peak and the air was too thin.

"You have no idea how long I've wanted to do that."

"How long?" she asked, a little afraid of the answer.

"A long time."

She shook her head, her nose rubbing against his. "You did not. You didn't even like me."

"You didn't like *me*."

"We didn't like each other."

He pulled back far enough to look at her. "You challenged me when I wasn't used to being challenged. I like that about you."

She laughed. "That's a nice way of saying I'm mean."

Smiling, he kissed her forehead, and then her temple. "I wanted to get to know you better. I wanted you to know *me* better."

"You had a funny way of showing it."

His nose pushed against her ear, making her shiver. "I was nervous." He kissed the corner of her jaw. "You made me nervous."

"I did not."

"I knew you didn't like me." He nuzzled against her neck, and she shivered again. "I didn't want to screw up in front of you, and I knew I was going to."

"I liked you once I got to know you." Her hands were on his shoulders, clinging a little bit, because he was making her feel dizzy.

"I wasn't sure." He tugged at her collar with his index finger, pulling it aside so he could kiss the top of her shoulder. "I thought maybe you were just tolerating me, just to be nice. The way you tolerate Nate."

"Ugh, no. I like you so much more than Nate."

Scott straightened so he could look at her and broke into a devastatingly sweet smile. "You have no idea how relieved I am to hear that."

"You really thought I didn't like you?"

A shadow clouded his expression as he turned his head to kiss her temple. "It doesn't matter." His hands came up to cradle her jaw, and his thumb dragged across her cheekbone.

"Scott." She reached up to take his hands, holding them in hers. "It does matter."

His mouth tightened. He wouldn't meet her eyes. There was something he wasn't saying.

She let their hands fall to hang at their sides, fingers still clasped together. "What is it? Tell me."

"You remember the very first time we met?"

Grace nodded. "In the production office."

His Adam's apple bobbed as he swallowed. "You were talking to Carmen, and I was early. I overheard you when I approached the office." His eyes locked on hers. "Talking about me."

"Oh god!" Grace covered her mouth with both hands. She couldn't remember exactly what she'd said, but it definitely hadn't been complimentary. "Scott, I don't know what to say. I'm so sorry. I didn't mean it."

The corners of his mouth curved in a rueful smile. "Yes you did. But it's okay."

"It's not. I never should have talked about you like that."

No wonder he'd been so combative that first day. As if he hadn't had enough to overcome, then coming in and hearing her talk about him like that. She was pretty sure she'd maligned his acting abilities, which was totally unfair and uncalled for, and knowing now how little confidence he had in himself, she wanted to hurl herself off the nearest freeway overpass.

"You only said what everyone thinks." He gave a sad little shrug that broke her heart into pieces. "I'm used to it."

"I don't think those things anymore. I only felt that way because I didn't know you. I was so wrong, Scott, so totally wrong about you."

He traced the edge of her jaw with his index finger. "It's really okay, Grace. I understand."

"Do you?" She searched his eyes, mentally twisting a knife in her own gut for every glimmer of doubt she'd ever seen in them. How could she have been so careless and cruel?

"Yes." He kissed her forehead.

"You should hate me. Why don't you hate me?"

"I did at first. Then I just wanted to change your mind. I've been trying to change your mind about me ever since."

She pressed her palms against his chest, curling her fingers into his shirt. "I can't believe, all this time—is that really how you thought I felt about you?" The idea of it was agony.

He brushed a lock of hair off her face. "When we were at the bar that night, I started to think maybe there could be something more there..." He dropped his hand to his side. "But you were a little drunk, so I wasn't sure you meant it. And then it felt like you pulled away from me after that."

She smacked him in the chest. "Only because I thought you were with Poppy!"

"Fair," he admitted, hanging his head a little. "I sort of fucked that up."

"Sort of!"

He caught her hand in his. "In my defense, I didn't know there was anything to fuck up. You haven't exactly been giving me a lot of encouragement."

"I was intimidated by you."

His thumb moved across the palm of her hand. "I don't believe you. You're not intimidated by anyone."

"That's an act. I was a nervous wreck around you because you're so, you know, *you*. And because I could never tell if you were really flirting with me or if you were just being friendly, the way you are with everyone."

He kissed her lightly on the lips. "I was definitely flirting with you."

"But you flirt with everyone."

He kissed her again, a little longer this time. "Not the way I flirt with you."

"Well, I couldn't tell the difference."

One of his hands slipped around her waist and the other came up to stroke her face. He kissed her again, his hips pressing against hers and his tongue sliding into her mouth.

She sank into him, tilting her head and opening up for him. She was clinging to him again, because she was in real danger of swooning at his feet, and she wondered if this was how he did it with all the other women. If he kissed them like this and did that thing he was doing with his tongue, and then they let him do anything he wanted to them. Grace wondered if she was going to let Scott do anything he wanted with her. *Probably*, as long as he kept kissing her this way.

"Grace," he murmured.

"Hmmm?"

His mouth moved to her ear. "Can you tell I'm flirting with you now?"

"Mmmm, yeah."

He laughed softly. "Good."

She took his face in her hands and tilted it down so she could look into his beautiful, bottomless eyes. "Can you tell I like you now?"

"I don't know," he said gravely. "I think I might need another kiss to make sure."

She pressed her lips to his, her hands on either side of his face, amazed that he was letting her do it after those things she'd said. One of his hands held the back of her neck and the other splayed against the small of her back, pulling her flush against him. He caught her bottom lip between his teeth and—

Someone knocked on the door of the trailer, and they startled apart.

"Hey, Scott, they're ready for you," Cal shouted.

"Okay!" Scott shouted back.

"I have to go," Grace said, stepping past him. *Crap*. They'd be looking for her on set, wondering where she'd disappeared to.

"Wait," Scott said.

She waited.

He kissed her again—gently, but taking his time. When he pulled away, he was smiling. "Okay, now you can go."

Grace ran back to the soundstage with a big dumb grin on her face.

14

G race couldn't stop touching her lips. They were still tingling from kissing Scott. She could still taste him too, on the tip of her tongue. The kiss—*all* of their kisses—kept replaying in her mind, every delicious second. Part of her still couldn't believe it had really happened.

Instead of dissipating, the butterflies in her stomach had multiplied exponentially. It made her feel intoxicated, but it was a dopamine high instead of an alcohol-induced one. She was having trouble sitting still. She kept squirming, like an impatient puppy who could see a treat just out of reach.

She couldn't quit smiling either. Every time she looked at Scott, her lips involuntarily curved into a grin. Which was a problem, because she had to look at Scott pretty much constantly. It was sort of her job.

"Someone's in a better mood," Joe observed, eyebrows raised, and Grace felt herself blush crimson.

"Finally got enough caffeine," she muttered, crossing and recrossing her legs as she looked down at her laptop to hide her face.

It didn't help that Scott kept smiling back at her. Every time he finished a take, his eyes found hers and went all crinkly. God, those crinkles around his eyes. She loved them even more when they were crinkling because of her.

He kept his distance though. Which was good, because she was having a hard enough time acting normal as it was. If he was actually close enough to touch, she wasn't sure she'd be able to control herself.

"What's with you today?" Carmen asked accusingly as they were perusing the craft services table.

"Nothing," Grace said, turning away to snag herself a blueberry yogurt.

"You're acting weird."

Grace reached for a spoon. "I don't know what you're talking about."

"Oh my god!" Carmen clamped her hand on Grace's arm, dragging her around to face her. "Something happened with you and Scott," she hissed.

"What? No." Seriously, how did she even do that? Was Grace really being that obvious or did Carmen have some uncanny sixth sense when it came to Grace's love life?

Carmen pulled herself up to her full five feet three inches and shook a finger that would have made her Mexican *abuela* proud. "Grace Speer, don't you dare lie to me."

Grace glanced around to make sure there was no one in earshot. "We may have kissed," she admitted quietly.

"I knew it! I knew he liked you!" Carmen bounced on her toes, her face splitting into a grin. "Oh my god, how was it? Tell me everything."

"It was nice," Grace said, smiling.

"Tell me about his lips. How do they feel? Is he a good kisser?"

Grace's smile got even wider. "He's a *great* kisser."

"Oh wow, you really like him, don't you?" Carmen's expression shifted to a concerned frown. "Promise me you'll be careful, okay? Men like that—" She stopped, like she was reconsidering what she was about to say. "Just don't let him hurt you."

"It was just a kiss," Grace said, rolling her eyes.

She wasn't picking out Save the Date cards or anything. She had no illusions about the likelihood this flirtation with Scott would turn into anything serious. At most, she was hoping to end her six-month dry spell by consummating their flirtation with a night of very hot sex. Maybe even more than one night, if things went well. But beyond that—beyond the end of the shoot—she had no expectations whatsoever.

Carmen shook her head. "It's never just a kiss."

GRACE GOT A TEXT FROM SCOTT TOWARD THE END OF THE shooting day.

Scott: Why did the chicken cross the playground?

She actually knew this one, so she texted him back the answer.

Grace: To get to the other slide.

A text bubble popped up to let her know he was typing a reply.

Grace waited.

And waited.

And waited some more.

Scott: Can I come over when u get home tonite?

The butterflies in her stomach started doing coordinated

aerial maneuvers, with, like, Delta rolls and Yo-Yos. Her fingers trembled as she typed her answer.

Grace: Yes.

OF COURSE SHOOTING RAN LONGER THAN USUAL THAT DAY. OF course it did.

And of course Ed Dudley decided tonight after they'd finally wrapped for the day was a good time to talk Grace's ear off about the dangers of pulling focus with a Cine Tape instead of an old-fashioned tape measure. Of course he did. And then Joe wanted her to look at some of the dailies with him, because sure, why not? It wasn't like she had any reason to want to get out of here tonight.

All of which meant Scott made it home well before she did.

Grace let herself into her house at ten thirty, dropped her bag on the floor by the door, and sprinted upstairs to brush her teeth. Once she'd taken care of her coffee breath, she applied a fresh coat of deodorant and tried to finger-comb some order into her hair, which by this point in the day had begun to resemble a Bichon Frise overdue for a grooming.

Before she had a chance to do anything else, there was a knock on the door downstairs. She'd been home for all of a minute and a half.

Hurrying back downstairs, she opened the door to a smiling Scott.

"Hi," she said, a little out of breath.

His smile got wider. "Hi." He was wearing a plain white T-shirt and jeans that looked like they'd been painted on, showing off every bulge and striation. *Every* bulge.

Grace swallowed and stepped back to let him in, trying to project casual calmness and not the all-consuming panic she was actually feeling. Now that she had him here, she had no idea what to do with him. Drinks were out, obviously. Should she offer him something to eat? What was the standard protocol for booty calls? Because that was what this was, right?

God, she hoped that was what this was.

There wasn't much in the way of actual food in her house, so she settled on an uncertain, "Do you want some water or something?"

Instead of answering, Scott moved into her space, his hands landing on her hips and urging her backward until he had her up against the wall next to the stairs.

"Hey," he said, gazing down at her with an intensity that made her giddy.

Grace took a shaky breath. "Hey."

Nervous didn't even begin to cover her current state of mind. It had been about, oh, two hundred and seventeen days since she'd done this—not that she was counting or anything—and a *lot* longer than that since she'd done it with anyone besides Chris. She'd forgotten what it was like to sleep with anyone else.

Scott Deacon was not just some ordinary anyone else either. He was the equivalent of going from junior varsity soccer straight to the World Cup. It was terrifying, but also not an opportunity anyone in their right mind would pass up. This was one of those moments that demanded to be seized with both hands. When Scott freaking Deacon was looking at you with sex in his eyes, you'd have to be crazy not to YOLO that shit. Wouldn't it be a crime against all womankind not to ride him like a John Deere? *Carpe fucking diem.*

Also? He smelled really good, and at this point Grace was convinced it wasn't cologne but some kind of, like, natural pheromone that made women lose control in his presence. More particularly, it made *her* lose control.

So she grabbed him and kissed him. Hard.

His mouth was hot and tasted of spearmint and something

unmistakably Scott. She lapped it up, arching her body against his, and he pressed into her, pinning her against the wall as their mouths slid together. The man could kiss, that was for damn sure. Grace couldn't wait to find out what else he could do.

Her fingers dug into his sides, tugging at the bottom of his T-shirt, and he pushed away from her suddenly and reached behind his back, dragging his shirt off over his head.

Grace's brain fuzzed into static at the sight of his bare chest and shoulders and—*my god, those abs.* She was definitely going to lick those abs tonight. For science.

When he pressed into her again, and his bare skin touched her skin, it was like a religious experience. Her hands moved worshipfully over the hard ridges of his stomach, awed that she was actually allowed to touch.

She could feel Scott smile against her mouth when he kissed her again, holding her face in both hands. He nipped at her lower lip, then soothed it with his tongue, and she melted against him, knees weak, moaning into his mouth.

"Grace," he murmured in a voice rough with promise. "Do you want to show me your bedroom?"

She did. She really, really did.

Taking him by the hand, she led him up the stairs. When they reached the threshold of her room, she felt a little like a skydiver staring down the open door of an airplane. One more step and she would be in free fall, hurtling toward an unknown destination.

Scott eased up behind her, his hands flattening out over her stomach as he kissed the back of her neck. His body was solid and heavy against hers, radiating heat, and she leaned back against him, closing her eyes on a long, contented exhale as his hands roamed over her hips and rib cage.

Just when she was in danger of sliding to the floor in a dreamy puddle, he spun her around in his arms and lowered his mouth to hers. She made an embarrassing noise in the back of her throat, and he deepened the kiss, bending her head back as the sharp edges of his teeth grazed her lips.

Her hands groped his chest shamelessly, appreciating the way the muscles flexed under her fingers. Her plaid shirt was already hanging open over her tank top, and Scott pushed it off her shoulders, running his hands down her bare arms. She clutched at him as he kissed her again and again, bottomless, bruising kisses interspersed with lighter, broken-up kisses that left her limbs quivering.

His fingers toyed with the hem of her tank top for what felt like an eternity before he finally lifted it over her head. Grace's 34As weren't much to get excited about—especially not compared to the parade of busty Hollywood babes who'd undoubtedly passed through Scott's bed—but his eyes devoured every modest curve and valley that showed through her black lace bralette.

His Adam's apple bobbed as he slid a finger under one of the satin shoulder straps. Then his hand slid down her chest, his fingertips skimming over her breast. Testing. Exploring.

"I like this." He slipped a finger underneath and gave the elastic fabric a little tug. "Easy access." His voice sounded low and husky, and it did things to Grace's self-control.

Hooking her fingers into the waistband of his jeans, she tugged him closer and pressed her face into his throat, closing her eyes as she breathed him in. She kissed him just below the corner of his jaw and his pulse jumped under her lips, kissing her back. His bristly neck prickled her skin and she rubbed her nose against it, relishing the sensation.

They hadn't even made it into the bedroom yet.

Scott's hand cupped her breast, his thumb circling her nipple, and Grace clutched at him. Standing was becoming too much of a chore, especially when her bed was so near. She took a tripping step backward, dragging him along with her, and they shuffled into the room together. When the back of her legs hit the mattress, he guided her down onto the rumpled sheets she hadn't bothered to make up this morning.

He didn't seem to mind her poor housekeeping habits as he bent over her, caging her between his strong arms. She slid her hands up his biceps, enjoying the unyielding contours of muscle, then remembered her earlier promise to herself and scooted down on the bed until her face was lined up with his stomach.

Grasping his waist, she arched her torso up and pressed her mouth against his abdomen. A tremor shuddered through him and she wrapped her arms around him, holding him tighter. Pleased with the results of her experiment, Grace trailed her tongue over the grooves between his abdominal muscles, starting just under his rib cage and working her way down.

When she dipped below his naval, finding the light trail of hair that disappeared into the waistband of his pants, he gave another shudder and reached around behind him to capture her hands. Pushing her back onto the bed, he held her hands above her head, pinning them in place as his body pressed into hers, the full length of him weighing down on her.

She wriggled and squirmed beneath him—not to get away, but to feel the delicious grind of his body against hers, and the rasp of denim over denim as their jeans rubbed together like a pair of high-schoolers. He kissed her throat, his fingers tightening on hers, and she let out a shaky breath. His mouth was soft and wet as it trailed over her skin, his breath hot and lascivious, raising blisters of desire everywhere it touched her.

"You taste even better than I imagined," he whispered as his tongue dipped between her breasts.

"You imagined the way my skin tastes?"

His teeth nipped at her through her bralette, just the right side of rough. "I imagined a lot more than that."

Grace inhaled sharply, squirming against his hold on her, and Scott laughed as he easily held her fast.

"Too many pants," she told him, giving up her struggle. "I need to feel you."

"So impatient." He shook his head at her, but let go of her hands to unfasten her jeans and peel them off her legs along with her underwear.

"Now you," she said eagerly as she kicked them onto the floor.

Scott slid off the bed, unbuttoned his jeans, and pushed them down to his ankles, exposing thick, muscular legs. Grace went a little cross-eyed imagining those thighs between hers—along with what lay beneath the large bulge at the front of his tight-fitting black boxer briefs.

She tried to reach for him, but he crawled back on top of her, clasping both her hands in one of his and pinning them above her head again.

She blew a frustrated breath through her teeth. "Why won't you let me touch you?"

"I will." He slid his hand up the outside of her thigh, his callused fingers raising goose bumps as they dragged across her skin. "I just want to appreciate you first."

Fighting the urge to squirm, she lay still while his eyes raked over her, consuming every inch of her body in a thorough perusal that was as intimate as anything she'd ever experienced.

The real surprise was how unselfconscious she felt. How easy and familiar this felt. His expression was so eager, and his touch so tender, that she felt utterly comfortable spread out before him like this. Spread out *for* him. She was his, utterly, to do with as he pleased. Instead of making her uneasy, the thought excited her even more.

He licked his lips. "I could look at you like this forever."

"I hope you plan to do more than look." She wiggled her hips and spread her legs a little, hoping he'd take the hint.

A smirk danced at the corner of his mouth. "Don't you worry about that."

As they met each other's gaze, the tension ratcheted up

another few notches. Sparks seemed to jump through the air between them.

She reached up to touch his face, remembering all the times its frozen facsimile had stared back at her from a magazine cover, billboard, or website. It was so different in person. So much more human and vulnerable. The chiseled good looks were still there, but underneath was a tenderness she found far more attractive than any photo shoot pout or feigned bedroom eyes. She was so lucky to get to see this side of him. What a precious gift.

Scott released her hands and tugged her bralette aside, exposing one of her breasts. As he lowered his mouth to it, Grace curled her fingers in his hair, her nails scraping over his scalp as she sighed with pleasure.

He took his time with the first breast before moving on to the other. Only when they'd each been lavished with attention did he slide her bralette up, over her arms, and all the way off.

In the short time they'd known each other, Scott had surprised her at every turn. He'd been thoughtful when she'd anticipated rudeness. Insecure where she'd assumed arrogance. And now, in her bed, he was restrained where she'd expected impatience. Unlike so many other men, his seduction technique was not of the high-speed variety. He seemed much more interested in enjoying the journey than getting to the finish line.

"You're so beautiful." His voice was hoarse and raw, and she could tell by the way he was looking at her that he meant it.

Grace pulled him down for a kiss. Their tongues slid together, licking and exploring as the kiss grew deeper. He slid a hand up the inside of her thigh and she opened wider for him, needing his touch like she needed air to breathe.

When his fingers brushed between her legs, she jolted as the sensation shot through her whole body. Her heels dug into the mattress as he touched her with caresses so light she had to bite her lip to keep from begging him for release. He watched her, his eyes dark and gleaming as he weighed her reactions to his minis-trations. Studying her. Learning her body and what she liked.

"Scott," she moaned, tipping her head back.

"Grace," he answered huskily.

"Are you sure you don't hate me anymore?"

He answered by increasing the pressure right where she needed it. "What do you think?"

Her toes curled as her back arched with pleasure. She could feel the tension building inside her, but it remained just out of reach. She'd never been quick to orgasm, especially with a new partner, but she didn't mind. Everything Scott was doing felt so good, she wasn't in any position to complain.

Sensing she needed more, he slid down her body, kissing her stomach before nuzzling between her legs. A tremor ran through her as he looped his arms around her legs and spread her wider. His head turned to kiss her inner thigh, then he looked up at her, their eyes meeting and holding as his breath caressed her. A sound somewhere between a whine and a pant escaped her, and he smiled as he lowered his mouth to her.

Grace's ex had never been much into going down on her, which probably should have been a clue where things were headed, but the truth was she hadn't missed it that much. It had never been her favorite part of sex. There was always a sense that it was a duty to be performed, and in return she had a duty to enjoy it, regardless of how enjoyable it actually was—and too often it wasn't all that enjoyable.

She'd always thought it was her. That it just wasn't her thing.

She was wrong about that. *So* wrong.

When Scott swept his tongue across her, it was with a confi-dence and desire she'd never encountered before, and it lit up her pleasure centers in whole new ways. Her hips bucked uncontrol-lably, and he pinned them with a heavy forearm as his tongue worked its magic, kissing and sucking and swirling.

She lifted her head, entranced by the sight of him between her thighs, and he stared back at her, eyes gleaming with hunger. This was no duty. He was getting off on it as much as she was.

When he picked up the pace, she squeezed her eyes closed and tipped her head back. His fingers bit into her thigh as he worked up to a maddening rhythm, and she let her legs fall open even wider.

He added a finger, then two fingers, then his thumb, and she moaned as the tension built and built. Her whole body was crying out for release, but it wasn't enough. She needed more. She needed him to fill her up completely.

Grace's hands fisted in his hair and she yanked, dragging his head toward hers as she exhaled his name.

He came willingly, grinning up at her as he kissed her stomach. "You're a lot of work, aren't you?"

"I never claimed to be easy."

His grin turned wolfish. "That's okay. I like a challenge. Tell me what you want."

"You. Inside me. Immediately." She was panting and desperate, a sweaty, heaving mess, and she didn't care one bit. "I hope you have a condom." Because she definitely did not, and she might actually die if she didn't get to have him this minute.

Scott's lips caressed a spot behind her ear that sent a shiver rippling through her. "What do you think I am? Some kind of amateur?" Untangling himself from her, he crawled over to the edge of the bed and reached for his pants, extracting several condoms from the pocket.

What a good Boy Scout he was. Always prepared.

He shoved his underwear down and crawled back over to her, ripping one of the condom wrappers open with his teeth. Hot and impatient, she waited for him to roll it on before she gripped his ass and pulled him toward her.

Weeks of anticipation had brought them to this moment. After all the slow build-up, everything felt desperate, like she couldn't get close enough, fast enough. Grace had never felt this sort of frenzy before. This insistent, animal hunger for someone else. She didn't just want Scott inside her, she wanted him everywhere, in every possible way. She wanted as much of him as she could get and then she wanted even more than that.

It terrified her a little, how deep her need for him went, so she shoved it to the back of her mind, concentrating instead on the here and now. The physical reality of their bodies, and the places where he touched her, setting her skin ablaze.

Scott pushed into her with no preamble, filling her completely, then pulled out again before she'd had time to properly appreciate the sensation. She let out a frustrated whimper and his mouth curved in a smile as he bent his head to kiss her. "Shhh." His breath teased over her lips, warm and full of promise.

He sat back again, cupping one of her breasts with one hand while he palmed himself with the other, teasing at her entrance. Her fingernails dug into his flesh, urging him on as she let out a sound that could only be described as a growl.

"You want it?" he asked, taunting her. Tormenting her.

She writhed beneath him. "Yessssss." He was so damn close to sliding into her, and she needed him *now*.

"Say it. Say what you want." There seemed to be no limit to how long he was willing to draw out this torture.

She was out of her mind. Wild with desire. "You. I want you."

Watching her face intently, he pushed into her with excruciating slowness, inch by tantalizing inch. "Tell me what you want me to do to you, Grace. I want to hear you say the words."

"Fuck me. Oh god, please, just fuck me—"

He pulled out and slammed into her with a force that rocked her whole body.

Grace cried out in relief, clutching at him as his sumptuous thrusts filled her up, giving her exactly what she needed.

She was so sensitive by then and so amped up, as soon as his movements inside her started to find a rhythm, she was clawing at him and arching beneath him, pressing into him for more closeness, more friction, more of everything.

Then she was coming as she cried out his name, and he was watching her with those intense green eyes. She was a mess of raw emotions as she rode the crest, all her physical desires laid wide open for him. He peppered her with gentle kisses, and held her with strong arms until she'd come back down.

"Well," he said as he brushed the hair back from her face, "I guess I know what you like."

"You," she whispered, pulling him down for a kiss. "I like you."

He started to move inside her again, and this time she was able to more fully savor the experience. God, he was so unfairly sexy. The way he held himself above her, his weight on one massive arm, the muscles taut and straining. The way he stared down at the place where they were connected, watching as he slipped in and out of her. The way his abs contracted with every thrust. The way he bit down on his bottom lip, his eyes fluttering closed when she squeezed her walls around him.

Grabbing her suddenly, he rolled them over so he was on his back and she was straddling him. His hands massaged her ass, guiding her down onto him, and she threw her head back, grinding against him and reveling in the sensation.

"That's it," he said, his fingers digging into her flesh. "You're gonna come again, aren't you?"

The words spurred her to a new plateau of ecstasy, but she had another priority now. She could sense he was holding himself back, and she took it as a challenge. She wanted to see him lose some of that tightly wound control. She wanted to be the one to make him lose control.

She moved her hips, watching his reactions the way he'd watched hers. Learning what he liked. How much pressure, how fast, what angle made his eyes roll back in his head.

He tried to resist, to wrest back control, but she held him down with a hand on each shoulder as she ground harder, faster, until he was shaking and groaning, his breath breaking as he fell apart at the seams.

An unexpected rush of emotion clogged her throat at the sight of him like that, and she bent to kiss him. His hand tightened in her hair as she felt him heave and tremble beneath her, gasping as the aftershocks rolled through him.

Scott's arms tightened around her, and he pressed a breathless kiss to her temple. "I could never hate you, Grace."

15

G race jolted awake in the morning to the harsh, tinny sound of "Pocketful of Sunshine" blaring from her phone.

"Unnggg," she groaned, her leg rubbing up against a larger and much hairier leg as she rolled toward the nightstand. She felt around blindly for her phone, nearly knocking the lamp over with her flailing, but it wasn't where she usually left it.

"Make it stop," Scott mumbled into his pillow.

"Sorry," Grace said, sitting up and rubbing her eyes. She squinted in the direction the hateful sound was coming from and spotted a pile of discarded clothing on the floor. Right. Her phone had fallen out of her pocket last night when Scott peeled off her clothes.

She crawled down to the foot of the bed and fumbled around on the floor until she finally laid hands on the accursed device, breathing a sigh of relief as she silenced it.

Beside her, Scott lay on his stomach with the sheets tangled up beneath him, utterly, gloriously naked. Grace would have loved nothing more than to crawl back into bed and wrap herself around him, but she had a seven o'clock call time and she needed to get up and get moving.

Which was really too bad, because Scott Deacon was in her bed and...*damn*. She'd always been keenly aware of his attractiveness, but lying there all stretched out and naked, he was fucking breathtaking.

And she'd had sex with him last night.

This was the moment of truth. In the harsh light of the morning after, would they make vaguely apologetic faces as they thanked each other for a fun night—then spend the rest of the shoot pretending to be buds without dwelling on the fact they'd seen each other naked? Or would their one night of fun stretch out into multiple nights?

Grace certainly knew which option she preferred—the latter —but Scott's MO was as hazy as a Magic 8 Ball.

"Are you staring at my ass?" he asked without opening his eyes.

"Maybe," Grace said. "It's a really nice ass. And I like the way it looks in my bed."

"C'mere." Scott rolled over, reaching for her, and she let him pull her down for a kiss. "I have to tell you something," he said, pulling back and looking at her very seriously.

Grace froze, her heart stuttering to a stop. "What?"

"Your bed sucks. Next time we're sleeping in my bed."

Next time.

He'd said *next time*. Which meant there was going to be a next time. *Booyah.*

Grace crawled on top of him and kissed the ever-loving shit out of him.

"Don't you need to get ready for work?" he asked, shifting his hips suggestively beneath hers.

"Screw work," she said. "I can be late."

GRACE WAS LATE.

She hated being late. Not that it hadn't totally been worth it, but now she was paying the price, having to rush through all her preparations for the day's shoot.

"Morning!" Dominic said cheerfully, holding the door to the soundstage for her.

"Morning," she muttered, hurrying past him with her head down.

She couldn't shake the feeling that everyone could tell, that it was written across her face like a giant, blinking neon sign: *I slept with Scott Deacon last night, ask me anything!*

Also, she was pretty sure she was walking funny. It had been a long time since she'd been that...active, and she was definitely feeling it this morning.

Without making eye contact with anyone, Grace made a beeline for her chair and busied herself setting up her laptop and marking up the script pages for the first scene of the day.

Scott strolled in not too long after, and the first thing Grace thought when she saw him was that she knew what he looked like under his clothes. Every inch of him. Not only that, but she knew what his skin tasted like, and the sound he made when he came, and that he liked it when she used just a little bit of teeth.

Today was going to be...interesting.

He took his time making his way over to her, stopping to chat with a few people before finally heading in her direction. "Morning," he greeted her brightly, like they hadn't just seen each other an hour ago. Naked. Super naked. Totally, totally naked.

"Morning," Grace mumbled, feeling herself color as she ducked her head.

Thanks to their morning activities, they hadn't had a chance to talk about how they were supposed to act around each other at work. How to play this. What *this* even was.

She wasn't even sure what she wanted it to be. Scott was *sooo* not her type, and there was a lot of baggage there. It was difficult to imagine him in a long-term relationship. The chances of him wanting something like that seemed so remote as to be inconsequential, and after what had happened with Chris, Grace wasn't super keen to jump into anything serious again anytime soon.

"So..." Scott started uncertainly, and Grace looked back up at him. His eyes roamed over her face like he was trying to decide whether to say whatever was on his mind.

Then Joe walked up, clapped Scott on the back, and asked Grace a question about the first shot. Scott drifted away with an apologetic smile as she tried to concentrate on answering Joe's question coherently.

———

SCOTT WAS NINETY-EIGHT PERCENT SURE HE WANTED TO SPEND the rest of his life with Grace.

He'd never felt this way about any woman, ever, and it scared him shitless. Like, shook him right down to his core. His stomach had been doing all sorts of acrobatics all morning, leaving him pinging disconcertingly between nausea and giddiness.

But then he'd look across the soundstage at Grace, and he'd remember the way she'd felt in his arms, and the way she'd clung to him as she breathed his name, and he couldn't imagine ever letting go of her. He felt like a different person when he was with her. A better person. Stronger. More hopeful. She gave him a reason to look forward to the immediate future instead of dreading it. He liked his life a hell of a lot more with her in it. Also, he'd slept better last night in her crappy-ass bed than he had in the last three years.

Yeah, he was a goner.

What Scott was far less sure of was what to do about it.

A few short weeks ago, Grace hadn't been able to stand the sight of him. He suspected it would be a bad idea to go all in this early in the game. Life wasn't a movie with a happy ending waiting at the end of the third act, and problems didn't magically disappear with a dramatic declaration of love. If he pushed for too much too soon, Grace might just run like hell in the opposite direction.

Better to hold back, at least for now. Stick to the tactic that had gotten him this far: slowly winning her over until one day she looked up and realized she couldn't live without him.

Once more, his gaze found her across the soundstage. She was conferring with the on-set dresser, clutching to her chest the thick binder that held her copy of the script as they discussed some continuity detail. As if sensing his eyes on her, she glanced his direction and her mouth curved in a subtle smile. Scott's stomach did a somersault.

They hadn't had a chance to talk privately all morning, and it was killing him. He was itching to get her alone, even just for a minute. He needed to touch her.

As soon as Dominic called the next fifteen-minute break, Scott made a beeline to Grace's side before anyone else could demand her attention.

"Come with me," he said, taking her by the arm and sweeping her out of the stage, down the hall, and into an unused storage room. As soon as the door closed, he wrapped his arms around her and pulled her into a kiss.

Her mouth opened willingly for his, her arms winding around his neck. It was everything he'd been hungering for, until—

"We need to talk," she said, breaking off the kiss. "About work."

He stopped kissing her and swallowed. "Okay."

"I just want to make sure we're on the same page."

"Okay," he said again, keeping his expression carefully neutral. "What page are you on?"

"I just think it would be best if we kept this—whatever this is —to ourselves. For now. If we didn't bring it to work with us."

He let go of her and stepped back. "If that's what you want." He could go along with that. It was pretty much what he'd expected. Certainly he could understand why she wouldn't want herself romantically linked to him.

"I just don't want it affecting my job. People find out about something like this and they start treating you differently. They start thinking things and saying things—"

"I understand," Scott said, cutting her off. He didn't need her to go into a detailed explanation of how his reputation would tarnish hers. He was well aware.

She bit her lip, rubbing her palms on her jeans. "Do you?"

He reached for her hand so she'd know he wasn't angry. "I do," he said. "It's okay. Really."

She squeezed his hand, tugging him closer. "It doesn't have anything to do with you. You know that, right?"

He couldn't help the bitterness that crept into his voice. "It has a little to do with me."

"No," Grace said, meeting his gaze evenly, "it doesn't. I'm just trying to keep things professional when we're at work."

He nodded, trying not to take it personally. "I can be professional." It was the least he could do, really.

"Thank you."

"As long as you let me be unprofessional when we're at home." His hand skimmed up her arm, sending a shiver of goose bumps across the surface of her skin.

Grace launched herself at him and closed her mouth over his.

"I thought you wanted to be professional," Scott said when they came up for air.

"Well, we're already here," she pointed out pragmatically. "And we've got ten minutes left until we have to get back. We might as well make the most of it."

They did.

THEY WERE PRETTY GOOD AT THE PROFESSIONAL THING, AS IT turned out.

Grace already knew Scott was good at putting on masks and taking them off again, and she had a lot of practice with swallowing her feelings and operating on autopilot, so it worked out fine.

It was especially fine after work that night, when Scott knelt on the rug in front of his big leather couch, hoisted her legs over his shoulders, and went down on her until she came crying out his name. That part was extremely fine.

Also fine was the night after that, when he had his way with her on his kitchen island, although it left her with a few colorful bruises in interesting places.

Scott's bed was quite nice too. Grace loved how ridiculously soft his Egyptian cotton sheets felt on her skin as his hips pinned her against the mattress. She was also fond of his shower, which was big enough to fit like ten people. It even had a nice roomy bench, which they made copious use of.

That thing where she'd never been quick to orgasm? Not so much a problem with Scott. It was like he'd figured out the secret to unlocking her cheat codes and they'd hit the orgasm mother lode.

The sex part was excellent, was what she was saying. She had no complaints whatsoever in the sex department.

The part that wasn't quite so excellent was when Grace had to watch Scott film his scenes with Poppy.

There was always a weird sort of disconnect whenever Scott slipped into character. When he was in character, he wasn't the Scott she knew anymore—he was like a different person wearing Scott's face. It could be a little disorienting.

When he was in character acting affectionate with Poppy, and touching her, and gazing lovingly into her eyes, it was actively hard to watch, even if it was just acting.

Grace understood the difference between fiction and reality.

She knew it was all just pretend. But then she'd recognize an expression or a gesture that Scott had used with her. That was *his*, not his character's. Which only stood to reason because they weren't actually two separate people, so of course there was going to be bleed over. But it made her feel sick to her stomach.

She was a professional though, so she swallowed it down, along with all her questions about what exactly she and Scott were doing.

They never had gotten around to having any kind of State of the Relationship summit. Scott wasn't overly big on sharing or opening up in general, and Grace didn't feel like it was worth pushing it. She wasn't naive; she knew how these things tended to work out.

Scott was almost as notorious for his sleeping around as he was for his drug problem, but he was only in recovery for one of those things. He'd already told her he wasn't the commitment type, which was fine. Keeping it casual was A-OK with her. Relationships were about feelings and commitment and baggage, and that was not what she was looking for right now.

They didn't have to talk about it. If Scott didn't feel the need to put a label on it, neither did Grace. She was pretty happy getting sexed up on the regular by a man who looked like a Greek god, so she was just going to enjoy it. Live in the moment. Not think about the future.

Carmen was totally wrong about her. She *could* separate sex from emotion. She was totally doing it. Look at her, sleeping with Scott Deacon, notorious womanizer, and not feeling a thing— except the many, many orgasms. She definitely felt those.

The only serious relationship Grace was interested in at the moment was her relationship with the cup of coffee in her hand, because Scott had kept her up way too late again last night. She'd fallen so far behind on her sleep, she was considering having a central line put in for a caffeine IV.

Coffee was her one true soul mate, and their love would never die.

"AM I REALLY THAT BORING?" CARMEN ASKED, TOSSING A wadded-up napkin at Grace across the lunch table.

"Huh?" Grace said eloquently, looking up from her salad.

"That's like the fifth time you've yawned in the last two minutes. You're practically falling asleep in your radicchio."

"Sorry, it's not you. I'm just behind on my sleep."

Grace had spent every night that week with Scott. She kept waiting for him to say he wasn't in the mood to hang out, but every night, as soon as she got home, there he was at her door. Luring her over to his house with offers of fantastic sex. It was hard to pass up—not that she wanted to. She couldn't get enough of him. Spending a whole day at work carefully keeping their distance and pretending to be indifferent to one another left her aching to touch him, like a junkie going through withdrawal.

Which was probably not a great analogy to use around a recovering addict, and she made a mental note never to say it aloud.

"Scott keeping you up at night?" Carmen teased.

Grace stared at her plate and concentrated on stabbing a cherry tomato.

"Shut the front door! You're sleeping with him?"

"Shhh, keep your voice down," Grace hissed, glancing around the commissary to make sure no one had heard.

Carmen leaned forward. "Why didn't you tell me?"

"Because we're not telling anyone."

"Why?"

Grace shrugged. "Because it's no big deal, and I'd rather it wasn't common knowledge around the set, or, you know, on the front page of Perez Hilton."

"How can you say it's no big deal? You're sleeping with Scotty Deacon. Like, *Tiger Beat* Scotty Deacon. Did you know I had a poster of him in my room when I was twelve? Right above my bed, next to my Destiny's Child poster."

"I was more of a Nick Carter girl myself," Grace admitted. Her teenage obsession with The Backstreet Boys had overshadowed pretty much everything else happening in the pop culture landscape back then. "Anyway, it's not like we're dating or anything. It's all very casual."

Carmen lifted an eyebrow. "When have you ever been casual about a man in your life?"

"I'm trying something new. Like you said: no emotion, just sex."

"Yeah? How's it going so far?"

"Excellent, thanks for asking."

Carmen looked doubtful. "Okay, but is he actually good in bed?"

Grace couldn't help the smile that spread across her face. "Better than good."

"Really? Because usually when they're that pretty they can't find the G-spot with a headlamp and a map."

"He can find it just fine," Grace assured her. "Trust me."

Carmen shook her head sadly. "Girl, you are so doomed. No way you're not falling for him."

Grace rolled her eyes. "Whatever you say, glass house. How are things with Dominic?"

At the mere mention of his name, Carmen's face lit up in a giddy grin. "It's really great."

Grace had never seen her like this over a man. Carmen was supposed to be the cool-headed one. The tough, practical woman who didn't lose her senses over a guy. Going all sappy and goo-goo-eyed was supposed to be Grace's job. And now look at the two of them. How the turns had tabled.

"So you guys are really serious?" Grace asked.

"Yeah." Carmen nodded slowly. "I think..." She paused, and her expression turned adorably sheepish. "I think I love him."

Grace reached across the table to squeeze her friend's hand. "Carmen!"

"I know!" Carmen agreed enthusiastically.

"Have you told him?"

Carmen shook her head, still smiling. "Not yet. But soon, maybe."

Grace was so, so happy for her. And for Dominic. Genuinely. But she was happy for herself too.

She didn't need what they had. She was perfectly content with things the way they were between her and Scott. Everyone had exactly what they wanted.

Life couldn't be better.

16

"What are you in the mood for?" Scott asked Grace that night as he thumbed through a pile of takeout menus.

They were at his place. They were always at his place, because it was nicer and bigger than her place. It was hard to be annoyed about it, since her place was literally ten yards away, so she could always just run next door whenever she needed something. The only real time Grace had spent at her house this week had been when she was getting ready for work in the mornings.

She leaned against him, peering over his shoulder at the menus scattered across the kitchen counter. "We could always go out."

He made a face. "Eh."

"Or not."

He looked over at her, and his eyebrows scrunched together in a way she found completely adorable. "Did you want to go out?"

She shrugged. "It was just an idea. I'm not married to it or anything."

"Someone might recognize me, is the thing."

She nodded and leaned back against the counter beside him. "Right."

"Going out in public can be kind of a hassle."

"Sure." She actually forgot, sometimes, that he was a big famous movie star. He was just Scott to her now. Her Scott. At least for the time being.

His hand snaked around her waist, tugging her up against his hips. "Besides..." He bent his head and nuzzled against her ear. "If we stay in, we don't have to wear so many clothes."

"Mmmm," she sighed, shivering. "Good point. Very good point."

"I thought so." His tongue darted against her ear, and she shivered again. "But if you want to go out instead..."

Her hands curled around his upper arms. "Nope. I'm good."

"You sure?" he asked, sucking on the spot behind her ear. The one that made her knees wobble.

"So—so sure," she mumbled, clinging to him for balance.

Scott's hands settled around her rib cage. She loved his hands. They were big and warm and just the right amount of rough. She liked the feel of them on her body, and the things he did to her body with them.

"What do you feel like ordering?" he asked, his breath hot on her neck.

"Whatever you want." She was way too distracted by what he was doing with his tongue on her neck to think about food right then.

His hands slid down to her waist. "Are you hungry?"

"Mmmm." She was hungry, all right, but not for food.

He pulled back to look at her. "We can order something now if you want."

She reached up and threaded her fingers through his hair. She loved his hair. She loved that she got to touch it as much as she wanted, which was a lot.

He smiled. "Or..."

Her hand slid down to the side of his neck, so she could pet his scruff. He closed his eyes and made a purring sound, leaning into her touch.

"Or?" she prompted when he didn't say anything.

He opened his eyes, and his fingers dug into her hips. "Or we could order later."

"Definitely later," she said, nodding. "Later would be better."

"Later," he agreed, and kissed her, deep enough to bend her head back. His hands cupped her ass, and Grace wrapped her legs around his waist as he lifted her off the floor.

They didn't get around to ordering food until much, *much* later.

IS A SEX HANGOVER A THING? GRACE WONDERED ON MONDAY.

She and Scott had spent the entire weekend in a blissful sex bubble. It had started with several rounds of vigorous Friday night sex, followed up by sleepy Saturday morning sex, which had led to seductive omelet-making—Grace wouldn't have thought omelet-making could be sexy, but when Scott did that flip thing with the pan, whoo boy—then some lazy afternoon making out, which had turned into snuggly napping. After that had been a round of shower sex, followed by takeout and some quality cuddling in front of the television, capped off by yet another round of acrobatic sex. And Sunday had been second verse, same as the first.

But now it was Monday and she was paying the price for their mini-sexcation. She was *definitely* walking funny—the chafing situation was real, not to mention the beard burn in some...delicate places.

To make matters worse, they were on night shoots all week, and Grace definitely had not gotten as much sleep as she should have during the day today, thanks to Scott. Who was not even shooting tonight, so she was stuck in a damp, grimy warehouse at two o'clock in the morning—which technically made it Tuesday, but the important part was that it *felt* like Monday—paying the price for their folly all by herself.

The scene they were shooting tonight was super intense too. It was after Nate's character had abducted Poppy's character, and was trying to scare her into giving up the information he needed. Poppy was in her underwear again—thanks very much, male screenwriter—and Nate was screaming at her and punching his fist into the wall next to her head with such fury that Grace honestly didn't know how he hadn't broken his hand yet. Then he had to grab Poppy by the throat and throw her roughly to the ground, take after take.

Both actors had worked with the stunt team so they could do it without hurting themselves—or each other—but it was a little hard to watch. Nate was being genuinely scary, and Poppy was curled up on the ground with tears pouring down her face, shaking and crying and begging for mercy. Grace didn't know how she could dredge up all that emotion over and over again, but she did.

Every time they finished a take, Nate bent down and helped Poppy off the ground with an apologetic smile. Then they reset for the next one, and he went right back to being the scary guy screaming at her.

When they took their first break to reset the camera, Poppy shrugged into her robe and fumbled in the pocket for her cigarettes.

"You're doing great," Joe told her. "Really believable."

"Yeah, well, I've got some experience with it," Poppy said, lighting her cigarette with a shaking hand.

Back when Poppy was younger and her career was just starting to take off, there had been a lot of stories about her father in the press. He'd been the driving force behind her modeling career and had acted as her manager throughout her teenage years, but by all accounts he'd been a drunken bully. The police had been called to their home more than once over alleged domestic violence incidents, and he'd been arrested a couple of times for getting into fistfights, although no charges had ever stuck.

If that was what Poppy was channeling for this scene, Grace was even more impressed, and also heartsick for her. To go through such a horrific experience, and then to bring it to work and relive it for the sake of a scene in a movie took a kind of toughness Grace couldn't even fathom.

Joe wrapped one of his big arms around Poppy's small shoulders and gave her a fatherly squeeze. "Just a few more times," he said gently. "And then we'll be done."

———

When Grace finally got home at eight in the morning, she didn't have it in her to do anything but crawl straight into bed —alone. Because she had to get some real sleep or she might actually die.

She didn't see Scott until they were both on set that night. He teased her about how tired and cranky she was, and texted her dumb jokes and silly pictures to try and cheer her up, but in the morning, at the end of a long, brutal night of shooting an action sequence in a rail yard, they both went straight home and crashed in separate beds. Because night shoots were hell.

The problem was that Grace didn't adjust well to sleeping during the day, no matter how virtuous she tried to be about it. All the sleep masks and white noise machines in the world weren't enough to lull her into a deep, restful sleep when her body knew the sun was shining on the other side of the blinds. She only ever managed to get a few hours of fitful sleep, no matter how tired she was or how long she lay in bed. It was always like this for her though. Her body never seemed to get used to the new schedule until it was time to adjust back the other direction. She'd accepted the unpleasant inevitability of it, but if anything ever made her quit the business, it was going to be this.

Infuriatingly, Scott seemed to take it in stride, like it was no big deal to flip his sleep schedule one hundred eighty degrees on a dime. When she asked him about it, he simply shrugged and said he was used to dealing with insomnia, and it didn't much matter whether he was having it at night or during the day. She couldn't even be jealous of him, because that really sucked for him, but it was still annoying how revoltingly cheerful he managed to be on set.

Meanwhile, Grace spent the week in a zombie-like daze of exhaustion. The hours from five p.m. to seven a.m. were spent desperately mainlining coffee and trying to keep her eyes open at whatever unpleasant outdoor location they were occupying for the night, and the rest of her time was spent in bed, tossing and turning and trying to will herself to fall asleep.

Scott generously offered to tire her out, but on top of everything else, she'd started her period, and honestly? Even if she hadn't, she probably wouldn't be in the mood. Insomnia made her too tired for sex. PMS plus insomnia made her unfit for human company entirely.

Basically the only times she and Scott were together all week were on set, where they had to keep their distance and act like nothing was going on. Which wasn't doing anything to improve her mood, because she missed being close to him. She missed the smell of him, and the warm solidness of his body, and how safe and secure she felt in his arms.

She was suffering from Scott withdrawal—although again, probably not an analogy she should use around him—and the only solution was to grit her teeth and get through it. To make it to Saturday, when they were done with night shoots, and they'd have the whole rest of the weekend to spend together.

Thursday night they were shooting on a hotel rooftop in the Central Business District, which was at least an upgrade from all the gloomy industrial sites they'd been at this week. It was about two hours before dawn when Scott came up beside Grace as she was staring out vacantly at the cityscape.

"Hanging in there?" he asked, his arm brushing against hers as he joined her at the railing. He was dressed in a suit for the scene, and he reached up to loosen his tie.

She nodded half-heartedly, suppressing a yawn. "I really hate night shoots."

"Me too." His gaze drifted to the wide, dark river snaking through the city below them. "There's something kind of magical about being awake this time of night though. It feels otherworldly."

"It's a liminal space," Grace murmured.

Scott's eyes swung to hers. "What's that?"

"A place of transition. Reality feels altered because you're leaving the familiar behind and waiting for something new to begin, but you don't know what it's going to be yet. The hours before dawn are like that—yesterday's over, but tomorrow hasn't started yet, so you're hovering in this moment of ambiguity." She shook her head. "Or something like that, anyway."

Clearly, she was half delirious from throwing too much caffeine on top of too little sleep, otherwise she wouldn't be babbling at Scott about liminal spaces, of all things. But he just smiled at her fondly and said, "I never thought of it that way."

"It can be a trigger for anxiety. Not everyone's good at existing in ambiguity."

His hand closed over hers, squeezing gently. They shouldn't be holding hands like this where everyone could see, but she'd missed his touch so much she couldn't bring herself to pull away.

"You have to trust that the next step is going to be one you can handle," Scott said. "The program taught me that."

Grace leaned into him a little, and they watched the eastern horizon for the first glimmer of the new day's light.

By the time Saturday morning rolled around, and they were freed from the living hell of night shoots, Grace was so dead she actually slept for ten hours straight.

She woke at six in the evening to a text from Scott.

Scott: Going to dinner with Poppy c u later

So. Okay. Great.

It was only their first night off all week. And he'd decided to spend it with Poppy.

That was...fine.

Wasn't it?

They were being casual, right? That was what Grace had said. All sex and no feelings. Which meant Scott was free to spend his time however he wanted, with whomever he wanted.

So what if they hadn't been alone in days? That had been Grace's choice, not his. He wasn't obligated to spend time with her any more than she was obligated to spend time with him. It wasn't like they were actually dating or anything. Were they?

Grace stayed in her pajamas all night and ate a pint of ice cream for dinner while she waited for Scott to come home. Sometime after one a.m. she finally gave up on him and went to bed.

He texted her the next morning at ten o'clock.

Scott: U up?

When she opened the door to him, he stepped straight into her arms, bending her back a little when he kissed her. "I missed you," he murmured, burying his face in her hair.

Grace had missed him too, so she didn't ask what he'd been doing with Poppy last night, and she didn't object when he took her hand and led her upstairs to his bed.

"I'm sorry about last night," Scott said later, nuzzling the back of her neck as they were basking in post-coital contentment.

Grace couldn't help stiffening slightly. "It's fine." She was aiming for a breezy tone but it fell a little short of the mark.

His arms tightened around her, and his lips pressed against her shoulder. "It's not fine. I wanted to be with you."

She turned in his arms so she could look at him. "Then why did you go out with Poppy?"

He sighed, his palm skimming up the outside of her thigh and over her hipbone. "Because she needed me."

"What does that mean?"

He hesitated, like he was...not guilty, exactly, but definitely hiding something. "Poppy's not..." He paused, considering his words. "I know she struts around all the time like she's fine, but she's not."

"Okay," Grace said slowly. That wasn't what she'd expected to hear, and she wasn't sure what it even meant.

"Remember how I told you Poppy and I were a lot alike? Well..." He stopped, waiting for her to make the inference.

"Oh!" Grace said as she finally realized what Scott was hinting at. "Oh." Poppy had an addiction problem too. Only clearly she was not in recovery, because Grace had seen her drinking at Scott's party.

He ducked his head so Grace couldn't see his eyes. "I'm not saying she's—she's nowhere near as bad as I was, but...she's struggling with some things. Things I can understand better than most people."

Grace tried to reconcile her idea of perfect Poppy Carpenter with what Scott was telling her. It wasn't all that hard to do, especially after Poppy's comment on location last week. She could see how someone like Poppy, who'd found fame at a young age, might be just as damaged as Scott, even if she was better at hiding it.

The industry was brutal on its young stars, and very few made it through the gristmill without scar tissue.

"Is she okay?" Grace asked.

Scott let out a breath, nodding. "She and Sareh had a fight yesterday. Hopefully, it'll blow over." He looked so relieved that Grace wasn't mad. She felt like a first-class jerk for being upset with him last night.

She ran her fingers through his hair and over the stubble on his cheek. "I'm sorry to hear that, and I hope they work it out. I think it's really great that you're such a good friend to her."

Scott propped himself up on one arm and pushed Grace onto her back, kissing her. She sighed against his mouth, and he sucked her lower lip between his teeth before shifting his weight and curling his body around hers again.

"I'd rather have been with you," he murmured, resting his head between her breasts. "I'd always rather be with you."

Grace blinked, barely able to breathe around the lump in her throat.

Maybe what they had *was* real. She hadn't let herself think about what would happen after the shoot ended, because the idea of losing Scott terrified her. But maybe she didn't have to lose him. Maybe things could stay the way they were, even after they went back to LA.

He shifted, nuzzling his face into her breasts. "Oh! I haven't had a chance to tell you the good news yet: I might do a play in New York. Off Broadway, but it's real meaty stuff. I'm going to fly out there and take some meetings after I wrap here."

Or maybe not.

A play. That was like a six-month commitment or something, wasn't it? Maybe more.

In New York. The opposite side of the country from where Grace lived.

"That's fantastic," she said, wrapping her arms around him. "I'm really happy for you."

She had to be happy for him. He was excited about it, and he needed this. He'd been so down about his future prospects. This was great news for him, even if it wasn't so great for *them*.

Working on a film—especially on location—was like going away to camp. The relationships you forged on set could feel more intense because of the stressful schedule and the separation from friends and family. But more often than not, they were only temporary. Not many people kept in touch with their camp besties. Occasionally the odd relationship would last beyond the production, but usually people dropped right back out of your life again as soon as everyone went home.

Grace had always known there was a chance Scott would lose interest in her as soon as he went back to his regular life. More than a chance. A likelihood.

She'd been down this road before, and she knew how it usually turned out.

"Do you want me to make you mac and cheese for dinner?" Scott asked.

"Always," she said, holding him tighter.

17

"I went to the gym with Nate this morning," Scott told Grace on Monday night.

It was raining, and they were curled up together on his couch watching a basketball game. Well, *he* was watching a basketball game. Grace was only pretending to watch the game.

Her sleep schedule was still recovering from last week, so mostly she was trying to stay awake until they got to the sex portion of the evening. Honestly, what she really wanted to do was put on her pajamas and crawl into bed, but they only had so many nights left together, and Scott had wanted to watch basketball, so here she was.

"There's nothing like watching someone warm up with your max to make you question your manhood," he complained.

She hummed noncommittally in response, and he dug a finger in her ribs, homing in right on her ticklish spot.

"This is the part where you're supposed to reassure me that my manhood is unmatched, regardless of how much I can bench."

Grace pushed his hand away. "Your manhood is perfectly adequate." She meant it as a joke, but it didn't have quite the lighthearted zing she'd been going for.

Scott went quiet for a moment before he said, "Something wrong?"

"I'm just tired. Today was a long day." A long day of watching Scott and Poppy hang all over each other. Which might also have had something to do with Grace's mood.

They'd been shooting the emotional reunion scene where Scott finds Poppy after believing she's dead, and there'd been a lot of crying and hugging and kissing all day. Grace was still trying to shake the bad taste it had left in her mouth—and the guilt over letting it get to her in the first place. At least he'd taken a shower when he got home, so she didn't have to smell Poppy's perfume on him anymore.

"Is it the basketball? Because you said you didn't mind watching the game, but I'm happy to turn it off if you—"

"I don't care about the basketball," Grace said, more snappishly than she'd intended. *Oops.*

"Okay," Scott said slowly, recoiling a bit.

She pushed herself to her feet. "I think I'm just going to go back to my place and sleep in my own bed tonight."

"Hey, Grace! Hey!" He propelled himself off the couch and made it to the door at the same time she did, blocking her exit with an arm stretched across the doorway. "Will you please tell me what's going on? Did I do something?"

"No." She shook her head, feeling tears prick her eyes and not knowing where they'd come from. "It's nothing."

He cupped her face in his hand, tilting it up toward his as his eyes raked over her. "It doesn't seem like nothing."

"What are we doing?" she blurted out, defenseless in the crosshairs of his bottomless gaze.

Scott's brow wrinkled in confusion. "What?"

"You and me." She hadn't planned to have this conversation tonight, but now that she'd started it she might as well finish. "Is this just a hookup? Or is it something more?"

His face went blank, so she couldn't tell what he was thinking.

"What do you want it to be?"

"I'm asking you."

He gave her one of his smarmy movie star smiles. "I want whatever you want," he said, trying to use his charm on her.

It was the wrong move, because she wasn't in the mood for his games.

"Right," she gritted out and ducked under his arm, done with this conversation.

"Wait." He caught her by the wrist. "Please." His voice broke a little on the please, which was enough to make her turn around.

"I'm tired of not knowing what we are," Grace admitted with a sigh. "I don't know if we're dating. Or if you even date."

"I date," Scott said a little defensively.

"Are you dating *me*?"

"I kind of thought so, yeah." He sounded annoyed, like she was magically supposed to have known that somehow.

"It's a little hard to tell, since we've never actually gone anywhere together."

"*You're* the one who wanted to keep it a secret," he shot back resentfully, which was totally unfair.

"Because I didn't want to be judged at work for who I'm sleeping with! We're not at work twenty-four seven."

"Yeah, well, I don't have the luxury of living my life incognito. If we go out in public, we'll get spotted together."

"I don't care about that."

"You will when your picture ends up on TMZ and blows your cover at work."

"Wait," Grace said, as it finally sunk in what he'd just said. "So, we *are* dating?"

The defensiveness drained out of him, and in its absence his expression betrayed a heart-twisting uncertainty. "I mean...yeah? Assuming you want to be."

"I want to be." Finally saying it out loud left her a thousand pounds lighter. Grace hadn't realized how much it had been weighing her down, trying to keep her feelings for Scott to herself.

Scott let out a long exhale. "Okay."

"Okay."

His eyebrows scrunched in adorable befuddlement. "Why are we fighting?"

"We're not."

"Good." He wrapped his arms around her waist and buried his face in her neck. "I don't want to fight."

Grace held on to him as tight as she could. "Me neither."

He sighed against her, and she felt the tension in his muscles release.

"Scott?"

"Hmmm?"

"Are you going to keep dating me after we wrap?"

He lifted his head, and his eyes crinkled as he smiled at her. "I sure as hell hope so."

"What about the play?"

His smile faded. "I don't know." He pressed his lips against her forehead. "We'll figure it out though, okay?"

Grace reached for his face and ran her fingers over his stubble. She loved his stubble. She wanted to pet it always.

"Okay," she said, and kissed him.

MOST OF SCOTT'S LAST WEEK ON SET WAS DEVOTED TO shooting the big climactic action sequence that took place on the train the film got its name from. Shooting inside the out-of-commission passenger car set up in front of green screens was cramped, difficult work. Scott spent his days covered in fake blood, performing grueling stunt sequences that left him bruised and exhausted at the end of every day.

Not so exhausted they couldn't make the most of their

remaining few nights together though. Scott had been more amorous and attentive than ever, and Grace was having a harder time keeping her hands off him at work, which meant they got a little less discreet about their relationship.

"You've got something in your hair," Tamika said, reaching up to touch it. "Is that prop blood?" she asked, rubbing her fingers together

"What?" Grace grabbed the lock of hair in question and pulled it in front of her face. "Uh...oops?" She and Scott had been making out in his trailer at lunch, and she'd tried to be careful not to get any of the sticky red goo on her, but apparently she had not been entirely successful.

Tamika gave her a knowing smile and reached for her makeup remover. "Don't worry, your secret's safe with me."

Even though Grace was trying to savor every moment, the days seemed to pass at hyperspeed. Before she knew it, Friday was upon them and they'd called a wrap on Scott. There was a cake big enough for the whole crew, and a lot of hugging and picture taking, and it was all Grace could do to keep the tears at bay.

She had to stay in New Orleans for another few days of pick-ups next week, but Scott was leaving for LA on Sunday. What was worse was by the time Grace got back to Los Angeles at the end of next week, Scott would already be gone. He was flying to New York on Wednesday to take some meetings and do a photo shoot for a short *Esquire* profile, immediately followed by two weeks in Tokyo to shoot a commercial for some video game.

They were going to be apart for almost a month, which was longer than they'd been a couple. A separation that length would be a trial for even an established, solid relationship. Grace was terrified of what it would do to her and Scott.

But that was a problem for the future. First, there was a wrap party to go to on Saturday night.

Grace was *so* not in the mood for a party. There ought to be a word for that sense of nostalgia you got for something that wasn't over yet. There was probably one in German, or Japanese, or Danish. Her mother would just say she was borrowing trouble. Whatever you called it, Grace had a bad case of it.

Scott actually seemed excited about the party, so Grace tried to put on a cheerful face for his sake. She wasn't super successful, unfortunately.

"Hey, what's wrong?" he asked her the second time she didn't laugh at one of his jokes. They were in his rented Audi, on the way to the club the production had rented out for the party, and he reached across the console for her hand.

She laced her fingers with his and squeezed. "Doesn't it make you sad that tonight is the last time we're all going to be together? I'm not ready for it to be over."

He squeezed her hand back. "It does, but not sad enough to keep me from enjoying the time we have left."

Grace nodded. It was exactly what her mother would say. If only it was that easy.

"Besides, tonight's a big night," Scott said cheerfully. "It's our first official date."

They'd talked about it yesterday, and Grace had agreed there was no reason to keep hiding their relationship now that Scott was done shooting. They weren't working together anymore, so it didn't matter if anyone knew about them.

Which meant the wrap party would be their debut as a couple in front of their friends and coworkers.

It was possible Grace was a little nervous about it. But also maybe a little excited.

Scott brought her hand to his lips and kissed her knuckles. "Everything's going to be fine. You'll see."

As soon as they walked in the door of the club, Scott transformed into his genial party persona, but this time he kept his hand firmly on Grace's waist as they made the rounds of the room together. Instead of checking on everyone else to make sure they were having a good time, he only checked on her, giving her a smile or a light stroke of his hand every few minutes to let her know he hadn't forgotten about her.

It was a revelation, being around other people and having Scott pay more attention to her than to everyone else for once. Knowing that she actually *was* special.

"I knew it!" Dex exclaimed triumphantly when he saw them. "I knew there was something going on with y'all!"

No one seemed particularly surprised to see them together, as it turned out. Apparently they weren't that good at hiding it after all.

Joe didn't comment on it at all, but the smug look he gave Grace before he pulled her in for a hug spoke volumes.

There was an old-school photo booth set up for the party, and everyone took turns squeezing into it in different combinations, trying to see just how many bodies they could cram in there at once. Scott pulled Grace into the booth for a session with just the two of them, and kissed her the whole time the camera was flashing. When the machine spit out the strip of four black and white photos, he tore it in half, giving two of the snaps to Grace before tucking the other two into his wallet.

Poppy and Sareh showed up an hour later. Poppy had wrapped two days before Scott, but stayed in town for the party—and maybe also for Sareh. They arrived together, but Poppy wasn't out to the public, and the tabloids would have a field day if they got wind she was bi, so she and Sareh were careful not to engage in any PDA where someone might take a picture of them.

When the dancing started, Scott begged off, so Grace let Carmen and Tamika drag her away. She stayed on the dance floor through three songs before taking a break and making her way back to Scott.

"Your cheeks are all pink," he said, smiling at her.

"That's because I'm sweating."

"Mmmm, I know." He bent down to kiss her. "It's amazing."

She laughed against his mouth. "Weirdo."

"You should probably drink some water though. I'll get it for you."

She loved how he was always taking care of her. It was one of her favorite things about him.

While Scott was off at the bar, Poppy came bounding over and threw her arms around Grace's neck.

"I'm so happy for you," Poppy said into her ear, hugging her hard. Her skin was hot and sticky, and her breath smelled like whiskey.

"Thanks?" Grace hugged her back, not entirely sure what Poppy was talking about.

Poppy released her and grabbed both of Grace's shoulders, staring at her in that intense way drunk people had. "He's a great guy. And he adores you. I hope you know that."

"You mean Scott?"

Poppy nodded vigorously. "You've been really good for him. He's like a thousand times happier around you."

"Really?" Grace asked, feeling herself grin.

"Really." Poppy nodded some more.

"Hey," Scott said, coming back with Grace's ice water.

Poppy let go of Grace and gave Scott a big, sloppy hug.

His eyebrows lifted, and one of his arms wrapped around Poppy while he passed Grace her water. "What's up?"

"Nothing," Poppy said, grabbing Grace and pulling her into a three-way hug. "I just love you guys so much."

"We love you too," Scott said, frowning slightly. "Everything okay?"

"Yep!" Poppy said. "Fan-fucking-tastic." She released them and bounced off to join the dancing.

"Is she all right?" Grace asked, watching Poppy on the dance floor.

Scott shrugged and shook his head slightly. "Who knows?"

"Do you wanna—"

"No," Scott said, turning back to Grace and dropping a kiss on her lips. "Tonight's about the two of us. Poppy can take care of herself."

They spent the rest of the night glued to each other, until it was time for Scott to get up on stage, alongside Joe, Poppy, Nate, and Dex, to thank everyone for all of their hard work on the film. When they'd all made their speeches, Dex cued the DJ, and the same NSYNC song they'd lip-synched to at Scott's party started up. Scott rolled his eyes at Poppy, but he sang along like a good sport, even managing to look like he was having fun as they all did the dance moves together. Half the people there had their phones out, recording the performance, so video of it would undoubtedly be all over the internet by tomorrow.

As soon as the song was over, Scott fled the stage and sank gratefully into Grace's waiting arms. "You were amazing," she told him.

"That fucking song," he muttered. "So embarrassing."

"I thought you looked hot," she said, nuzzling against his neck.

He claimed her lips, and what started out as a soft kiss quickly turned heated. "Are you ready to get out of here?" he breathed when they finally broke apart.

She'd thought he'd never ask.

Grace's hand stayed tightly clamped on Scott's thigh the whole drive home. Every time he stopped at a red light, he covered it with his, stroking his thumb across her knuckles and casting fevered glances her way.

They barely made it inside his house before they were tearing at each other's clothes.

Their kisses were chaotic and bruising, their hands everywhere at once, like they couldn't get enough of each other. By the time they managed to stumble upstairs to the bedroom, they were already half undressed: Scott's shirt open and untucked, and Grace's dress unzipped and hanging off one shoulder.

Scott's hands roamed over her back, heavy and warm, before

plucking deftly at the clasp on her bra. She sighed as he freed her breasts and slid her dress down over her hips. As soon as it hit the floor, she surged toward him and shoved his shirt off his shoulders, pressing herself into him, desperate for more contact.

She needed him so much it was like a physical pain. An ache so deep it made her eyes sting. His name was on her tongue, but she couldn't form the word around the burning at the back of her throat.

Scott's hands cupped her face, strong and steady, his thumbs stroking her cheekbones as his lips soothed away her tears. "Shhh," he murmured, peppering her face with gentling kisses. "We've got all the time in the world."

They didn't. But at least they still had tonight.

Grace sank into his arms and tried not to think about the future.

EARLY SUNDAY MORNING, GRACE OPENED HER EYES TO THE sight of Scott's phone hovering in front of her face. "What are you doing?" she mumbled, batting it away. She felt hungover, even though she hadn't had a drop of alcohol at the wrap party.

He smiled at her. "Taking a picture so I can remember how you look first thing in the morning." He'd already gotten dressed in jeans, a hoodie, and a baseball cap—the official low-key celebrity travel outfit.

"Ugh, why?" Grace groaned, running her hands through her tangled hair.

"Because it's my favorite sight, and I'm going to miss it for the next three and a half weeks."

She felt a fresh pang of sorrow at the prospect of their separation, and rolled toward him, making grabby hands. "C'mere."

Scott leaned over and indulged her with a kiss before he went back to packing his bags.

Grace had offered to take him to the airport, but he had to turn in his Audi, so there wasn't much point. Besides, Scott had said, better they say their goodbyes at home in private than at the airport in front of gawkers with camera phones.

She got up and got dressed, then sat on the edge of the bed uselessly while he moved around the room, stuffing the last of his belongings into his suitcases: his toothbrush, his phone charger, his flip-flops. There was a cleaning service coming to the house tomorrow. He'd already told her to help herself to anything she wanted in his pantry or his fridge before then.

When he was done, Grace followed him downstairs and stood around while he went from room to room double-checking things, before carrying his bags out to the car.

Too soon, he was all packed up and it was time for him to leave for the airport.

"I'm going to miss you," Scott said, pulling her into a hug and pressing his face into the top of her head.

Grace held on tight and nodded into his chest.

His arms clenched around her, hard enough to make her ribs ache. "It's only three weeks."

"Three and a half," she mumbled.

"We're gonna be fine." He lifted her chin and kissed her, slowly and intently.

It ended before she was ready, and then he was walking away from her and getting into the car. Grace stood just inside the doorway, waving as he backed the car out and drove away.

She didn't cry. Not when his car turned out of sight, or even when she went back inside his empty house to gather up her things. She felt pretty proud of herself for that.

She did spend the rest of the day on her couch, feeling sad and trying to cheer herself up by bingeing TV shows on Netflix.

Scott texted her from the plane.

Scott: Miss u already

She sent him back a string of sadface emojis.

"My house feels weird," he told her when he called that night. "Emptier than it did before."

Grace knew the feeling. Her little rental house felt barren without Scott right next door. Her heart felt barren too.

"I don't even know where you live in LA," she said.

"Laurel Canyon. What about you?"

"Culver City."

"That's not too far. When I get back from Tokyo on the twenty-sixth, I'll make you dinner at my place."

"You'll be too jet-lagged."

"I'll sleep on the plane."

"You won't have any food in your house."

"I'll go to the grocery store."

"On your first night home?"

"For you, I will."

"All right, then," she said, smiling. "It's a date." Their second real date. And only twenty-five days away.

Grace tried to picture their life together in LA. Driving back and forth from her apartment to his house in the hills. Shopping together at Trader Joe's. Going out to restaurants. Dodging the paparazzi.

It was difficult to imagine. It didn't feel like something that belonged to her life.

"I'll call you tomorrow night," Scott promised before he hung up.

Apparently Grace had already forgotten how to sleep alone, because she spent half the night tossing and turning in her stupid lopsided bed.

When her call time rolled around on Monday morning, she was not ready for it. It was hard being on set without Scott there. Knowing that he was two thousand miles away in Los Angeles while she was still stuck here in New Orleans, working. It sucked that she couldn't look forward to spending the night with him at the end of the day—that she wouldn't be able to look forward to it for nearly a month. Over and over, she found herself staring at the spot where his chair used to be, missing him.

"Hey," Carmen said, stopping by to check on her. "You okay?"

"Fine," Grace said, forcing a smile.

Carmen saw through the lie, of course, and gave her a sympathetic hug.

As a thank you to the crew, Scott had arranged for Grace's favorite food truck to visit the set at lunch. It only made her miss him more.

"Did you like the empanadas?" he asked that night when he called.

"Yeah," she told him. "They were great. Everybody loved it."

"I miss you," he said. "LA sucks."

Grace rolled over and hugged one of the pillows to her chest. "I miss you too."

He must have been able to hear the rustle of the sheets. "Are you in bed already?"

"Yeah." It was only ten, but she hadn't seen any point in staying up.

"What are you wearing?"

She couldn't help laughing. "Are you serious right now?"

"Deadly serious." His voice sounded low and rough, and it sent a shiver of desire down her spine.

"What are *you* wearing?" she asked him.

"Hang on." She heard him fumbling with the phone for a second and then: "Not a damn thing."

Well okay, then.

"I'm wearing your T-shirt," she said. "It still smells like you."

"Nice," he breathed. "Underwear?"

"The polka dots." He was intimate with all of her intimate apparel by now, so he'd know which ones she was talking about.

"Mmmm, my third favorites. Take them off for me."

Jesus, they were really doing this. Grace hadn't had phone sex since high school, and she felt a little silly, but she played along. "Okay."

"Touch yourself for me, Grace." The huskiness of his voice sent goose bumps shivering over her skin, and she let out a little moan as she pressed her hand between her legs. She was surprised to discover how aroused she was already.

"That's it," Scott said, his breath coming in rough pants that didn't leave any question about what he was doing on his end. "Let me hear you."

"Scott," she sighed, her hand moving faster.

"God, I miss the taste of you," he said. "I wish I had my tongue inside you right now."

"Oh, god." She pressed harder.

"If I was there with you, I'd spread your legs and go down on you until you screamed my name."

Shit, she was so close, past the point of being able to form coherent sentences. All she could do was gasp into the phone as she chased her release.

"Is that what you want, Grace? You want my fingers inside you and my tongue on your clit?"

"Yes," she panted.

He drew a shaky breath. "Say it."

"I want—oh, god, Scott—ahhhh." As she fell over the edge, she heard a telltale grunt that meant he was right there with her.

For a while, there was nothing but the sounds of their breathing as they both came down from the high.

"You okay?" Scott asked eventually.

"Mmmm," Grace sighed. "Yeah. I'm good."

There was a moment of quiet and then, "Grace?" He sounded uncertain. Almost shy.

She sat up a little. "Yeah?"

"I—" She could hear his breath stutter as he hesitated. "I *really* miss you."

18

The next time Scott called it was Wednesday night, just as Grace was getting home from work.

"Shouldn't you be heading to the airport?" she asked as she toed off her shoes and dropped onto the couch. He was supposed to be catching a red-eye to New York in two hours.

"Car's on its way, I'm just finishing up the last of my packing."

"The car is on its way and you haven't finished packing?" she repeated in horror. Just the thought of it gave her a stomachache. She wasn't leaving New Orleans for two more days, and she'd already packed and repacked her bags twice. "Are you out of your mind? You shouldn't be talking on the phone right now, you should be packing."

He huffed out a soft laugh. "It's fine, I'm almost done."

She heard him pop his gum and frowned. "Is everything okay?"

"Yeah, fine, I'm just running late."

"As usual."

"Pretty much, yeah."

There was a series of shuffling sounds on his end as he shoved things in his suitcase, and she wondered what his house in LA looked like. It bugged her that she didn't know.

"What day is your meeting about the play?" she asked, chewing on her lip.

"Monday."

"Are you nervous?"

"Nah. It's just a meeting. I've done a million of them." She didn't believe him, but she didn't push. She knew he hated to admit when he was stressed out, and now, when he was distracted and rushing, wasn't the best time for a heart-to-heart about his state of mind.

"You'll call and let me know how it goes, right?"

"Sure—oh, shit, that's the driver, I've gotta run."

"Okay. Have a safe flight."

"I will. Talk to you soon."

"I miss you," Grace said, but he'd already hung up.

She got a text from him in the morning after he landed in New York.

Scott: The weather sux here

Grace: Here too.

It was her last day on set, and it was raining.

They finished up early, and afterward she went out for celebratory drinks with Joe and some of the crew. Grace kept her phone close in case Scott called, but he didn't.

Instead, he sent her a selfie of himself all dressed up for his *Esquire* shoot. They had him in a button-down shirt and tie with a suit vest and no jacket. His hair was slicked back, and he was freshly shaven. Even though she missed the scruff, there was no denying it was a good look on him. A *really* good look. Seeing it made her chest ache with longing.

Scott: Thumbs up or thumbs down?

She sent him back a whole row of thumbs-up emojis, followed by a bunch of heart-eyes.

Scott: How was ur last day?

Grace: Not bad. Short.

Scott: R u sad?

Grace: A little. How's the shoot going?

Scott: Ok I guess I hate these things.

Grace: Call me when you're done?

Scott: Dinner with Paige tonite I'll try to call tomorrow?

Grace: Sure, have fun. I miss you.

Scott: Miss u more

"PAIGE, CAN YOU PLEASE RETURN ONE OF MY CALLS SO WE CAN talk?" Scott squeezed his phone in a white-knuckled grip, pacing across the theater office waiting room as he spoke to his sister's voicemail. "I'm sorry, okay? I shouldn't have criticized you. You're absolutely right, I have no leg to stand on. I just worry about you. I'm your big brother, I can't help it. Please, *please* call me back."

It was Monday, the day of his big meeting with producers of the play he was up for, and this was the third voicemail he'd left for his sister since their fight Thursday night.

When he'd arrived at Paige's apartment to take her out to dinner last week, it had reeked of weed. His baby sister, the one who'd watched drugs ruin his life and begged him over and over again to get clean, had turned into a burner.

He knew it was just pot, and it wasn't even illegal most places, but he didn't give a shit about the legality. It had just been a little weed when he'd first started using too. A little weed here, a few drinks there. Then some speed to help him focus, anti-anxiety drugs to take the edge off, and sleeping pills at night. The more drugs he'd tried, the more his body had craved them.

With his brain chemistry, there was no such thing as "just a little weed." And Paige was his half-sister. What if she shared his susceptibility to addiction? Their mother certainly did.

Maybe he'd overreacted a little. He hadn't meant to yell. He'd just smelled the pot and freaked out.

Scott just didn't understand how Paige could be so cavalier about it. Getting high wasn't worth playing Russian roulette with her life. He'd thought she was smarter than that. Especially after everything he'd put her through.

So yeah, he'd yelled. Because he'd been scared. He was fucking terrified Paige was going to throw her life away like he had.

Instead of going out to dinner, they'd had a huge fight that had ended with Scott slamming out of her apartment after she'd told him she didn't need a lecture on good life choices from an addict.

And ever since, Paige had been screening his calls.

Scott had originally thought he might use the weekend here in New York to try to catch up with some old friends, but as soon as he'd set foot in the city he'd changed his mind. Who was he kidding? He didn't want to see anyone from his past any more than they wanted to see him.

Instead, he'd spent the whole weekend holed up in his hotel

room, replaying the argument with Paige in his head and trying to figure out what he should have said or done differently. When he wasn't prepping for this damn meeting, that is.

He'd decided he wasn't going to do the play, but he still wanted to wow them today, because he needed to know that he could. Sabrina had sent a recording of an intern reading the script for him, and he'd been listening to it obsessively for the last few days as he prepped for the meeting. He knew everything there was to know about his character: his relationships, motivations, background, and how he fit into the dramatic action and broader thematic context of the play.

This time, Scott wanted to be the one to say no instead of the one begging for a chance. He wanted them to *want* him.

But he definitely wasn't taking it. New York wasn't good for him. He'd felt it seeping into his bones as soon as he stepped off the plane, like a poisonous fog. It made his limbs feel heavy and his brain itch. The crowds that packed the streets made him tense, the constant clamor of sirens and construction set his teeth on edge, and the weight of the buildings looming overhead constricted his chest.

Scott had done his first hit of heroin in New York ten years ago, and now he understood why. Everything about this city made him feel like a raw, exposed nerve. He couldn't stand the thought of being here for as long as the play would require—and he especially couldn't stand to be away from Grace that long.

He felt a sharp pang of guilt at the thought of her. He'd been avoiding talking to her all weekend, because he didn't want her to know how nervous he was about this fucking meeting. He hadn't even told her about the fight with Paige, because he didn't want her to worry.

He needed Grace to believe he was okay, because if she knew how not-okay he really was beneath the surface, she'd run the hell away from him as fast as she could. That was what the majority of his friends had done—not that he could blame them for ghosting.

He'd been a real nightmare. Why would anyone want to put up with him at his worst?

He just had to get through this one meeting. Then he'd call Grace. Once he had some good news to report.

"Mr. Deacon?" He glanced up at the assistant who'd just stepped into the waiting room, and she gave him a practiced smile. "We're ready for you now, if you'll follow me."

———

"WHAT THE *FUCK*, SABRINA?" SCOTT WAS PRACTICALLY shouting into the phone as he walked past Union Square Park on the way back to his hotel. "Do you have any idea how completely humiliating that was?"

One good thing about New York: no one paid the slightest attention to a celebrity yelling obscenities into his cell phone as he walked down the street.

"I can imagine, darling, and I am truly, deeply sorry. I had no idea."

Scott's meeting had lasted exactly ten minutes—nine of which had been spent making uncomfortable small talk with the casting director while they waited on Adrian Terry, the play's director. When Terry had finally showed, he shook Scott's hand, thanked him for coming, and told him they were going another way. Scott hadn't even been allowed to do a reading. He'd simply been dismissed out of hand.

"He said I was only there as a favor to you."

"Well, yes, I did have to call in a chit with Elise to get you a face-to-face, but it was meant to be a serious meeting. I expected them to keep an open mind until they'd actually met you."

"I spent a week prepping for this. I fucking flew all the way out here, and it was for nothing. They were never even going to consider me for the part."

"I am sorry, and you can believe Elise will be getting a piece of my mind, but these things do happen."

Not to me hovered on the tip of Scott's tongue. But that wasn't true anymore. He was exactly the sort of actor these things happened to.

This was his new reality.

When he got back to his hotel room, he changed into workout clothes and headed straight to the nearest gym to work out his frustration. He pushed himself to muscle failure, and then he got on the treadmill and pushed himself some more.

He took a roundabout route back to his hotel, insinuating himself into the rush-hour crowds that packed the sidewalk as he wandered the streets in aimless circles. It was past seven when he finally let himself into his park-view hotel room and collapsed onto the king-size bed in exhaustion.

All that exertion did the trick, because within minutes Scott had fallen into a blessedly dead sleep, still wearing his sweaty gym clothes.

GRACE WAS HAPPY TO BE BACK IN HER OWN APARTMENT, IN HER own bed. She loved Los Angeles. She'd missed it.

Part of her missed her little house in New Orleans though. She missed coffee on the balcony, and the view of the park. Her skin had gotten used to the Gulf Coast humidity, and now it felt parched and too tight. She even missed the smell in her old refrigerator. After nine weeks, it had started to smell like home.

Her refrigerator in LA had a smell too, but it was different. It used to smell like home to her, but now it didn't.

She'd get used to it again, she supposed. Or maybe she should scrub out her fridge and invest in some Arm & Hammer. Refrigerators probably shouldn't have smells, ideally.

Scott had texted to check that she'd gotten home okay, but

they hadn't talked in several days. She tried not to be disappointed by that. He was probably just busy. He knew a lot of people in New York, and he'd said he was going to try to do some catching up and networking while he was there. Plus he was probably trying to spend as much quality time with his sister as he could.

Grace didn't want to cramp his style or be the nagging girlfriend who expected him to stop living his life in order to check in with her. He'd call when he had a chance.

She really missed him though. Being apart was even harder than she'd anticipated.

The last thing she'd ever meant to do was fall in love with Scott Deacon, but that seemed to be exactly what had happened, against her better judgment. So much for her great experiment in casual sex without feelings. There was nothing casual about this hollowness in her chest, or the fact that she couldn't seem to sleep without his body next to hers, or the intensity with which she craved the sound of his voice.

He texted her a couple times on Saturday, but Grace didn't hear from him at all on Sunday. The jokey meme she sent him didn't get a response. Neither did the good luck text she sent before his meeting Monday morning. He hadn't posted on any of his social media accounts since he'd left New Orleans, but she checked them obsessively, just in case he updated again. He didn't.

She'd put the strip of pictures from the photo booth on her bedside table, so it was the last thing she saw before she turned out the light and the first thing she'd see in the mornings. It wasn't the same as actually having Scott there, but it was all she had for the time being.

On Monday night, when she still hadn't heard from him, Grace tried calling him, but got his voicemail. "Hey, it's me. I was just calling to see how your meeting went. Call me when you have a chance."

He texted her back the next day.

Scott: Sorry got busy. Meeting ok. Don't know anything yet.

He was just about to board his flight to Tokyo, so that was all she got out of him.

They texted back and forth a few times over the next week, but the time difference was a serious impediment, and they never seemed to be able to connect.

Grace resorted to watching his old movies for company, but found it difficult to reconcile the version of Scott captured on film—young, manic, and carefree—with the serious, scarred, more subdued man she'd come to know. It was like watching a stranger on-screen, and it made her feel even farther away from him.

As the days wore on and their separation stretched out, Scott texted less and less frequently. Grace tried not to panic. He was busy working. Long-distance was hard. There were a million perfectly innocent reasons he might not have as much time for her, and she refused to let herself think the worst.

Until eventually his texts stopped altogether. One day, then two days, then three days went by without a word.

Grace kept texting him anyway, asking if everything was okay. She tried calling a few times too, and left voicemails, but it all went unreturned.

After ten solid days of radio silence, she couldn't make excuses for him anymore. It was time to face facts.

Scott had moved on.

What happened in New Orleans stayed in New Orleans, apparently.

19

Scott felt like he was wading through a swimming pool filled with shit. It required every ounce of energy he had just to keep his head above the surface and avoid being sucked down into the dark, choking depths.

He'd thought things would get better once he got to Tokyo, but they were worse.

Tokyo was as bad as New York, only cleaner. Too many people, too much noise, not enough space. And this commercial he'd signed on to had turned out to be a fucking nightmare.

Series of commercials, really. It was six interconnected one-minute spots. There was a vague storyline set in a vaguely sci-fi future that vaguely resembled a video game universe. On paper, it had seemed like a pretty cool idea. In execution, it was a staggering embarrassment.

The sets were cheesy as hell, the costumes were even worse, and the director was some kind of deranged auteur who liked to improvise and experiment on set. Every day, Scott was asked to do increasingly ridiculous things in order to hawk some Japanese sports drink he'd never heard of. Today it was line dancing in a hot pink leisure suit alongside a bunch of people in cardboard robot costumes. Thank god the damn thing would never show back home in the States. Except for the internet, of course. Everything made its way onto the internet.

Scott couldn't even object or complain when the director asked him to wave his arms like some sort of demented scarecrow while shouting along with the Japanese jingle, because he needed this job to help prove he was a good little soldier who showed up and did what he was told—no matter how fucking stupid it was.

At the end of every day, Scott crawled into bed and stared at the ceiling of his hotel room, too numb to do anything but lie there and wish he was somewhere else.

The numbness had taken over both his limbs and his mind, making them feel heavy and unwieldy, like something that belonged to someone else. Everything was an effort: eating, sleeping, showering, getting out of bed in the morning when his alarm went off. He tried to pretend everything was fine when he was around other people on set, but the exertion of all that pretense left him drained and useless at the end of the day.

He hadn't talked to Grace in two weeks. He hadn't even been able to make himself reply to her texts, much less answer his phone. She'd left him a series of increasingly worried-sounding voicemails and he hadn't responded.

He'd meant to. He'd *wanted* to.

But he was so exhausted and numb all the time, and with the added complication of the time difference it was more than he could manage. Every day he'd stare at his phone's screen willing himself to touch the call button but unable to actually do it.

So he put it off for another day. And another. And another after that.

Until it got to the point where he'd waited too long, and he knew she'd be upset with him. His dread of her well-deserved reproach only intensified his inertia. The guilt over not calling her was eating him alive, but he couldn't seem to do anything about it.

It wasn't just Grace he was avoiding either. He'd been dodging

Robbie and Alfie's calls too. He couldn't face anyone right now. But Grace was the one he missed so much he could barely breathe when he thought about her.

Scott knew, somewhere buried deep down in the rational part of his brain, that talking to someone was exactly what he needed. But the rational part of his brain wasn't in control at the moment. The numbness was, and he couldn't seem to shake it.

He was terrified to let anyone know how much he was struggling, because if he said it out loud it would be real. He wouldn't be able to lie to himself anymore and pretend he was okay.

He *would* be okay though. This fucking commercial wasn't going to bring him down.

He just needed a little more time. Tomorrow would be better. It had to be.

He just needed to get through today first.

If he could get through today without getting high, that would be enough for now.

———

GRACE COULDN'T EVEN PRETEND TO BE SURPRISED SCOTT HAD ghosted on her. She'd always feared he would lose interest in her once the shoot ended and they went their separate ways. It had been delusional to hope otherwise.

In a way it was almost a relief to let go of all the uncertainty, stop trying to rationalize his behavior, and admit that whatever short-lived connection they'd had was over—had never even been real in the first place.

They were too different, and they hadn't had enough time to build a solid foundation before they'd been separated. If it hadn't happened now, it surely would have when he moved to New York.

Better to tear the bandage off sooner rather than later. Maybe that was even why Scott had distanced himself. Because he'd signed on to the play in New York, and hadn't wanted to be encumbered with a long-distance girlfriend he barely knew.

When you looked at it like that, she couldn't even blame him, really. Although it would have been nice if he'd had the guts to come right out and say it.

Grace let herself mourn the passing of their brief relationship that barely even qualified as a relationship by drinking a bottle of wine, flipping through all the photos of Scott on her phone, and sobbing into the T-shirt he'd left her.

But she'd be damned if she was going to let him break her.

Once she'd had a good cry about it, she picked herself up, stuffed Scott's T-shirt in the washing machine, hid the photo strip from the wrap party in the back of a drawer, and moved on with her life.

For the next few days, Grace tried to distract herself by catching up with her LA friends. But she didn't tell any of them about Scott, and if they noticed there was anything wrong they didn't comment on it. When Carmen texted about getting together, Grace put her off. Carmen had warned her about Scott, and Grace wasn't ready to face her yet and admit that Carmen had been right all along. Even though Carmen would never say "I told you so," it would be hanging there between them, and the wound was still too raw.

It was hard work, pretending to be fine. Pretending not to miss Scott with every cell in her body. Her chest hurt all the time, like something had tangled itself in knots around her heart. It hurt even more than her breakup with Chris had, and she didn't understand why.

Grace had been with Chris for *two years*, and she and Scott had only been a couple for a few weeks before their separation. They'd barely been a couple at all. It had been more like a temporary delusion than an actual relationship.

So why did it hurt so damn much to lose him?

She could survive it though. She *would* survive it. She could still breathe around the pain, most of the time. She could learn to live with it.

But then the twenty-sixth rolled around. The day Scott was supposed to get back from Tokyo. The night they were supposed to have had their second real date.

The knots in Grace's chest got a little tighter, a little more difficult to breathe around. And yeah, maybe she dug the photo booth strip out of the drawer and cried over it a little—but only for a few minutes. She was coping. She was getting through it.

Until she got a text from Scott.

Scott: Can I see u?

The sight of his name on the screen nearly stopped her heart. She'd assumed he was done with her for good, that she'd been relegated to history as just another woman he got bored with after a few weeks and stopped calling back. She thought she'd reconciled herself to never hearing from him again, but now here he was asking to be admitted back into her life, and she didn't know what to do.

For a good two minutes, Grace tried to talk herself into telling him to fuck off. But her heart was racing in her chest so hard her limbs were trembling. She *needed* to see him again. Desperately.

Even if it was just so she could have a little closure before he exited her life for good.

Grace: OK.

Scott: What's ur address?

She gave it to him, then went into the bathroom to wash her face. No way in hell was she going to get dressed up for him after he'd dropped out of her life, but she could at least face him with clear eyes and clear skin.

When she was as ready as she could be, Grace went into the living room and sat on the couch to wait. Thirty minutes later, there was a knock on her apartment door.

Stand firm. Don't let him off the hook—no matter how much you want to.

She took a steadying breath before opening the door. Despite her resolve, Grace's heart betrayed her by skipping a beat at the sight of him.

Scott.

Standing on her doorstep in a leather motorcycle jacket she'd never seen before. His hair had been cut shorter, almost into a buzz cut, and it made his face seem gaunter. He was still devastatingly handsome, but he looked haggard. There were dark circles under his eyes and a defeated slump to his shoulders.

Good, she couldn't help thinking.

He blinked at her and ran his hand over the top of his head, like he wasn't used to his hair yet either.

"You're back," she said when he didn't speak.

He nodded uneasily, as if he wasn't sure what kind of reception to expect.

Grace wasn't sure what kind of reception she was going to give him, so that made two of them. Her hand hovered at the base of her throat, tugging at the collar of her T-shirt as they regarded one another.

"Do you want to come in?" she said finally.

"If that's okay."

She stepped back, and Scott walked into her apartment. It was his first time seeing where she lived, but he didn't look around. He only had eyes for her. "I missed you," he said in a voice so quiet it was almost a whisper.

The bitterness clogging her throat leaked into her voice. "Did you?"

"I'm sorry," he said, hanging his head a little.

"For what?"

"For letting you think I didn't miss you."

Grace crossed her arms across her chest. "Then why did you?"

Scott stared down at the floor, shifting his weight. "I had a bad few weeks."

"You could have called and told me about it."

"I didn't want to whine at you."

"So you thought it'd be better to let me think you didn't like me anymore?"

His expression turned pained. "I wasn't exactly thinking clearly."

"What happened?" Grace asked, suddenly afraid of what his version of a bad few weeks might look like. "You didn't—"

"Fall off the wagon? No, but thanks for the vote of confidence." He sounded resentful, which she didn't feel like she deserved after what he'd put her through.

"Then what?" she snapped, losing patience. He was the one who'd asked to see her. Whatever the reason was, she needed him to get on with it.

He shook his head, clenching his jaw.

"Was there someone else?" she asked, giving voice to the fear that had been haunting her since he'd stopped calling. That he'd traded her in for someone new as soon as he got the chance. Someone more his type—more in his league.

He actually managed to look horrified. "God, Grace, no. There's no one but you."

"How am I supposed to know that?" She took some satisfaction in the way he flinched.

"There was a lot going on. I wanted to call you but...things just started piling up on me and I got buried under it."

"Like what, Scott? What happened that you couldn't talk to me for almost three weeks? That you couldn't even return a text to let me know you were okay?"

"I wasn't okay."

Grace swallowed as a tight ball of dread settled in the pit of her stomach. "What happened?" she asked again.

He stared down at the floor, grimacing. "I had a fight with Paige in New York. I didn't get the play. The commercial turned out to be a humiliating piece of crap, and I was miserable every second I was in Tokyo."

"That does all sound pretty sucky." Grace had been so busy feeling rejected and convincing herself Scott had replaced her that she'd never considered what else might have been going on—that he might have been lying when he'd told her everything was fine. "But you still could have talked to me about it."

It wasn't like avoidance was a new behavior for him. Scott had never been the world's greatest communicator, and he had a maddening tendency to shut down and try to hide it when things got difficult. She knew all of this about him, but she'd naively assumed they'd moved past it. She'd thought he would turn to her if he was having a hard time, and it hurt that he hadn't.

"I know." Scott inhaled a ragged breath and blew it out slowly. "I've been kind of a mess. Mostly because..." He finally looked up at her, and his eyes were shining and so vulnerable it made her breath catch. "I didn't know how to get through my days without you."

Grace felt some of the knots around her heart start to loosen, and couldn't decide if that made her a sucker. She wasn't sure she cared if it did.

"I fucked up," Scott said, taking a stuttering step toward her. "I'm sorry." He started to reach for her, then seemed to think better of it, his hand hovering uncertainly in the space between them. "Please just give me another chance, Grace. Please." He sounded destroyed, and it was enough to melt the last of her reservations.

She nodded, and he fell into her arms, wrapping her up tight.

God, she'd missed this so much. She'd missed *him*.

Now that she knew what had been going on, she felt guilty for abandoning him—for letting him abandon her. She should have tried harder to get through to him. She should have guessed that something was wrong. She should never have given up on him like that, not when she knew how precarious his sobriety was. She should have found a way to get through to him and make sure he was okay, even if it had meant flying to Tokyo and tracking him down herself.

She'd been so afraid of losing him to distance or disinterest or another woman, she hadn't even considered the much bigger threat: Scott's own mental state.

"I'm so fucking sorry," Scott muttered into her hair. "You don't even know."

Grace's hands roamed across his shoulders and over his head, getting used to the spiky, velvety feel of his shorter hair. He smelled the same as she remembered, only better, because of the leather jacket, and she breathed the scent of him deep into her lungs, feeling her chest expand without pain for the first time in two weeks.

"I thought—" She faltered, blinking hard as she held him tighter. "I thought you'd lost interest in me."

"I didn't," he said miserably. "I couldn't."

"Then why did you stop calling? Why didn't you answer my texts? I don't understand why you couldn't just talk to me."

His arms constricted around her, and she felt his chest hitch. "I didn't want you to know how bad it was. I was afraid if you knew you'd leave me."

"So instead you left me?"

He shook his head, nuzzling deeper into her hair as he held her tighter. "I didn't mean to. I just felt like such a fucking failure, and I didn't want you to see me that way too."

"Okay, but you know that's stupid, right?"

He huffed out a soft laugh against her neck. "I do, actually, but I guess I've still got some work to do."

"Clearly," she agreed. They'd never talked about his mental

health, but if he wasn't already seeing a therapist she was going to insist that he start. "What happened with your sister?"

He drew in a breath, and his shoulders stiffened against her. "I found out she's been getting high. It's just weed for now, but I didn't handle it very well, and she wasn't in the mood to be lectured by her addict brother."

"I'm so sorry." Grace rubbed her hands over his back, trying to tease out some of the tension.

He sighed against her shoulder. "And then I found out they weren't even considering me for the play. They only agreed to the meeting as a favor to my agent. I spent a week prepping for it and it was over in five minutes."

"Oh, Scott."

"The thing is, I didn't even want it, because I didn't want to be away from you for that long—I'd already decided I was going to turn it down—but it was humiliating to find out I wasn't even in the running."

Grace clasped her arms around him, swallowing around the burning in the back of her throat. She'd had no idea he was planning to turn the play down for her. If only he'd *told* her that.

"And then I got to Tokyo, and everything was a disaster there too. The commercial was an embarrassment—taking that job was a huge mistake. It felt like I couldn't do anything right anymore. I kept telling myself I'd call you as soon as things got better, but everything just kept getting worse. And then so much time had passed that I knew you'd be mad, and I couldn't face it. I didn't know if you'd even want me anymore."

Grace pulled back, not all the way out of his arms, but far enough that she could look him in the eye. "I wasn't mad, Scott. I was hurt."

He nodded slowly, shouldering that. "I never meant to hurt you, I just—I was a mess. I wasn't thinking straight."

"Tell me the truth. How bad was it?"

His eyes met hers. "I didn't use, if that's what you're asking."

"But you thought about it."

His jaw tightened. "I think about it every single day. But that's not a mistake I plan to make again, no matter what happens. I don't want you to think I'm going to go back to using every time I get depressed or we have a fight."

She was going to worry about him anyway, there was no getting around that, but his determination was reassuring.

He searched her face, trying to gauge her reaction, so she gave him a small smile and pressed her palm against his cheek. "You can't shut me out when things start to get hard," she said, because apparently that was something he needed to be told. "You have to talk to me. I'm not just here for the good times, okay?"

His fingers dug into her waist as he nodded again, swallowing thickly.

"And I need you to be here for me too."

He bent down and kissed her softly—carefully—on the lips. "I will be," he promised. "From now on."

"I mean it," she said, blinking back tears. "You can't just disappear on me like that. It hurts too much. I can't take it."

He hugged her close and kissed her forehead. "I won't. I swear. Never again."

She wanted to believe him, but she knew there were no guarantees. There was nothing he could say to prove it, no words powerful enough to serve as collateral against future mistakes. There was only trust. And hope.

What she did believe was that it was a promise he wanted to keep. And that was good enough for now. They both had a ways to go if they were going to get this right, but as long as he was willing to put in the work, so was she.

Grace kissed him—not softly or carefully, but fiercely, with all the longing she'd felt since he left. Scott kissed her back with equal urgency, his mouth opening to hers as his hands tangled in her hair. Warmth flooded her body, and she pressed into him, desperate for more. He sighed into her mouth, then his arms tightened around her and he lifted her off the floor, spinning her around.

She let out a startled squeal, and Scott set her down again, both of them laughing and gasping for breath.

"God, you're beautiful." He reached up to trace her lips with his thumb, and she felt her heart flutter, unrestrained, for the first time in weeks. "I missed your smile. I missed trying to make you smile."

"I missed your face." She ran her fingernails through his stubble. "And your beard."

His hand curled around the back of her neck and he pulled her in for another kiss. "I missed this," he murmured against her lips.

Grace shuddered with pleasure as he left a trail of tiny kisses from her mouth to her ear. His lips skimmed down to her throat, and she felt him smile against her pulse point before his teeth gently nipped at the sensitive skin, making her wriggle against him.

One of his hands slipped under her hoodie, searching for bare skin, and she moaned when he finally found it. "I missed touching you," he breathed, spreading his fingers out over her back to pull her flush against him. His breath tickled her ear as his teeth grazed her earlobe. "I missed the taste of you," he said in a low, throaty voice, and Grace lost all higher brain function.

"Scott," she murmured, clinging to him. Her legs were in very imminent danger of giving out on her, and she was thrumming with desire, her breath coming in short, uneven gasps.

"Grace," he said as he cupped her face in a tender hand. His eyes were dark and intense, and as green as she'd ever seen them. "Do you want to show me your bedroom?"

Oh, yes. She did. She definitely, definitely did.

20

"You know," Grace said as Scott kissed her on the way to her bedroom, "if I'd known this was how today was going to go, I'd have worn better underwear."

Well, shit, Scott thought.

He'd been planning to take his time and kiss her for a while longer before venturing into her pants, but now he couldn't wait to find out what she was hiding under there.

Hiking her up on his hips, he carried her over to the unmade bed and tossed her into the middle of the mattress. Grace threw her head back, laughing as she bounced, and the sound of it loosened something deep in his chest. It had been too long since he had heard her laugh.

Fuck the hopeless spiral that had caused him to push her away. *Never again*, he vowed silently as he knelt on the edge of the mattress. *Never, ever again.*

Grace lifted her hips for him as he hooked shaking fingers under the waistband of her yoga pants. Once he'd stripped them off, he paused to appreciate the view. "I missed your polka dot underwear," he said, running his fingers over the thin white cotton. "You have no idea how much."

She huffed in feigned indignation, her kiss-swollen lips forming a pout. "You've missed my underwear? Really? *That's* what you've missed?"

He locked eyes with her, one hand smoothing up the inside of her thigh as the other traced the edge of her underwear. "I never said that's all I've missed."

He'd missed *everything*. Every inch of her, every second of every day. He'd missed her so much there were times he'd felt like he would suffocate from it.

And now, by the grace of some miracle he was afraid to examine too closely, she was inviting him to touch her again, and he was awed by the abundance of riches. Scott slid his hand inside her underwear and—*fuck*, she was so wet already, like she'd been aching for him as much as he'd been aching for her.

Grace shuddered and tipped her head back, exposing her throat to him as she ground against his hand. "*Oh my god,*" she moaned as he slipped a finger inside her. "I've missed this."

"This?" he said, adding a second finger. "Or *this?*" He dragged his thumb across her clit, loving the way it made her whole body tremble.

She answered with an incoherent moan, and he lunged forward to bury his face in her neck. Her pulse fluttered beneath his lips as he sucked hungrily at the delicate skin.

Her hands found his face, tilting his head up to hers. "I missed *you,*" she said, cheeks flushed, gazing at him with eyes that were dark with desire.

It was almost too much to bear, how much he loved her, how he'd never stood a chance without her. "Grace..." He blinked hard, trying to form the words hovering on his tongue, but she cut him off with a kiss.

"Scott," she mumbled into his mouth, arching against him. "I'm going to need you to fuck me now. Like, right"—her hands found their way to his belt buckle, tugging him closer—"now."

He had no idea what he'd done to deserve her, but he didn't

need to be asked twice. Eagerly, he yanked her underwear down her legs and tossed it to the floor behind him.

Grace pushed herself upright, kneeling in front of him on the mattress as she unfastened his pants and slipped her hand inside. The edges of his vision whited out as she wrapped her fingers around him, and he heard himself stutter her name.

Her mouth covered his as she stroked him, pushing his pants down his thighs for better access. It was all Scott could do not to come right then and there, but no way was he letting that happen. Not yet.

"Please tell me you have a fucking condom," he said, because he'd shown up at her door empty-handed. He'd actually thought about sticking one in his wallet, just in case, but it had felt too much like tempting fate. He hadn't been that confident she would forgive him. He'd been too afraid to even let himself hope she'd ever be his again.

"Good thing one of us is prepared." Grace smirked at him as she withdrew her hand from his underwear and disappeared into the bathroom.

While he waited, Scott stripped off his clothes and lay down in the middle of her bed. It smelled like Grace—like *home*, even though he'd never set foot in her apartment before—and it made him want to roll around on it like a dog in a pile of freshly raked leaves. More importantly, he wanted her to roll around *with* him.

She laughed when she returned with a strip of condoms and found him waiting for her completely naked. "Made yourself comfortable, I see."

"Now you," he said. "Take off your shirt."

Mischief curved her lips, and she tossed the condoms onto the bed as she turned her back on him, reaching around to grasp the hem of her T-shirt. Slowly, teasingly, she raised it, exposing the lush perfection of her ass. Throwing a sultry look over her shoulder to make sure he was properly appreciating the show, she lifted it over her head and tossed it to the floor.

"Now your bra," Scott said, swallowing.

He watched, transfixed, as she reached behind her back and unfastened the clasp. Turning to face him, she smiled and let her bra fall to her feet, baring her breasts.

Fuck, they were so beautiful. *She* was so beautiful. He wanted to devour her whole. Speaking of which...

"Get up here and sit on my face."

Grace's eyes widened for a moment before her smile turned saucy. "If you insist."

Oh, yeah, he insisted.

Scott's muscles quivered with anticipation as she crawled up the bed toward him and threw her leg over him, straddling his face. His mouth watered as her heavenly musk filled his senses, and he grasped her hips, greedily pulling her down to his mouth.

Bliss bubbled inside him as he closed his lips around her, lapping up the heady, familiar taste. Grace shuddered above him, moaning as he licked a path from her opening to her clit, and he sucked the sensitive nub between his teeth, glorying in every sound he drew from her, every movement she made, every shaking breath she drew as he pleasured her.

When he slipped a finger inside her, she threw her head back and squirmed against his face, whimpering. His hand tightened on her hip, holding her firmly in place while his finger curled inside her, and he stroked her with the flat of his tongue, increasing the pressure just the way he knew she liked it, until she came with a loud cry, stuttering his name.

"Oh my god," she sighed, slumping forward to brace herself on the headboard. "You are so good at that."

Christ, she looked radiant with her chest flushed and her eyes heavy with desire, so beautiful it stole the breath from his lungs. Scott's hand came up to her face, cupping it tenderly as he was overwhelmed by a wave of affection.

The sly smile she gave him set his pulse racing as she clambered off him and slid down the bed to position herself between his legs.

Her hand glided slowly over his torso and down his abs, her tongue darting out to wet her lips as her gaze came to rest on his dick.

"Your turn," she said, making his cock twitch in anticipation. Gazing at him with dark, lusty eyes, she took him in her hand.

His fists clenched in the comforter as she tipped her head down and ran her tongue over his slit. As her lips closed around his shaft and her hand stroked up and down his length, he groaned in ecstasy. By the time her head started to bob up and down, he was a whimpering mess.

"Gr—grace," he stammered. It was taking every ounce of his willpower not to come in her mouth.

She hummed in response, and *holy fucking shit*, it almost undid him.

His hands curled in her hair, tugging her head back. "Stop."

Grace pulled off him with a pop and looked up with half-lidded eyes, her lips swollen and wet.

"I want to come inside you." He wanted her tight, hot walls around him. He wanted her to ride his cock until she came. He wanted to feel her orgasm pulsating around his dick. He wanted her so much he couldn't think straight. "Please."

"As you wish." She reached for a condom and he strained to hold himself still as she rolled it on.

Every muscle in Scott's body tensed as she climbed on top of him and guided him to her entrance. When she sank down on him, he moaned in grateful relief, tipping his head back into the pillows as her slick heat enveloped him.

Her breath caught as she took him all the way in, then she settled her weight on his legs and stilled, watching him with mischievous eyes. "How's that?"

It was—*fuck*—it was all he could do not to come right then and there. It had been so long and he'd thought he'd lost this forever. He'd dreamed of it, ached for it, and now that it was happening it would be so easy to let go and lose himself in her.

But no way was he going to let that happen, so he clenched his teeth and held fast to the fraying threads of his control.

Then she started to move.

Oh, Jesus, yes. Just like that.

His hands splayed over her ass, enjoying the feeling of being buried inside her and the sight of her writhing in his lap. He arched his back, and Grace sucked in a sharp breath as he matched his rhythm to hers. They moved in blissful unison, slow and steady, enjoying the feel of each other and getting used to having this again.

Scott reached a hand up to palm her breast. Grace's eyes fluttered closed when he dragged his thumb across her nipple, and she threw her head back, moaning.

"That's right," he said. "Let me hear you."

God, she was majestic. In the soft lamplight her skin glowed as golden and silky as her hair. He ran his hands over the perfect curve of her hips and her thighs, marveling at this gift he had been given. This second chance.

How had he survived all those years before he met her? How had he ever lived without this woman in his life? It didn't even seem possible now.

"Fuck," he said. "Fuck, I missed this."

A feeling of perfect, transcendent completeness filled him. Being buried inside her, surrounded by her, set every nerve ending in Scott's body aflame with sensation. He didn't know how much longer he was going to be able to hold out.

Grace's movements started to speed up, her fingernails digging into his skin as she braced herself on his shoulders. Scott ran his hands down the backs of her thighs and then up again, his fingers digging into her ass as he urged her to go harder, faster, his hips rising up to meet hers, increasing the friction right where she needed it.

"Oh god," she gasped. "Yes, that's it. Please, just—more." She was so close, trembling with exertion, and he was determined to get her there or die trying.

Scott lifted her up and slammed her down on him. Once. Twice. On the third time she threw her head back and cried out his name.

Her orgasm thrummed around him, nearly driving him over the edge, but he set his jaw and gentled his movements, coaxing her through it and drawing out her pleasure. His hands stroked up and down her back as her breathing slowed and her shoulders sagged bonelessly.

"Wow," she said. "That was...wow."

Scott pushed himself upright and wrapped his arms around her, gathering her into his chest. She leaned into him and pressed her forehead against his, their breaths mingling as their noses rubbed. Her fingers slid into his hair, curling at the nape of his neck and sending shivers down his spine.

Carefully, he lifted her legs, one at a time, and brought them around his waist so she'd be more comfortable. Grace hummed approvingly at the change of angle, then clenched around him, drawing a groan from him.

"Scott," she breathed, her mouth moving to his ear. "You feel so good."

He rocked his hips, driving up into her, and she hissed with pleasure, her fingernails digging into his scalp. It was intense and intimate, their bodies completely wrapped up in each other, so close it was impossible to tell where she ended and he began.

Scott gasped her name, trembling against her. His heart was overflowing with joy, with love for this woman, and with gratitude that she'd taken him back. "I missed you, Grace. God, I missed you so much."

"I know," she murmured, and held him tighter as they rocked together. "I'm here now. I'm yours, Scott. You don't have to hold back anymore."

A shudder traveled through him. He dropped his head against her shoulder and finally let himself go.

It hit him hard, crashing over him like a storm surge, carrying him away on a wave of pleasure that left his muscles weak and his eyes burning with tears.

Grace rocked him through it, dragging her fingernails over his scalp in soothing circles. "I'm here," she whispered, over and over. "I'm here, I'm right here."

When he opened his eyes again, she was gazing at him with a soft, watery expression that made his heart clench. He reached for her face with both hands, and pulled her lips to his.

"I missed you too," she whispered between kisses. "So much."

His hand smoothed over the back of her neck. "You don't have to miss me anymore. I'm right here."

GRACE DRIFTED SLOWLY TO CONSCIOUSNESS IN THE DARK, AND for one disorienting moment was convinced she'd only dreamed that Scott had come back to her.

Until she felt the weight of a muscled arm draped across her waist, and the warmth of a hard body pressed against her back. He was really here, in her bed. He hadn't left her after all.

Scott's fingers moved over her stomach. "You okay?" He sounded wide awake, and she wondered if he'd just been lying there listening to her sleep.

Grace laid her hand over his, as much to reassure herself as to reassure him. "Yes. Why?" She wondered how long she'd been out, and how long he'd been awake.

"You made a sound."

Definitely listening to her sleep, then. "A sound?"

"An unhappy sound."

"Bad dream." It was an easier explanation than her mind

256 | SUSANNAH NIX

playing tricks on her, making her think he'd been a figment of her imagination.

"Want to tell me about it?"

"I really don't."

"You're not having regrets, are you?"

Her fingers twined with his. "About what?"

"Me."

Grace's heart clenched, and she rolled over to face him. In the dim glow of the streetlights leaking in through the blinds, Scott's eyes looked dark and troubled, so she reached up to touch his cheek. "Never."

Maybe she should be. The road that lay ahead of them was unlikely to be an easy one. Scott had a boatload of issues that weren't going to magically vanish overnight. She didn't know the first thing about being in a relationship with an addict, which was probably something she should have started educating herself about before now.

They were going to need to communicate better, and admit when they were feeling scared or insecure—which was something they were both terrible at. It was going to take a lot of work, and a lot of patience.

But Grace couldn't imagine letting Scott go, given a choice. She wasn't willing to give up on him yet.

"Come here," he said, giving her waist a rough tug. "I need you closer."

Fitting herself against his side, she laid her head on his chest and wrapped her arms around him. If she could have held him tighter, she would have. "Comfortable?"

"Perfect." He stroked her hair. "You're perfect."

Grace pressed her face into his neck, inhaling the soothing, familiar scent of his skin. Luxuriating in this moment of peace and comfort.

"I love you," Scott said. Just like that. Like it was easy.

The words hung in the air between them, stealing all the breath from her lungs.

"I should have told you sooner," he went on, pressing a kiss to the top of her head. "I should have told you before I left New Orleans and every day while we were apart."

Grace squeezed her eyes shut and swallowed around the lump in her throat. "Scott—"

"You don't have to say it back. That's not why I'm telling you. It's okay if you don't feel the same way. I just wanted you to know how important you are to me."

She did feel the same way though. If she was being honest with herself, she'd loved him for a long time. She'd just been too afraid to acknowledge it. Too wary of being hurt again if she let herself fall. So she'd kept her feelings locked up in a tiny box, and buried the box at the bottom of her heart, where no one could find it or even know it existed.

Scott was damaged, and closed off, and kind of infuriating sometimes, but he was trying. He loved her even though he thought she might not love him back.

He deserved to know how she really felt.

"I love you too," she told him, letting the words wash over them like a wave, filling in all the cracks.

This thing between them wasn't a dream, and it wasn't a fantasy. It was scary and imperfect and wonderful.

It was real.

EPILOGUE

TWO MONTHS LATER

G race was back at work, on the set of some abysmally unfunny comedy that would probably end up going straight to On Demand. She liked the director though, and the crew, and most of the cast, with only a couple of exceptions.

It was a good job, and she was happy to have it.

They were shooting on the Fox lot, which was nice. Convenient parking. Decent commissary. Not a bad commute, as Los Angeles commutes went.

She felt her phone vibrate with a new text message, and as soon as the director called "cut" a few minutes later, she dug it out of her pocket to see who it was from.

Scott: U want takeout tonite?

He was shooting a movie just a few miles away at Sony. Tyler Posey had dropped out at the eleventh hour, and Scott had snagged it by being both available to step in at the last minute and willing to do it for cheap. It wasn't a huge role, but it was a major studio production, and a chance to show the world what the new improved Scott Deacon could do.

It was a job, and he was grateful to have it.

Grace: Sure, whatever's fine.

She and Scott had been outed by the paparazzi a few weeks ago when some creep with a camera had spotted them coming out of a Mexican restaurant in Studio City. For twenty-four hours, pictures of the two of them walking across a parking lot carrying their leftovers in styrofoam to-go boxes had featured at the top of every gossip site on the internet.

Until Hollywood darling Kimberleigh Cress had obligingly and very publicly started "dating" up-and-coming action star Griffin Beach. After that, has-been Scott Deacon and his nobody girlfriend had been promptly forgotten. Grace had wanted to send Kimbergriff a cookie bouquet to say thanks, but Scott had talked her out of it.

Even though she knew better, Grace had made the mistake of peeking at some of the comments about her online. Ugly didn't even begin to cover it. Ever since, Scott had been even more nurturing and protective than usual. Which was saying something.

Scott: Or would u rather I make mac & cheese?

Grace: Your mac & cheese. Always.

Scott: Heading home soon.

They'd been alternating between each other's places since he came back. Grace loved relaxing at Scott's gorgeous Laurel Canyon house on the weekends. With its swimming pool, huge kitchen, and whirlpool tub in the master suite, it felt like vacationing at a resort. But Scott seemed to prefer Grace's cramped apartment for reasons that eluded her, so that was where they spent most of their weeknights.

She sort of missed the days when they were neighbors, but there was something to be said for having Scott's things mingled with hers. His toothbrush and his hair product had a permanent place in her bathroom, he had shoes and clothes stowed in her closet, and he kept buying pots and pans and knives for her kitchen, because, according to him, all of hers sucked. They hadn't spent a single night apart since he'd come back from Tokyo, and even though they didn't technically live together, they were effectively cohabitating.

Scott kept making noises about selling his house and looking for a new one. He talked about it like it was something they'd do together. Like it would be *their* house.

It was still just talk right now. It wasn't like they'd actually started looking or anything. He hadn't officially asked her to move in with him yet. But she was pretty confident he would. And when he did, she was definitely going to say yes.

Grace: Still got a few hours left here. Home by 9 maybe?

Scott replied with a thumbs-up, a string of hearts, and the cheese emoji.

He was seeing a new therapist and had started going to his twelve-step meetings again. Grace had been doing a lot of reading about addiction and attending some Al-Anon meetings of her own to better understand her role. At her urging, Scott had agreed to see a psychiatrist, who'd started him on antidepressants. He hadn't wanted to at first, because he was afraid mood-altering drugs would undermine his sobriety, but the psychiatrist had assured him SSRIs wouldn't get him high and were much less dangerous for his recovery than letting his depression go untreated.

So far the results had been mixed, but it was early days. Hopefully they'd find the right dosage of the right meds, and in the meantime Scott was working hard on his therapy and taking other steps to stay healthy.

It was something they were working on together. No more hiding his struggles or pretending everything was fine. He'd gotten better at opening up about his feelings, both the positive and the negative.

Grace was trying to get better about it too. She still had a hard time putting her faith in other people, but it was getting easier to do it with Scott. Finally having some honest conversations about their fears and expectations helped. Trust wasn't quite as scary when you understood the other person's shortcomings and knew when you could rely on them—and when they needed to rely on you.

The two of them were a team now, and whatever lay ahead, they'd face it together.

Scott: Knock knock

He texted her the exact same joke every day. It had become their daily ritual, sort of like an affirmation—a way for Scott to let her know that he was still here, that he was okay, that he was thinking of her.

Grace smiled as she typed her response, playing along as if they hadn't had this same exchange fifty times. She liked to think they'd still be having it fifty years from now.

Grace: Who's there?

Scott: Olive

Grace: Olive who?

Scott: Olive u

ABOUT THE AUTHOR

SUSANNAH NIX lives in Texas with her husband, two ornery cats, and a flatulent pit bull. When she's not writing, she enjoys reading, cooking, knitting, watching too much television, and getting distracted by Tumblr. She is also a powerlifter who can deadlift as much as Captain America weighs.

www.susannahnix.com